One man's progress in troubled times

Ernest Dyer

Published by New Generation Publishing in 2023

First Edition

ISBN: 978-1-80369-922-6

www.newgeneration-publishing.com

New Generation Publishing

Chapter One

The route through the gently sloping valley being taken by the traveller followed a track that had been used to carry people, trade goods and stock animals for centuries, if not for millennia. Although spotted with flecks of white-foamed sweat the traveller's horse maintained the steady gait that had taken them twenty-five miles that day. A day that had started at a busy coaching inn located on the outskirts of the hilltop town of Shaftsbury. Where their overnight stay had been but a staging post on the journey that had begun three days earlier in London.

The warmth of the animal beneath him and the early spring sunshine of the warming day on his face, caused the traveller to draw the horse to a halt and dismount. Making it easier to remove his heavy coat and to take a short pause in the journey in order to absorb the beauty of the blossom-fringed fields lining the predominately green valley. The reflective moment progressed from his taking in various mainly farming-related aspects of the scene to his comparing this timeworn peaceful outlook to the horrors of the military conflicts that had been part of his experience for the past twenty-five years. But which had dominated his life during the last five years of service in the British Army during the Peninsular campaign, leading up to the bloody engagement that was becoming known as the Battle of Waterloo.

Parts of this experience floated with harsh impact into his mind. The images of rows and rows of worn-out troops trudging along seemingly endless dusty lanes. Being followed by sad groups of even more exhausted camp-followers - the wives, girlfriends, and occasionally a child, the prostitutes, some older soldiers fallen behind, along with men urging along the lines of pack-mules laden with ammunition and other supplies. Then there were even more dramatic images of the wounded and the dead strewn over battlefields that echoed with the piteous cries of the semi-conscious wounded men. The terrified eyes of fearful horses locked in an inhuman world their animal natures could not comprehend. The bloody nastiness of close combat, the destruction of body shredding cannonade, the limb removing carnage of a sabre-slashing cavalry charge, and the general chaos of battle.

These were the more immediate thoughts of progressing military conflict. But then his memory turned to the impact on the Spanish towns and villages passed through by men charged with the thought of recent engagements and seeing their comrades killed. Men filled with anger (as well as for some greed) intent on taking this out on villagers and townsfolk most of whom had no hand at all on either side of any conflict. Firstly, it would be the stolen wine and spirts that would fuel the anger and release the controlling influence of conscience. This would then soon lead to the raping of women and to men being beaten or even stabbed or shot down, along with the theft of valuables and much of the foodstuffs required by the population for their survival.

He was reminded that war is such a terrible expression of human activity, but his despair was somewhat tempered by the thought than not all soldiers indulged in such disgraceful behaviours. Some, indeed most, did try to maintain a certain dignity during the bloody business of waring.

The process of moving from the enhancing contemplation of the valley to scarred memories of past conflicts left the traveller in a subdued mood as he remounted his horse and gently urged it into movement. It was a mood that continued with his following the winding track as it climbed toward the head of the valley. But on such a day as the pair crested the hill our traveller could see set before him the countryside that was to be his new home – warring was now behind him, and farming was to be his future.

The man's horse had been his companion for some years and between them there was a level of understanding and of trust that made for a comfortable pairing. The tall chestnut-brown bay had three white ankles and a distinctive strip of white blaze running down its head from eyes to nostrils. This was an animal descended from a linage designed more for stamina than outright speed – being deep in the shoulders and sturdy in the legs.

As the pair crested the hill the traveller could see not just the farmland and occasional patches of woods stretching into the distance, but also a substantial manor house about half a mile further on. Even from this distance he could see that what had obviously been a run down, bordering on derelict, building was now undergoing some substantial work. With much of the roof having been retiled and with wooden scaffolding enclosing the walls. Half a dozen men could be seen working on the roof and front of the building where a couple of the first-floor windows were being replaced and the face of the house was being rendered. On two sides of the main house a range of neglected outbuildings could be seen, and at the rear there was a red-brick walled garden covering about two acres.

It was encouraging for the traveller to see the progress that had already been made in preparing the house and outbuildings for his moving in. He had bought this large but much neglected estate and had spent many weeks planning how he would bring the house and the 42 farms spread across the 3,000-acre, Downland Park Estate into the nineteenth century. A century that, today in 1820, had seen the impact of a precocious revolution in industry but also a range of significant changes in farming methods – not just in terms of mechanisation, but also in the understanding of soil conditions and in animal husbandry. The intensity of his study and planning for this project had served to distract him from the memories of warfare – the nightmares still stirred the bloody images of war to the surface but were now occurring less often.

The traveller drew his horse to a halt within the spacious forecourt at the front of the house. As he dismounted a broad-shouldered individual, clearly dressed for rough work, came hurrying down the main steps and the two embraced as would two very good friends.

'Well Joe, we are back together at last' said the traveller 'How are you and Mary, have you both settled into life in the country?'

'It is so good to see you sir. Yes, these last few months have been quite a learning experience for me, but even more so for Mary. At first, she very much missed the neighbourly hustle and busy vibrancy of life in London, but we have both been made very welcome by the local farming community and even more so by the villagers down the way in Cerne Parva. Such that, I am thinking it would now be quite a wrench to part Mary from the kitchen and neat front parlour of our lovely cottage. And for both of us the garden, the chickens and pigs, along with our cow, has so improved the way we live. The smell of the domestic animals is rich and warming compared with the raw stink of the city.'

'That's good Joe, and for our new lives drop the 'sir', it's just James from now on.'

These friends had been together for much of the past ten years. James working his way up through the officer ranks of the army to reach the rank of colonel and Joe starting as a private rising to become a colour sergeant. These being in effect the two key components of the head (James) and the spine (Joe) of their regiment.

'Right let's have some lunch Joe, then you can show me round the Hall, the garden, and some of the Home Farm, and as we go along, please update me on work done and work still to do.'

The two men climbed one of the two curved sets of steps leading up to the large oak double doors at the main entrance to the house. Passing through the hallway they entered a naturally lit room at the rear of the house where they could see Joe's wife Mary standing beside a small table on which was set out a selection of cold meats, cheeses, buttered bread, along with a bowl of watercress, and a good-sized flask of ale.

James insisted on Mary joining them for lunch and noted how well she was looking with a newly sun-browned face and some additional weight since he had last seen her when she had been pale and rather thin.

After they each served themselves, they sat overlooking the walled garden to the left of which was the modest cottage shared by Mary and Joe. The white walled, thatched building was fringed by fairly well organised clusters of daffodils, bluebells, lupins, cowslips, and lily of-the-valley, in colourful bloom, and these being interspersed with green shoots of hollyhocks, corn flowers, and stocks, trailed over by pastel coloured rambling roses and sweet-scented honeysuckle that would come into flower as the spring merged into summer. The land adjacent to the cottage extended to about half of an acre or so of well-kept vegetable garden.

'Now Mary, apart from the toil of having to care for our Joe, how have you settled to your new life in the country?'

Mary's open face set into a warmly creased smile.

'I would admit that I could hardly imagine that I would

settle here in Dorset. I felt that the ways of country people and the wildness of the land would not suit a town-girl like me. But these initial doubts have gradually eased over the past couple of months and have now reduced to a point where I am coming to believe that I belong here. I feel the aura of the land is seeping into my very being sir. And seeing how Joe has taken to life here, even accepting the responsibility of managing the estate, has been so uplifting – his military service left him spiritually wounded, but I can already see that life here is having a healing affect. I would never have thought that I would see him milking a cow but now he does this with practiced ease, and I have even caught him talking to the pigs!'

James reflected that Mary's articulate speech, in contrast to a relatively lowly social position prior to Joe's recent appointment to estate manager, was a legacy of her lower middle-class upbringing. An upbringing that she had been separated from due to parental opposition to her marriage to Joe.

'That's good to hear Mary and as I have just told Joe, from now on it is James rather than sir. Together we are going to build something to be proud of as we progressively bring this estate back to financial health and take it into a modernised future.'

Following lunch the two men worked their way from room to room assessing the progress that had been made to the internal renovations. The newly papered walls covering smooth plasterwork and lined at the ceiling level with tastefully finished cornices. The more substantial fireplaces of the day rooms and the more modest ones in the bedrooms were part of a newly constructed internal heating system designed for efficiency as well as comfort. And the richly varnished stair-risings and bannisters enhanced moving between floors, adding to the pleasure of the overall experience of the being in the building.

Satisfied with progress within the house, the two then made their way out into the garden area. Much of it still quite overgrown, at least up to the substantial gateway leading to the extensive walled garden. Here progress was more obvious, with the two young gardeners – Jake and Michael – being determinedly bent to work, showing why this was the case.

'I can show you the plan of how this will be laid out sir, sorry James. We haven't settled on the details yet as we are trying to assess soil conditions and exposure to wind in different areas. But of course, the primary aim being to create a plot that will be able to provide most of the salad, fruit, and vegetables, required for the main house throughout each year. For the fruit, so far we have just pruned some neglected espaliered apple, pear, and plumb trees, and planted some new varieties, along with half a dozen quince bushes.'

While Joe was talking James had noticed a small head peering at them from the top of the west wall.

'Who is that over there, Joe?'

'Ah, we do not yet know his name but over the past couple of weeks that lad has been taking a keen interest in the work that has being taking place out here. If we call out to him, he runs away as fast as his skinny little legs can carry him. At a speed that easily outpaces us and is surprising given how undernourished he looks. In the last few days Mary has been putting out some bread and cheese and after waiting for her to return to the cottage he quickly snatches it up and is off. He is either very scared or very shy.'

Noticing that their attention had turn to him the boy ducked down, climbed back down the tree that had provided his observation post and was soon on his heels. Taking a slight detour to see if any food had been left outside of the cottage. When he saw that there wasn't any his heart sank. He had been feeling so proud at being able to bring some food home to his mum. He lived in what was not much more than a neglected hovel on a patch of scrubland situated on the outskirts of the village of Cerne Parva – seen by some of the more socially aspiring villagers as something of an eyesore. This young boy, Jude, was the youngest member of a household containing his now disabled father, his mother and his two elder sisters, the oldest of which, Tess, had a six-month old baby. The family had fallen from just manageable poverty into near destitution since his father had his accident and had been unable to continue with his one-man haulage business and having to sell his old horse and time-worn cart.

The fear that pervaded the very air of the cottage was the mostly unexpressed thought of having to appeal to the Poor Law institution that was the Workhouse. A place where families were torn apart and the shame of poverty marked, more scarred, the reluctant residents.

Tess's baby was a something of a mystery to the boy. He knew that eighteen-year-old Tess had left home about two years ago to work as a companion to an old lady in a large manor house about ten miles away, and had last year returned home with a swollen belly and in a very sad state. Since then he had occasionally noticed a smartly dressed young man riding slowly past the cottage which seemed in some way to connected to Tess. His mum had urged Tess to go out and talk to the stranger and on more than one occasion he had overheard her say 'It is his fault Tess, he owes you.' But his sister would just gaze moodily at the earthen floor.

Meanwhile back at the manor-house the evening was drawing in as James and Joe completed their inspection of the walled-garden and had continued on to the Home Farm that Joe directly oversaw as an aspect of the estate management. The farm employed four full-time agricultural workers and Joe had been endeavouring to encourage them to work more as a flexible team rather than each just getting on with their own quite narrow idea of their work. Although all were involved with the annual harvest in late summer, for the rest of the year the stock-man managed stock, the pig-man the pigs, with the other two working the land. This silo-like job distinction was generally inefficient and could often serve as an excuse to take it easy.

'Well Joe, it's been a long day and I am impressed with the progress that you have made. I need another day to move beyond our interest in the estate in order to discuss the other business that we are endeavouring to progress further west. I guess that you will be pretty busy tomorrow but can you and Mary come to lunch again, after which we can focus on our post-service organization.'

'Yes, that's fine James – I do know that Mary has taken on a cook for the house and she, Jane Goodall, will be moving in and starting work tomorrow. In the meantime, Mary has made a meat pie and as soon as you are ready to eat this evening, she will heat it up and bring it across to the house.'

After enjoying the substantial meal provided by Mary, James settled down for the night in the main living room warmed by a wood-log fire that had been set by the live-in housemaid, Susan, who was another new servant taken on by Mary. Joe had delegated the selection of staff for the house to his wife knowing that she would have a much better understanding of the suitability of candidates for house-based work. The house was too big for just a cook and one housemaid to manage, so more would be needed, not least, someone who can take charge of running the house and so relieving Mary of the additional work. But this was for another day and tonight was a time to relax, drink a glass of wine and to look forward to all the tomorrow's yet to come.

It was bright sunlight streaming though the wide windows, as well as the hammering of stone masons working on the walls, which woke James. And by 10 o'clock he was sitting down to coffee on the sun-warmed terrace running across the back of the house. Susan had brought the silver tray of coffee, milk, and sugar from the kitchen and as she poured, he could see how unsettled she seemed to be.

He gestured for her to take the vacant chair next to his. This unexpected gesture only added to her nervousness. She had not been used to such treatment from her employers. In that past, she had been expected to move aside and look down when passing or being passed by members of the families she had served. So, when invited by James to sit she gingerly perched on the very edge of the chair as she nervously twisted the apron covering her dress, unsure what the problem might be.

'Susan, please relax, you have done nothing wrong I just want to gain some idea of why you wanted to work here.'

'It was the advert in the local newssheet for work close to the village that my father read out to me that I responded too. My first employment was with a family over Steepleford way where I had to live in. I had been told that I would be able to spend Saturday night and all-day Sunday back home with my family but once I started, I was expected to work seven days a week and was fortunate to be able to get home just once per month. I was so unhappy. The job itself was wearing me down with having to run up and down three flights of stair with heavy buckets of hot water and being on-hand for any requirements of the family or even of the more senior servants. I only lasted for six months and one day I was so tired that when cleaning a valuable vase, I fell asleep and knocked the vase off the table. The master was furious and ordered me to my room. The next morning I was sacked without any of the pay owing nor even a reference.'

She stopped talking and her face flushed as she realised how much she had said, but James just smiled at her and said 'That's fine, go on Susan.'

'I should not be talking like this sir, but the experience was horrible. Mother and father were so understanding and, although I knew that they would be struggling to feed me, they welcomed me home. The chance of working so close close to family was too good to miss. I thought that the lack of any reference would result in my not getting the job here, but my father said just be honest Susan and tell whoever you have to see the truth of what you have experienced. If they reject you, it might well be because they would have been similar employers to your last one, but if they are sympathetic towards you then it looks like they might be good people to work for.'

'Your father seems pretty wise to me Susan, what does he do?'

'Father's a carpenter, a really good one, you should see the furniture that he has made for our cottage and for many others in the village. But he has always struggled to gain regular work due to his having lost a leg when serving in the navy. Having a wooden leg means his can't travel far and so can only seek work locally and there is only so much of this available.'

'Hm.....it might be that I could offer your father some work. I need quite a bit of book-casing fitted along the walls of what will be my library. Thank you Susan for sharing your recent experience with me and I hope that you will be very happy here. If you do have any problems, then start by talking with Mary.'

By lunch-time James had already spent a couple of hours pouring over a series of maps spread out on the living room floor. He knew that there were 42 farms whose tenants paid rent twice a year to the estate. The farms varied in size, with most being about 50 acres but there were four farms of over 300 acres. Presumably, these larger farms had grown as the tenants took over adjacent farms when they became vacant. These would be tenants belonging to the rising breed of more affluent Yeoman farmers becoming more common in England. James was thinking that the farmers running these larger farms might have already taken steps to modernise their farming methods and so had become more efficient. He had mixed feeling about the larger holdings. Were they the result of tenants of neighboring farms taking over the tenancies for which new tenants could not be found or had they simply bought out tenants whose circumstances had made them vulnerable. This perhaps being due to sickness of a farmer or following a series of poor harvests. Yes the larger farms might provide the necessary economic conditions suitable to accumulate the capital required for modernisation, but on the other hand they would reduce the number of individuals able to become tenants and so have their own farms as an alternative to paid employment.

This did not seem to be such an issue on the estate as it was only four farms that had grown so far, and he would be able to monitor how he would best manage vacated farms in the future.

Later at lunch, as the food was being enjoyed, the conversation during the meal was generally a repeat of the previous day, but as soon as they had finished eating Mary returned home, having been forewarned by Joe that they would need to focus on estate and some other business for much of the afternoon. The two men moved from the dining area to an adjacent living room where the maps were still spread across the floor.

'Right Joe, I would like to call a meeting with all of the estate's farmers next Sunday afternoon. I will then set out my initial thinking on how we want to run the estate.'

Joe had already been informed about James's intention to reduced rents in the short-term in order for the mostly neglected farms to accumulate capital, and for groups of the smaller farms to see if they could form some co-operative groups able to jointly purchase and share new machinery.

Joe had reservations about reducing rents. He had already come to learn of the cost of running a large country house, but he also knew that James had substantial financial assets so could subsidise the estate, at least for a few years.

'Over the next few days, I will walk round the farms and ensure that each individual tenant will receive an invitation to the meeting.'

'Thanks Joe, now let's move on to our project based down in Devon.'

James was now referring to an agricultural community that he had been instrumental in setting up. It was when serving in India as a solider in the employment of the East India Company (EIC) that he first came to realise how badly the Company and later on the British government treated ordinary soldiers.

The EIC had initially been set up as a private company with a royal charter from Queen Elizabeth I, and an army of 260,000 men. It became notorious for the excess cruelty employed as it endeavoured to maximise profits from exploiting the people of the Indian sub-continent. To the extent of using slave labour and in trading in these, along with the drug opium.

For the company's soldiers the low pay was obvious,

especially when compared to the fortunes made by those at the head of the Company, such as Robert Clive and Warren Hasting in the previous century who had been able to leave India as very rich men. Two individuals that had set the acquisitive tone associated with service for the Company. If at a more moderate level James, as a captain rising to become a major, had also benefited from the 'rewards of battle'.

Such rewards were added to when he went on to serve as a colonel in a British Army fighting its way through Portugal and Spain. The difference in rewards between commissioned officers and the men of the line was significant. At the Peninsula War's end, most of the surviving officers were able to return to a Britain offering comfortable lives and to their being feted in the glamourous setting of country house balls and garden parties.

Amongst other valuables Wellington himself was gifted the 5,000 acre 'Strafield Saye Estate in Hampshire at a cost to the British government/people of £260,000. An estate he was able to leave to his family, along with the then fortune of £400,000. Whereas most soldiers discarded at the war's end were left to pretty much fend for themselves. At best some were able to gain low paid labouring-type work and for those unable to obtain even this, there was some parish relief and other very meagre, and always demeaning charitable support, or worst still there was begging or theft. Groups of the 'heroes' of Waterloo were left to roam the roads unwanted in most of the towns and villages they passed through.

For James this situation played on his conscience and the first action he took on leaving military service was to compile a fairly detailed report – including actual examples of the lived experience of individual soldiers and sailors

- that in carefully measured language, set out the harsh reality of post service life facing demobbed military men, and arguing for a decent veteran's pension. In the winter of 1818 he had sent copies of the report to the future George IV (who, due to his Father George III having gone mad, had been made The Prince Regent in 1811), The Prime Minister the second Earl of Liverpool, the Foreign Secretary Viscount Castlereagh, and the Secretary of State for War and the Colonies the fourth Earl of Buckingham. Thinking that surely one or more of these dignitaries should be motivated to progress the cause of ex-soldiers and sailors. But all that he received back was a couple of obviously hastily scribbled letters offering sympathy, with one pointing out the high level of national debt that the government had to address. James was aware that the national debt had increased to about £900 million by the War's end. And that even just meeting interest payments was taking up about half of the total national income. But he was also aware of the vast personal fortunes that had been made from the war by bankers, miliary supply merchants, and large landowners...... a collective from which most members of parliament and all of the government were drawn. James reflected on an essay he had recently read written by the German philosopher Immanuel Kant, who observed that: 'One must understand that the greatest evil that can oppress civilized peoples derive from wars, not, indeed, so much from actual present or past wars, as from the never-ending and constantly increasing arming for future wars.'

Frustrated by the lack of interest from government he decided to use some of his own fortune to support at least some ex-military. This was a fortune gained partly from his service in India and Spain, but more so from careful investment in construction and in dealing in the London property market. With these being further increased by an inheritance gained on the death of his widowed mother. His father, as well as being a quite substantial farmer had also been an early and very successful investor in canal companies and himself owned a fleet of about 50 barges built to carry manufactured goods, and the raw materials necessary to make them, to and fro across the country.

Initially James had set up an agency that would offer to pay the fare and provide some modest seed funding to help settle ex-servicemen prepared to emigrate. This being primarily to Canada but also Australia and the United States. But this only helped a relatively small number of those willing to leave their county of birth and begin again.

He then started purchasing farmland in the county of Devon and began a process of resettlement based on self-supporting smallholdings. He also had ambitions to open factories come training schools, where ex-soldiers and sailors could gain the mechanical skills sought in industrializing Britain.

The issue he soon had to face was the realization that even using all of the interest paid on investments from his own fortune the costs would become unsustainable within but a few years. His thoughts had turned to a means of gaining funding that would take him outside of the law. Whilst he had been brought up to have a certain level of respect for laws – he knew that the laws made by the elite group primarily made up of aristocrats, powerful merchants, and lawyers, who served as M.P.s in the British Parliament were invariably laws that favoured their own class. Laws that more often bore down oppressively on those lower down the social scale. From his experience of life in London he was aware of how many of the very poorest were reduced to having to steal just to survive. And if caught being imprisoned, with some even hung, for the crime of simply trying to stay alive. For James, the law and justice rarely coincided in the British legal system. And the crime of the government's neglect of ex-servicemen was for him obvious.

It had been during the time that he was considering how to develop his ambition to assist those cast aside after serving their country that James had taken to making long circular walks from his London town house in Hanover Square. A favourite route taking him past the wealthy residential properties lining and adjacent to the Square, then south through St. James Park and across the expansive area of stabling known as the Kings Mews which was then being suggested as a site for a spacious piazza-type monument to The Battle of Trafalgar, centred with a substantial column to Horatio Nelson, an admiral who had been ennobled following his success at the battle of the Nile in 1798. His route then turned north at the Charing Cross, along St. Martin's Lane to the area of slum housing lining three of the seven cobbled streets running from their confluence at the Seven Dials. Here the rising affluence of the more central parts of the fast-growing city most obviously met the abject poverty of the outer areas. The narrow lanes and alleyways, being jam-packed with rickety buildings some with ill-fitting doors and most lacking glazed windows, with only strips of pre-used tarpaulins serving to block the gaps at night.

Children of various ages played in muddy, cobbled streets littered with all sorts of discarded rubbish along with horse and even some human waste. The heady smell of this mixture turning the stomachs of the more genteel who had mistakenly turned into one of the fetid lanes but being unnoticed by the mostly barefoot ragged-clothed urchins who played there. This being the type of housing whose residents lived in streets, that later in the century William Booth in his surveys of London districts coloured black on his class-based maps. Black representing residents noted as being the 'lowest class, vicious, semi-criminal', or the slightly, more respectable (or slightly less disreputable) dark blue as 'very poor and in chronic want'.

The level of poverty appalled James, but the shear vibrancy of the people and the colourful street scene of musty shops and overloaded stalls drew him to include at least one of these lanes in his weekly walks. On one occasion when he had ventured along one of the wider of these lanes the hawkers and pedlars were raucously plying their wares, with loud calls intended to inform residents of both their presence and of the goods on offer. One deep voice stood out, causing James to look toward its source. If he had first reacted to the voice, he then recognized the hawker selling bundles of chopped firewood from a creaky barrow. He crossed the short distance between them and grabbed the man by the shoulder. 'Ezra what a surprise to come across you'.

As James looked at his old companion he took in the shabby condition of his clothes and the fact that he looked to be at least a stone lighter than when they had served together. This, Ezra, had been a sergeant major in the Grenadier Guards. The two men, if unequal in rank, had been equal in terms of the respect they had for each other. After the initial friendly greetings, it was clear that Ezra wanted to move on. He was a proud man and did not want James to judge him for being in near poverty. James picked up on this, but it only served to make him want to learn more about Ezra's circumstances. He took his friend firmly by the arm and guided him into a public house situated towards the Seven Dials end of the lane.

'No excuse Ezra, I am buying us both a decent lunch and I am insisting that you bring me up to date on your experience since being demobbed.'

They entered the Three Tuns public house after James ensured a tough-looking street-boy that he would be rewarded with a penny if the cart they parked out-side was still there with goods intact when they were ready to leave. The two men settled into a corner table within the saloon bar, ordering pale ales to go with their roast beef dinners. As they waited for their meal the talk was mostly quite general, mainly about the better days that Ezra had experienced when he first left the army – a few months during which he was able to support himself fairly comfortably as he used up his accumulated service pay and some small amount of savings. When the steaming plates of meat, potatoes and thick gravy had been served James couldn't help but notice how enthusiastically Ezra was eating. Finishing the food and wiping his plate clean with a thick crust of bread when James was only about half-way through his.

'Look Ezra, it does seem that you have fallen on hard times recently, and this reinforces my own view of how badly ex-servicemen are being treated. Cast off when no longer required or are too ill or injured to man-the-line. I have established an organization that might be able to help you. But also, one where you might be able to help other old soldiers.

In his recent walks James had been slowly fermenting an idea about how he might finance his veterans support project in the longer-term, and perhaps even expand its work. It would require men like Ezra to progress this – it was this coincidental meeting that had brought the strands of the idea together.

He would form a gang of ex-servicemen prepared to step outside of the law in order to progress the, for him, noble cause of supporting veterans. He was aware that the lives of the men as well as his own, would be on the line. If they were caught when engaging in what would be 'crimes' such as bank, warehouse and highway robbery and possibly some smuggling, they would face capital punishment. A cold fact that he would need to make all those recruited fully aware of.

'I admit am pretty desperate now colonel, I can't seem to make a living out of the job of buying logs out in Epping Forest then chopping these into firewood to be sold in small bundles. The poverty gradually seeps into your soul. Fortunately, I don't have any dependent wife or children. My beautiful Molly withstood the hardships as she followed in the regiment's supply train throughout the Peninsula Campaign but within two months of returning to England she caught cholera and died.'

'Yes Ezra, I remember Molly, a real driving force amongst the women who followed husbands and lovers across much of Portugal and Spain. I am sorry for your loss.'

Ezra wiped his eyes with a sleave of his threadbare jacket, sniffed loudly, and looking James direct in the eye asked:

'Right colonel, what's ye plan? What's this 'organization' thing that ye mentioned just now?'

'Well, over the past year I have established a London-based emigration agency to channel ex-service men who want to start new lives in the United States of America, or in one of the colonies of Canada or Australia. Paying fares and providing sufficient funds to last for a year, so allow the time to settle into new lives. I have also been buying land in the county of Devon and have been able to settle more men down there. Single men more often favour emigration, but those with families mostly prefer to start a small holding on the land in Devon. We currently have 1000 acres under cultivation down there, divided into about 200 tenanted small holdings of 5 acres each. The rents have been set at a minimum level, pretty much 'pepper-corn', just to ensure the legality of the tenancies. New tenants have been provided with additional funding to build their own houses – we have encouraged a co-operative approach to building, so settled tenants are expected to pitch in and help newcomers build a cottage. This settlement seems to be working well and a self-supporting community is being formed.'

'Ha colonel, that is really impressive.'

'Yes, but as yet Ezra we have only helped 200 ex-servicemen to establish small-holdings and about another 300 to emigrate, not that many when you consider the tens of thousands cast aside at the end of recent wars. There are many more that need, indeed deserve, help to start viable new lives but the funding has been stretched and more money is required if we are to continue the work.

Now Ezra this is where you can help – I want to form a group ideally made up of ex-soldiers and sailors. Men prepared to break the law by committing capital offences and so place their lives on the line. A fundamental condition would be that minimal physical harm should come to any person being robbed or to those protecting them.'

James paused to allow Ezra to absorb the ambition and the seriousness of his words.

'Well Ezra, we have been back together for just a few hours, and I have given you a great deal to think about. I have been very open with you due to my trusting that you will at the very least keep my intentions to yourself. Even if you decide not to get involved in fund raising activities there will be a place for you on my own estate in Dorset if you want to take up agricultural work.'

'That's kind colonel but I suspect my skills are more towards relieving the rich of their money than in turning the soil or herding animals.'

'Don't make any hasty decision on this Ezra, here is

sufficient money to keep you in a decent lodging house for a week or so. Let's meet up in this pub in one week's time and you can let me know what you have decided.'

The two parted, each with a lot to think carefully about – Ezra about an opportunity to gain self-respect, if at the possible cost of swinging his life out at the end of a coarse-threaded length of rope – James to consider a similar end for himself but also having the responsibility of others losing their lives because of him.

It was in a light drizzle the following week when James set off to meet up with Ezra. The weather suited his subdued mood as he still had doubts about the enterprise he was planning. By the time he turned into Little Earlum Street and entered the Three Tuns the rain had as least cleaned some of the accumulated horse and donkey manure from the pavement.

Once his eyes became accustomed to the dimly lit bar, he could see Ezra hunched over a glass of ale at the table they had shared the previous week. He ordered a small beer for himself and another pint of ale for his friend.

Well Ezra, have you been able to decide on our conversation of last week and remember that I made two different offers each involving a possible future for you. There is the task of leading a gang of tough ex-service men on activities taking you beyond the law and in which you will be risking your life, and the other offer involving your moving down to my Dorset estate where you can meet up with an old comrade, Joe Campion, and take up work on the home farm. Whatever you decide would be fine by me.'

Ezra took a deep drink of his beer, sat up, ran his hand down his face and was looking at James as he said:

'For the first few days of this last week I had been wandering around areas of the city, mostly along the river, trying to compare the advantages and disadvantages of each offer. On these walks I was repeatedly distracted by individuals begging or selling cheap wares by the roadside, much as I have been doing with the firewood. I had previously taken this street-life for granted as being but an aspect of the fate of the poor. Our conversation last week spiked my interest and I began to ask the beggars and hawkers for their stories. Some just told me to bugger off but most seemed happy to share their stories and I was surprised just how many of them had served in the military. Then walking along roads like Piccadilly, The Strand, and Drury Lane, there were those many rheumy-eyed men huddled in shop doorways, gathering in the nearby park areas, and lying in gin assisted semi-consciousness on the pavements. After what you have highlighted I was thinking that this is probably the sad plight of many of our ex-comrades.

I have been hearing about the monument for Lord Nelson to be constructed near to the Charing Cross and I compared this to the expected monuments to ordinary servicemen – all that many of us could expect is a pauper's grave, for most unmarked, or at best having the 'monument' of a cheap wooden cross.

I am sorry to go on colonel, but I wanted you to understand some of the background to my decision on your offers.'

'That's fine Ezra, you do seem have been progressing similar considerations to my own. It will be interesting to hear your conclusions.'

'Well my conclusion is that I fully agree with your comments about the injustice of men who have served the nation being ignored by the Government. One that always wants us to fight its wars but then just discards us, as if embarrassed by our presence. I am angry, but it is an anger that I really would like to channel into the fund-raising scheme that you suggest. If the first few days of last week allowed me to come to this decision, then the past couple of days have been spent trying to track down some of our old comrades. Many of these have ended up in London – all at the very bottom of the social scale. I had occasionally met with Tom Pearce and Caleb Standing in pubs around the Dials and it was easy for me to find them. Tom was on the run after deserting from the navy. It seems that he had been press-ganged into service during a drunken evening in Portsmouth but, being prone to sea-sickness and resenting the poor food and low pay, he had scarpered when his ship put in at St. Katherine's Dock.

Caleb had been earning good money as a prize-fighter but due to injury to the knuckles of his right-hand this source of income had pretty much dried up. Just now he is having to get by on the odd shilling earnt from gentle sparing with novice fighters and some casual work as a Smithfield slaughterman. He felt the sparing more as charity than an activity he could take any pride in and the bloody work of slaughtering brought back memories of the worst of battles.

I set out your plan to Tom and Caleb, but I have only identified you as ex-military and a loyal friend to servicemen. They are both unsure that we can achieve much but they are definitely in. Caleb said that he had seen John Kent in Hyde Park and he was in very sorry state, having to doss down in a bushy area of the park. He had been engaging in some petty criminal activities. But he had heard that since then John has been caught during a street robbery and was currently serving a one-year sentence in the newly opened Millbank Prison. A sentence less than it could have been due to the Judge acknowledging John's fine military record; a rare act of leniency. He will not be released for a couple of months, but I will visit him next week just to see if he is interested in joining us.'

James past two guineas across the table. 'Take these Ezra and give them to John. This should at least help him to obtain something more than basic prison food.'

'So, in sum colonel, we do seem to have a basic gang ready and willing to get started on progressing your plan.'

'You have been busy Ezra. For now I will set up a bank account in the name of Felix Hardy. If you remember Felix was a young corporal who sacrificed his life to save his men at the battle of Coruńa when he charged into a group of Frenchies about to sneak up on our rear-guard. I think the account will in a way link to a soldier whose memory we all hold dear – one of the dead now buried in the silent debris of history. Since we returned to England I have been trying to find his family but as yet no success with this and I still have his service and other identity papers. So, we can raise Felix from the dead to join our gang in absentia.'

James had a sense of things really moving forward now and he could see the enthusiasm for the cause in Ezra's face. The somewhat depressed sad-eyed expression of a week ago had been replaced by a look of bright-eyed determination.

'I will arrange to have 20 pounds paid into the new account, and you can access this as required. The first task is to rent and furnish a house and move the men into it. Ideally this will be in a quiet road in somewhere such as Highgate or Camden on the northern outskirts of London as I think that most of your actions will involve the main routes to the north. I assume that this will take up most of the next week for you and in turn I will spend the week planning the first action.'

And so began the next stage of James's ex-servicemen's support plan. With the first action by the newly formed gang being to hold up a stagecoach traveling between London and Birmingham carrying bullion between banks. The action netted 2,000 gold sovereigns with the pre-agreed division being %5 for the gang members straight away and 5%

invested for them in government bonds. The remaining 90% being for funding the purchase of land in Devon and paying emigration fares and settlement grants. The combination of interest on James's own capital and the income from 'crimes' of robbery and perhaps some smuggling, should be sufficient to help a steady stream of ex-servicemen, and if appropriate their families.

Following the first couple of actions James decided that he could leave the running of the legitimate side of the agency to a manager assisted by a clerk in a small office in near Soho Square, and the illegitimate fund-raising side of the business to Ezra assisted by an ex-payroll soldier. With these two these being informed of possible targets by a number of well-placed bank clerks and customs and exercise officers susceptible to bribes.

It was then, during early May when James had taken the two-day journey down to the Dorset Estate, pleased to have left behind the noise, dust-laden air, and the rank smells of London.

Chapter Two

It was on a warm Sunday afternoon when the estate farmers, some with wives or older sons, came up to the Hall for what would be for most of them a chance to meet their new landlord and to give all of them the opportunity to learn about his plans for the future of the estate. Or at least those aspects of any plan that would impact on their farms.

The spacious and airy Home Farm barn situated adjacent to the east wall of the walled garden had been prepared for this gathering. Hay bales made up much of the seating and down one side of the barn a row of trestle tables was just about supporting the weight of the food-stuffs laid along them. Stacks of crusty rolls alongside a row of cottage loaves, blue china bowls of deep yellow butter, solid blocks of cheddar cheese lightly dusted with flour, plates of cured ham, pork pies, and a range of pickles and chutneys. At one end had been placed large bowls of apples, pears and plums that had been stored over the winter. On the straw strewn floor beneath each table had been placed two earthenware flagons, one containing small beer and the other fairly weak cider. These weaker brews were preferred over strong ales and the coarse scrumpy-type cider, due to the meeting being intended to be a social opportunity for those committed to the agricultural work of the estate to come together, but also to be a meeting where serious business would be discussed.

'Well, if nothing else comes of today Ned, we will at least be well-fed.'

This observation being made by a surly-looking red faced individual whose dull red waistcoat stretched over an ample belly and from which hung a length of solid gold chain. At one end this being attached to a buttonhole and the other to a gold hunter watch nestled in a pocket of the waistcoat. A watch that when the owner was in company was taken out and ostentatiously considered much more often than knowledge of the time required. Farmer Bedlow as he was known was the tenant of the largest farm on the estate. An outcome that had been due to a series of careful acquisitions made over the past 20 years. Years in which Henry Bedlow had managed to cheat the frail widowed owner of Downland Park out of the true rental value of the farms he took over when these became vacant. He had established a mutually agreeable arrangement with the previous estate land agent. An arrangement that included the agent employing a bribeable land-valuer to undervalue a vacant farm when Bedlow negotiated, but grossly overvaluing it when an outsider expressed an interest. This suited the manager, and their dubious business arrangement became a family relationship with the marriage of the farmer's son to the daughter of the agent.

The vaulted-roofed barn was increasingly providing a warm smoky atmosphere as the number of clay-pipe smoking locals increased. Most of the farmers knew each other and, after helping themselves to generous portions of food, were sitting in groups, within each of these the conversation being about one or other aspect of what the new owner might have planned for them. In one group were some older more affluent farmers aspiring to join the yeoman class. A group rising in Georgian England, gaining wealth as they benefited from the high war-time price of food and for some the additional land provided by the Enclosure Acts. These were a series of legislative measures denying access to land previously held in common and in effect just giving it to the already well provided for, the wealthier classes of farmers and landowners. A process of denying the means of subsistence to many lower- class peasants who had relied on the sharing of common land set in time-divided strips on which to grow vegetables for their table or a crop for sale. Or perhaps an acre or two of open land shared by villagers on which to graze a cow or horse. Access to common land made the difference for many families between having sufficient to at least get by or, if deprived of this, of falling into poverty. For many of those in the latter group it gave them the unattractive choices between seeking the charitable if meagre support of the parish, entering the degrading family-separating setting of the workhouse, or of moving to the nearest city in order to gain work in the factories that were the focus for industrializing Britain. A twentieth-century historian would describe enclosure as: *'...a case of plain class robbery, played according to..........law laid down by a parliament of property owners and lawyers.'*

As James and Joe entered the barn the conversation in the groups gradually ceased and heads turned towards them.

James spoke first.

'Firstly, thank you all for coming along today. My intention is to set out my plan for the estate but it is a plan for our future that will require your enthusiastic support if it is to be a future based upon the successful management of the land in our care. My use of the word 'care' might seem odd, but I ask you to consider that the land is eternal whereas we are but temporary custodians of it – it is land that yes, we hope to gain a reasonable living from, but it is also land that I am sure you would want to pass on to the next generation in good heart.

The Downland Park Estate runs from here at the top of the Medlum Valley, so north to the edge of Blackdown Chase. It is an area of farmland benefiting from the shelter of the sloping valley sides and a generally predictable and temperate climate. We are fortunate to be here. But Joe and I have during that past week spent some days walking between your farms. During these walks we have been able to meet most of you at your work, but we have also been able to see that on too many farms the land and buildings have been neglected. I do accept that the recent past management of the estate has been lax to say the least and responsibility for drainage and buildings in tenancy agreements is not nearly as clearly set out as it should be. If the condition of buildings is a cause for concern, then even more worrying is the condition in which we found some of the fields used for grazing the animals and the state of the soil in fields used for growing corn, wheat, barley, and animal winter feed, as well as vegetables for the local markets. The buildings can be repaired, ditches can be cleared, drainage can be dug, and these fairly easily. But if we are to improve the primary resource that underpins the productive potential of the farms then this would need to be based on the longer-term task of soil improvement. A doable task, but one requiring determination and knowledge.

As to this knowledge, I am sure that most of you are becoming aware of changes taking place in agriculture elsewhere in England. This is not just about mechanization such as improved iron-bladed ploughs able to open up heavy clay soils, or mechanical winnowing and threshing machines, but it is also about how to improve soil fertility and animal husbandry.'

James could see that a couple members of the audience were shifting their feet and casting glances at their fellows – a sign that there were questions to be asked.

'I will pause now and invite you to comment on what I have said so far.'

A tall thinnish young man stood up, somewhat nervously indicating the wish to speak.

'My name if Christian Greenwood sir and I have held

the tenancy on a 50-acre farm for three years now. I would say that I agree with your assessment – and am keen to learn more about what can be done. With respect sir, diagnoses is easy compered to addressing the issues.'

During his initial speech James had noticed that this blue-eyed, straw-colour haired, young man had been the only member of the audience taking notes during his presentation.

'Thank you Christian, I suspect that you have voiced a concern held by others, and I would say that the basic requirement in relation to addressing the problem is one of identifying the capital funding needed to implement modernization.'

There were a series of grunt and some nodding heads throughout the audience to affirm this as a common view.

Then farmer Bedlow rose ponderously from his seat.

'With respect sir, talk is all very well but will the necessary capital you talk of be gained by raising rents?'

'Well, the honest answer to that question would be yes but……. And it is the conditions of the 'but' that I now want to set out. I did just now say that capital is required but I also mentioned the need for knowledge, so I will come back to this once I have dealt with the finance.

I propose a five-year farm development plan – For year one I intend taking only a peppercorn rent of one penny, for year's two and three the rents with be set at a quarter of what you currently pay, and for years four and five it will be set at a half of what you currently pay. Then from year six onwards the rent will be as now plus an agreed annual rise based on the estate and yourselves equally sharing the benefits of the expected increase in productivity of each farm.'

Most members of the audience looked quite confused, as they endeavoured to absorb the implications of James's proposal – Rents were probably the most sensitive factor for tenant farmers. Set two high they could barely subsist but set too low was something they had never experienced – so James's no to low rent plan first was more confusing than informative for them.

Christian again stood up.

'So sir, the idea being that we can set aside the money that we would have been paying in rents for the next five years and invest this in machinery and land improvements.'

'Yes, thank you Christian, you have simplified the basis of the plan. But I also want to offer the possibly of non-interest bearing loans made from the estate and intended to provide seed-type funding for specific equipment that the tenant can show will be of immediate economic benefit. It might be that for an expensive piece of equipment a group of you together take out a loan and then share use of the machinery on a co-operative basis.

Obviously, what I have said so far and what I will be saying next does need to be carefully considered by each of you individually and no doubt discussed with your wives and each other. I would say that the progress being made in relation to low rents and any improvement loans will be generally monitored and more formally assessed annually just to ensure that we are effectively working towards the same ends.

Now let's move on to the knowledge mentioned earlier. Included in my plan is the intention to employ an individual who has just retired from farming a large farm in the midlands. This man, Arthur Gordon, although now sixty-odd years old has been at the forefront of agricultural innovation. He was an engineer before taking over his father's 300-acre farm and his modernizing initiatives have resulted in significantly higher crop yields, and his animal values have increased markedly. I won't go into detail, but

Arthur has agreed to spend one week every month for the next six months living on the estate and will be available to advise each of you on how you might innovate. Since his wife died he has handed the running of his farm over to one of his sons and he has been traveling the country acting as an agricultural adviser. Indeed, he has recently been granted a stipend by the government for his progressing this work.

So, there we are gentlemen - a lot for you to think about. I suggest that if there are no more immediate questions let us enjoy the rest of this gathering - the food, the drink, and of course the company. Then over the coming weeks each of you can arrange to meet Joe to see how the plan I have outlined will impact on your own farm in terms of rent levels and the more obvious improvements required.'

And so the farmers regrouped into pretty much the same small groups has had been together before the meeting started. But now the discussion in most of these was focused on attempts to identify problems with the plans – many were suspicious of James's motives, after all, what kind of landlord actually cuts rents!

Throughout the weeks of late spring the estate was, if only very slowly, being returned to at least something resembling its former glory. Work on the exterior of the main house had been completed, outbuildings repaired, and much of the decrepit frost damaged brickwork of the walls enclosing the garden had been repointed or replaced. On days when not occupied on other business James would change into workman's clothes and join the gardeners, Jake and Michael, working in the garden. It was nourishing to his spirt to get the feel of the soil running through his fingers, even if it was soil that would benefit from generous amounts of organic material being dug in. Like the farmland, the condition of the soil in the garden had also been neglected. When James commented on this Jake spoke up.

'It has been dispiriting for us sir, to see how the garden has been getting ever less productive. We have practised composting, but this has not been anywhere near enough to put back all of the goodness being taken out in the process of growing fruit and vegetables. The previous estate manager wouldn't allow us to buy in the manure or seaweed that was needed. The old master would never have allowed the garden to get into the state you saw when you first arrived here. But on his death the mistress employed a land-agent who, in my view sir had little interest in the long-term health of the garden.....sorry to go on sir'.

This speech was probably the longest continuous passage of words that the generally mono-syllabic gardener had spoken outside of the small cottage shared with his wife and two children for some time. It was the release of thoughts that had been at the forefront of his mind each time he had contemplated the decline of a garden in which he had spent seven years working as an adult, years that followed a childhood during which he had often helped his father who had been the senior gardener before his retirement.

'That's fine Jake, I appreciate your honest view, especially given that it reinforces my own thoughts about the garden's recent past – together we are going to change how the garden is managed. Let Joe know who used to supply the estate with manure and seaweed during the old master's time and give him some general idea on the amounts of each that you consider we need. It is a shame that all of the horse, cow, pig, and chicken manure from the Home Farm is required for its own long neglected soil, otherwise this would have been a useful source of organic material.'

As the day continued the three men bent to the tasks of digging, weeding, raking, and the particularly satisfying one of planting a variety of vegetable seeds. This involving using a hoe to draw a long shallow channel in the finely tilthed soil, then pressing each of the larger seeds, suitably spaced along the channels, then drawing a trowel along the line to allow the soil to be folded over the seeds. The process being completed with the firm but gentle pressing by the palm of the hand, just to ensure the seeds were comfortable nestled into the surrounding soil.

Rising up from having planted a row of carrot seed James looked up to see the young boy Jude again peering over the wall. As before the boy dropped from the top of the wall and ran towards the front gate. But this time as he rounded the corner of the garden he ran straight into a surprised Joe. The pair tumbled over, the nimble boy was soon back on his feet but Joe reached out and grabbed his thin ankle, bringing him down again.

'Now boy' said Joe as he stood up 'What's all this about?' he asked and as he lifted him by holding the boy's coarse sacking shirt some shinny apples fell to the ground, bouncing and rolling in different directions across the stoney path.

Having heard the commotion James had arrived to find Joe holding the boy by the scruff of his quite dirty neck.

'Leave me alone mister I ain't doing nothing wrong.'

'So, when was stealing apples not wrong?' asked Joe – 'These have obviously been taken from our winter store of fruit. And this perhaps explains why I have been noticing the stock of stored fruit and some root vegetables kept in the shed had been reducing more that we would expect since Christmas.'

At this point the group was joined by Mary who has been busy feeding her garden chickens on the other side of a nearby hedge.

'Hold on you great lump Joe and you also please sir

– you are both scaring the boy witless' she said, pushing her ample bulk between the two men and placing a meaty protecting arm around the boy's narrow shoulders.

'He is shivering from fear and just look how thin he is. Come with me my lovely. I have a nice warm meat pie cooling on the kitchen table, and we can start by your eating a decent portion of this. Then you can tell us why you have been taking the apples and other vegetables.'

As she turned to go, she looked back at the surprised pair looking on.

'I think there might well be more to this than meets the eye.' she said.

As Mary disappeared into the cottage with her small charge James said

'Well Joe, I am not sure quite what happened there…. the boy's fortune seems to have changed from being a condemned thief to becoming a spoilt guest!'

'I am sorry James but we both know that it's best not to challenge Mary when she is in one to her protective of the weak moods.'

'Your Mary is truly a force of nature Joe and no need to apologise for her. I remember that even in the worst of times during the recent Iberian campaign she stood out as a light of defiant and obstinate beauty in what was the harshest of worlds. Her determination offered an example that helped to keep the morale of many of the camp followers from sinking into despair. Let's leave them together for now. I suspect that in due course we will know everything about the boy. And we can then decide how we might deal with the miscreate.'

The next day James was sitting on the terrace reading the Times newspaper as Susan was setting out coffee and crusty buttered rolls on the wooden garden table. He could see Mary, followed at a few yards by a pensive looking

Joe, crossing the short distance from their cottage and then climbing the ten stone steps leading up to the terrace.

'Can I have word please sir?'

'Of course Mary, sit down here next to me. Joe, can you go into the house and ask Susan to bring more coffee and rolls and then the three of us can hear whatever it is that Mary has to say.'

Mary did not wait for Joe to join them. Over their breakfast he had already been forcefully made aware of what she was going to talk to James about.

'Sir the boy Joe caught taking the apples yesterday is named Jude Clare. He lives with his family at the other end of the village. A family that seems to have fallen into destitution after the father was injured and so unable to work. He has heard them talking about the possibility of the family being turned out of the cottage and being placed in the workhouse. From his upstairs bed, which in fact seems to be just a pile of straw, he has listened to his parents arguing about this and his mother always endings up in tears. He scems to have taken it upon himself to try to provide at least some food for his family. A family including himself, his mother and father, two older sisters, with the eldest, Tess, having a young child. Jude has been able to obtain some work scaring crows from the fields of a couple of farms, but this is paid in farthings an ha'pennies rather than anything more substantial. So, it was poverty and a sense of responsibility that had driven the boy to stealing sir.'

James took in the concerned look on Mary's face.

'I can only thank you Mary for your sympathetic investigation. I wasn't' sure what we would have done with him other than a boot up his rear end and giving a warning to keep off estate land.

But what you have discovered does make a difference.

The village generally seems fairly prosperous, but clearly there is at least one family that is struggling. Leave it with me Mary, I will have a think about this.'

''I have asked the boy to come back this afternoon sir, he wants to apologise to you, and I am baking a pie for him to take home.'

James spent some of the rest of the morning contemplating the young boy's situation. What would he have done thirty odd years ago if his family had been near starvation? Pretty much the same as this young lad he suspected.

'Of late I have been attempting to address the plight of soldiers following their being demobbed from the army, but there is a much wider problem of poverty in general and more specficllay how this impacts on children. I have one crusade already going on and, what with the added need to develop the estate, I am not sure that I can do much about poverty on a wider scale. But perhaps I can at least do something locally. I wonder how involved the village church in the form of its clergyman has been in supporting the weaker members of its flock.'

He was carrying these thoughts in his mind when later than day Joe arrived at the hall with Jude in tow.

The boy was obviously nervous but there was also a glint of determination in his brown eyes.

'Sit down Jude, Mary has been telling me more about the very difficult circumstances of your family and, although stealing is wrong, I can now understand why you have been taking food from our stores. Now we have to decide what we might do as an alternative to your having to resort to stealing.'

Inwardly Jude was surprised and very relieved that it seems he would not be going before the magistrate. He had been frightened by stories of people being hanged for stealing goods over the value of five shillings and he did not know the value of the fruit and vegetables that he had taken from the estate stores over that past year or so, but he thought that it might have reached the 'hanging' level.

'I have an idea Jude, how about you come to work here for a wage – I would prefer boys of your age to be at school, but it seems that the nearest school to the village is at least 20 miles away and this is just a small charitable institution.'

'But I can read a bit master' interrupted Jude.

'That's good to hear, who taught you to read?'

'It was my sister Tess, I think she learned a bit from the Sunday school teacher and then more when she went into service in the big house over Brockhampton way. Tess has always been the clever one in our family. Oh, and what's a 'wage' please master?'

'A wage Jude is where a person works for another person, an employer, and at the end of each week he is paid a sum of money.'

'So that must be what I get for the bird-scaring.'

'Yes, that's about right Jude, but I was thinking of something more longer-term. More of an agricultural apprenticeship. Joe will in effect be your employer. You will present yourself here at sun-up throughout the year. For four days per week until you are 12 years old and then it will be 5 days a week, and up to seven days during harvest. Each day Joe or one of the gardeners will set you to work. Until you are about fourteen the work should be fairly light, but it will be demanding, and you will be expected to do as you are told and to learn to become a journeyman gardener so gain a wide knowledge of gardening.'

'I am not afraid of hard work master.'

'We will see about that Jude, your starting pay will be four shillings per week

Now I want you to have a think about what I propose and if you are interested then Joe and I will come to your home to have chat with your mother and father because they will also have to agree to our arrangement.'

About an hour later Jude was walking back toward his home in something of a daze. Had he really been offered a proper job? Was he really to be paid two whole shillings a week? If he was unsure about this, he was pretty certain that the thick-crusted meat pie that was warming his hands as he walked along was real.

When his family had gathered in the small kitchen of their cottage, they listened as Jude excitedly outlined what had happened to him since leaving home that morning. His mother, Joan, was so relieved that he was not to be taken up for stealing food. She had been preparing to beg the new master or his agent to have mercy on her son. If hearing that this would not be necessary was a relief then she could hardly believe what Jude was saying about the offer of work made by the new master of the Hall. It seemed to be too good to be true.

'This would make us a bit less dependent on parish relief.' said Tess 'But is it fair for us to deny Jude his childhood?'

'Don't' worry about me Tess. I like the master; I think he is a fair man. And I really like Mr Joe and his misses. She makes such tasty pies and cakes. And taking up this offer means no need to pilfer, and working for this thing called a 'wage' makes me feel grown up. I also like gardening so becoming a gardener seems just the job for me.'

Jude had told Mary something of Tess's situation. That there did not seem to be a father for her child. Although having a baby before marriage was not uncommon in the countryside, marriage usually soon followed, So, when Mary past on the information about the absence of a father, this seemed for Joe to have perhaps been an outcome of her working away from home in service. These young women, forced by economic circumstances to leave home, could be lonely and vulnerable – Mary had often railed about this hidden scandal of how the master or the sons of the big houses take advantage of pretty servant-girls. Then, when the most likely outcome become obvious the girls are sent home in disgrace with the parentage being denied, often without a reference.

Joe wasn't aware that this was not the case for Tess. Although her pregnancy was the result of an unwanted liaison with, Alex Cranfield, son of the Dowager mistress who had owned 'Cranfield Hall' in Brockhampton, such was Tess's emerging womanly beauty that Alex had wanted to keep her on as a sort of easily available mistress. But he had insisted that the baby be placed in the Foundling Hospital that he knew had been established by the philanthropic Thomas Coram in the east end of London.

Tess was not only repelled by the slightest touch of Alex but would not be prepared to part with the baby. It was the first beautiful thing in her life that was properly her own. Tess was seventeen years old when she had been sent into service to be able to send at least small amounts of money home and also to remove the burden for her parents of having to support her. The new mistress had been very demanding – even when the long hours of housework undertaken under the gimlet eye of the principle housekeeper had been completed, Tess was still expected to read to the aged mistress until late into the evening. Only rarely did she get a day off and the fifteen miles each way of mainly muddy lanes that she had to traverse to get home for the day left her quite exhausted.

Whilst living at the Hall she had been able to nimbly avoid the unwanted roaming hands of Alex when they past in a corridor. This was as far his liberties had gone during the first six months of her time there. But one Sunday evening, tired after a visit home, she was in her small bedroom tucked into the eaves of the large house and she heard a soft knocking on her bedroom door – she had by then changed into her night-clothes so she only opened the door just a fraction.

There she could see Alex swaying slightly and obviously in drink, with a bottle of brandy in one hand and a small jug of milk in the other.

'Hello my lovely Tess. I am so miserable, and I desperately need someone to talk to, will you let me in?'

'But master it is late, can we please talk in the morning?'

Alex lent his weight to the door and pushed his way into the room. The only furniture was a dressing table, a rickety cane chair, and the bed. And it was the bed on which he sat, more fell, down upon, patting the bed-cover beside him.

'Come and join me shy Tess and we can cosy up and chat. Have a drink of this fresh milk. I brought it specially because I thought than you would not enjoy the brandy.'

In order to give herself time to think she accepted the milk and took a drink. It tasted a little odd but her thoughts were racing and were more focused on thinking about what she should do next. She wasn't to know that Alex had laced the milk with gin thinking that this concoction might relax Tess and so make their evening more conducive, at least for him. He casually rested his hand on her bare arm and started to talk about his problems, mainly focused on gambling debts and wishing his elderly mother had looser purse strings. He repeatedly urged Tess to take a drink as his hand moved down to her thighs.

As this was the first alcoholic drink that she had experienced Tess began to feel rather dazed. Alex sensed this and began to push her down onto the bed with one hand as he unbuttoned his trousers with the other. He was beathing heavily and sweating as he layover her slim body.

Tess did try to twist away from him but by now he had lifted her nightdress and was lost in his own moment of selfish sensual distraction. The tears that had been forming in Tess's brown eyes began to slide down her soft cheeks as she focused on a fine crack in the yellowed plasterwork of the ceiling. She forced herself to take her mind away from the immediacy of the violation of her body, back to her childhood home. She remembered waking up in the tiny loft room shared with her younger sister. Then stepping out of bed and tiptoeing into her parent's room where she would carefully lift the bed-cover and slip into the warm bed and cuddle up to her even warmer mother – she recalled the loving arms gently enfolding her. A moment fixed in memory, with her enmeshed in the rich smell of her mother's comfortably sleep-drawn body.

After Alex had left, Tess lay still unsure quite what had happened but knowing that her life had changed forever – she was now a sinner. And sins had to be atoned for.

In the following weeks Alex repeated his violation of Tess on a number of evenings. She became resigned to his attention as she felt there was little that she could do. She did approach the housekeeper and asked if a lock could be put on her bedroom door, but this was dismissed out of hand. The women well knew what was happening but felt this was just something to be accepted by the lowest class of servants.

As the months past Tess's belly grew and she let out her smocks so that the other servants and the mistress would assume a general increase in weight rather than advancing pregnancy. But the real cause of Tess changing appearance became obvious to Alex. This was when he made the suggestion of her returning to her family in order to have the baby away from the Hall, giving the reason as the need to care for a sick parent. Then having the soon to arrive baby placed into care with Tess returning to work and their, for him, cosy arrangement continuing.

It was a month later that Alex took her home in a fashionable light trap pulled by a fine pair of horses. Throughout the journey Tess was sunk in thought, concerned about how her family would manage without her wage. As they drew up outside of the cottage she turned to look directly at Alex determined to raise the issue of financial support. But before she started to talk he drew a leather purse from his overcoat pocket and handed this to her.

'There are sufficient coins in there to last for a few months Tess. I will send someone so that it can be taken to London and the Foundling Hospital, where I am sure it will have a good life Tess – it might even be adopted. She simply nodded, if she also noted his repeated use of 'it'. Whereas for her 'it' was a flesh and blood boy or girl baby whose life she could feel moving inside her. As she walked towards the cottage door, she did not turn to look at the departing Alex and although she was unsure of the greeting she would be receiving she was very pleased to be home.

She need not have worried as both parents warmly embraced her, their being resigned to accept, if with hindsight, that Tess's looks had made her downfall pretty much inevitable. Although it wasn't voiced, each of them felt a certain amount of responsibility for letting Tess go into service. They were determined not to allow her young sister, Elsa, to have to repeat Tess's experience.

In due course a baby boy joined the Clare household, this being a joyful addition. Although there was also concern about how they would manage once Tess's money had been used up. All they would have was the small income gained by Joan taking in washing, some vegetables from their small garden and the odds and ends that Jude brought home. What minimum parish relief they occasionally received was given with reluctance and received with embarrassment.

It was about two months after Thomas's birth that a male servant from Cranfield Hall arrived to collect Tess and the baby. He had been ordered to drop Tess off at the Hall before travelling on to London with the baby. But by now Tess had been growing ever closer to her nursing child and she was determined to keep Thomas at any cost. She was thinking that once she had recovered from the birth she would be able to at least gain some field or dairy work in a local farm. Lower paid and less certain than the regular work of being in service, but possibly just sufficient for the family to get by.

On hearing of her decision not to return with him the servant was quite angry, his being aware that the master would not be happy. And an unhappy master more often took his feelings out on a servant. But Tess was adamant, so he had little choice but to return to Cranfield empty-handed and at least he had a couple of hours of journey time to work out how to plead his case, one based on Tess's obstinacy.

During Tess's absence from Cranfield Alex had been spending much of his time in London. Rising at lunch time, drinking with rowdy friends throughout the afternoons, and spending the evenings in one of the many gambling clubs in the Whitehall area or the brothels of Shepard's Market. The clubs were those of the so called 'Golden halls' and included Almacks, Brooks, Whites, and The Cocoa Club. The brothels were those frequented by the upper-class's, ones where most sexual tastes were catered for and a degree of discretion was maintained. Alex was a poor card-player, and his gambling debts had been slowly mounting. Creditors were generous and fairly patient, due to their knowing that Alex was to inherit a fairly substantial country estate, and meanwhile their high interest rates nicely inflated the debts.

It was one lunch time during this London sojourn that Alex sat taking a late breakfast as he desultorily opened the day's post that had just be delivered by the GPO uniformed postman. A door-to-door delivery service began in1793 and linked to the royal mail livered coaches that sped, bugle -horns blowing, between towns and cities carrying the day's letters. One letter was from the managing agent containing a quarterly report of the estate's business. This information was a copy of the original provided for his mother. Alex barely looked at such reports, it was only the annual rental incomes minus all costs i.e. any profit available, noted at the bottom of the final page that held his attention. As he had pulled the report from the envelope a folded note fell onto the floor. On picking it up he read that it was from the housekeeper and he frowned as he read that Tess would not be returning to employment at Cranfield.

'Dam her', He said, casting the note aside. He was a man used to getting his own way, especially in his dealings with members of the lower classes. Time spent at Cranfield was rather a trial for him – He reluctantly accepted that he had to accommodate his mother's wish for him to at least have some involvement in the running of the estate. A practical aspect of this being that he had to spend more time there than in his much-preferred London haunts. He had assumed that during his presence at Cranfield he would find compensation and indeed sensual comfort by being able to have easy access to the lithe body of Tess. Yes, there were other maids, and indeed at least one of these was actually willing to enjoy his favour. But there was something about Tess, something more intriguing in her manner. This partly perhaps due to her being better educated than the other maids, but it was more than this, she emanated an inner light that drew him in. The thought of Tess not only fired his loins, there was also the additional attraction of her company.

At Cranfield he did have the country pursuits of fox hunting and shooting parties, and there was the occasional ball. But mannered flirting with the daughters of aristocrats and professional people was tiresome and very rarely went beyond suggestive looks and a stolen kiss. His anger rose at the thought of the loss of Tess. But his thinking deviously progressed to a consideration of Tess's family circumstances. He assumed that like many families in the lowest class, the Clare family were probably also in poverty. And now, with the addition of Tess and presumably a baby to support, then the dark shadow of the workhouse might well be an everyday consideration for them. He knew little and cared less about the workhouse system, but if this was a fate casting its dark shadow over the Clare family then perhaps there was a way of persuading Tess back to Cranfield. Her marital prospects would be slim given the obvious sign of her past clinging to her skirts.

It was with this more optimistic thought in his mind that he travelled down to Cranfield a week later. And once settled in and having spent an hour or so in the main sitting room in the company of his mother, he ordered the stable-lad to saddle up his favourite horse and lead it round to the front of the house. After mounting up he urged the animal into a trot, happily reflecting that his mother was looking even more frail that when he last saw her a couple of months previously. There was not even a twinge of conscience at the thought of wishing her dead. He was longing to take control of the estate, pay off his debts by selling some land, then enjoying a comfortable life spent mostly in London or perhaps in traveling to somewhere fashionable in mainland Europe. A Europe, now more settled since the demise of Napoleon and experiencing a rapid growth in upper-class tourism. Particularly to the more attractive locations such as Southern France, the Amalfi coast of Italy and for the more active, the Swiss Alps.

On arriving at the Clare family home, he was pleased to note the obviously run down condition of the small cottage. The warped window frames, the tatty condition of the thatched roof and the general air of neglect pervading the property. He dismounted, tied his horse to a gatepost, and sauntered up to the paint-peeled front door, on which he rapped with his silver handled riding crop.

The door creaked open to reveal the face of a pretty young girl and after taking in his appearance she looked at Alex as if he just fallen from the sky. She had only ever seen such assumed to be important people passing by on horseback or seated in a stylish carriage – to see one of these exotic creatures at their front door was approaching the mysterious.

'Is Tess Clare here?' he asked.

The child quickly shut the door. It was a few minutes later that the door was reopened and this time by Tess.

On seeing her Alex's felt a strange feeling in his stomach and a sense of need almost overpowered him. But he was able to take in the challenging look that Tess was giving him.

'I left your employment over two months ago now master and I never want to see you again. You mistreated me and you should not have come here.'

'But Tess, I need you at Cranfield, my life there is miserable without you. I realise that I have been rather mean in the past and now see that I should have done more to help you support your family. Let me make up for past mistakes.'

He was surprised at his own approach of persuading rather than his assumed right to order.

'Come back and I will immediately get the estate's managing agent to contract a local builder to work on repairing this cottage and in addition I will double your pay so that you are better able to provide for your family.'

Just then Tess's father pushed the door fully open. In his working life he had had some experience of dealing with the upper classes and he was not intimidated by the aura of entitlement that they generally assumed. Indeed, he was endeavouring to control his anger at what he suspected was the cause of his beloved daughter's current difficult circumstances. He might be unsteady on his legs and breathless when he moved too quickly, but he was the head of the Clare family and he felt a duty to protect them.

'He pointed a gnarled fist at Alex and shouted. '

'You clear off and stop bothering my daughter.'

Alex felt that he had left a message for Tess that would perhaps cause her to consider a responsibility towards her family – by committing herself to a future with him she could lift her family out of poverty. And what alternative prospects would she have on the marriage market as 'used goods?'

Satisfied that he could do little more for now, he decided it best to placate Tess's father.

'I am very sorry to have bothered you sir.' He said turning to untie his horse and lead it away from the house.

As he mounted and moved off he could see Tess starring at him from the doorway.

'I think I have sown a seed that will flower in due course' He smirked as he spurred his horse into a gallop.

'In the meantime I will have to satisfy myself with some night-time frolicking with a couple of other servant girls.'

In the following weeks Tess took to leaving the baby Thomas with her mother and walking along the hedge-lined lanes and muddy tracks threading through the village.

Her thoughts followed a repeated pattern – Starting out determined to reject Alex's offer – The memory of his hands

49

crawling over her body, the sweaty coming together.......
the guilt that followed. But then seeing her family struggling
so badly, with little prospect of improvement. She was
especially concerned about Jude and Elsa, both so thin. And
both she knew going to bed hungry most nights yet never
complaining. Similar to Alex, Tess was also aware that no
decent man would want to marry her now.

'What alternative do I have?'

By the time she arrived home she would invariably still
be unbale to decide between a future with the intensely
hated Alex and the best interests of her beloved family

'During one of her walks she had paused before the grey
stone village Church in order to retie her boot-lace. Just as
the parish curate was passing through the Lynch-gate. As
she stood up he saw her and, obviously recognising her, he
turned away with dour look of distain on his face.

'So even the Church rejects me – I suppose I am a sinner
and the fate of burning in hell forever awaits me.'

'I just pray that the same fate will not fall on my baby.
When I feel bolder, I will apply to have Thomas baptised.
Perhaps in a month or two the Vicar's Christian duty to save
sinners will have overcome his obvious dislike of one.'

And so began a period, already noted earlier in our story in
relation to Jude's experience, of Alex riding to the village
and lingering close to the cottage until Tess emerged for a
walk when he would approach her with entreaties for her
to concede to his wish for her to return to Cranfield. The
constancy of his attentions was wearing her down, and this,
along with the agitating conscience about her responsibility
for the Clare family's par-less situation, led her to finally
agreeing to Alex's entreaties.

'Right my lovely Tess, I will send Jackson in the gig to
collect you in two days' time.'

As he rode home satisfied that he had won his way at last, he was reflecting that what he had assumed to be lust for Tess's body had been transformed into a confusing type of love. Confusing because it was the experience of feelings that he had never had for anyone. If it was a form of love then it was one based only upon his own emotional needs, lacking much consideration of the needs of the object of these feelings.

It was drizzling with rain two days later when Jackson arrived to take Tess to Cranfield.

She walked towards him with Thomas bundled in her arms. Jackson was expecting her to hand the baby to her tearful mother who was beside her carrying a small bag. But instead, Tess began to step up into the carriage with the baby still in her arms.

'No' said Jackson. 'Due to the confusion the last time I was sent to collect you, I asked the master if you would be bringing the baby with you this time. He got really angry and shouted that I was specifically only to bring you.'

'Well, if that is the case you have had another wasted journey. My baby and myself are one.'

Jackson's comment had caused her to remember the 'its' that Alex had used about the baby before it was born. It made Tess realize that he would expect to have her at the end of a cord of dependency that he could pull toward himself anytime he wished for her company. And she supposed that even if Alex allowed her to keep Thomas with her he would hold an animosity towards his bastard son for the rest of their lives together – and indeed, she thought that the same would apply to any future children that would almost certainly be the outcome of the new arrangement.

She turned back towards the cottage feeling guilty at the relief she felt of having a good reason not to return to her old job. But thinking that perhaps the coming summer would offer more field or dairy work and in the meantime she could continue to help her mother with taking in washing.

On this same afternoon one of the estate gardeners had called in to see if the boy's mother and father would be available to meet the master and his estate manager later that day. When they intended to discuss the possibility of Jude being employed as an apprentice gardener at Downland.

The thought of an unprecedented visit from the master of Downland threw much of the Clare household into a mostly ineffective storm of work. Lots of activity and bustling around but little achieved other than objects that had been in one place were moved to another. And dust on some shelves was dusted just enough to settle on the shelf below. Albeit some surfaces were a little bit cleaner, and the floors were perhaps a bit less dirty. But a sense of trepidation was clearly etched on the faces of Joan and Tom Clare as they past a nervous hour or so waiting for the visit.

In due course James and Joe arrived at the Clare family home, ducking their heads to enter and being invited to sit on the rustic chairs pulled up at the time-worn wooden kitchen table. The visitors could not fail to notice the obvious poverty of the family. The cracked kitchen sink, sacking curtains, chairs with obvious repairs but still leaning at awkward angles, and a general air of wear and tear.

Through the misted summer sun and winter frost aged glass of the small window James could see the girl/woman Tess tending to some flowers that served as a colourful border to the family's onion, potato, and turnip plot.

After he had introduced himself and Joe, and Tom had called Tess in and, in turn, introduced all members of the family, with each of the girls effecting a pretty curtsy, James suggested that they all step out into the garden.

'Good idea.' said Joan indicating for Tom and Jude to

take out the four chairs set around the kitchen table.

Once the family and its visitors had settled in the garden James set out his plan for Jude. A plan for a type of apprenticeship that he had been thinking about.

'Mr and Mrs Clare, I can see that Jude is a bright lad and included in my idea of an apprenticeship is an intention to see if we can send him away to one of the farms I know of in Essex that are in the vanguard of modernization, or even for him to spend time in London working the park gardens at Kew where Sir Joseph Banks had been managing the growing of plants from across the world before his death last year. I want Jude to learn as much as possible about modern farming methods so that he will be able to learn about the type of gardening and farming that will take English agriculture into the nineteenth century. The methods that will increase the productivity of farming and so provide the food to feed our country's fast-growing population. He will also learn about the craft of caring for a large garden.

Seeing the frown on Joan's face he added that.

'He will not be sent from home until he is older Mrs Clare – probably around fifteen years. But if he is to get the best out of these times away he will need to learn to read and write at least to a reasonable standard. Right so that's my plan, what do you think?'

It was a lot for Tom and Joan to take in – but from what they could understand it seemed to be a real opportunity for Jude.

'Look' said Joe 'Why don't you two have a think about what we have said and let us know your decision over the next couple of days.'

Joe's own childhood was not dissimilar to Jude's in terms of economic conditions so he was aware of the way Tom and Joan would be struggling to take on board what had happened in the past hour.

Their complete surprise at the master of a substantial estate coming to their door at all and then actually offering them a genuine say in their son's future. Rather than being told by a farmer or head gardener at best that: 'This is the job, this is the pay, take it or leave it.' style they would have expected. But here on their small patch was the master himself.

Tess, who had been gently bouncy Thomas on her knees spoke up during the pause in conversation.

'I can teach Jude to read and write. I had already started before I went into service, and we have returned to some lessons since I have been home.'

James could not have failed to notice such a good-looking young women, and he now could also see that there was an intelligence beyond the beauty. He had a natural curiosity about why a baby for one so young and seemingly unmarried. Perhaps Joe, or more likely Mary, would know the story.

The two men left the family still in something of a collective daze, but both Tom and Joan already had a sense of something good being on offer for Jude.

Chapter Three

The next morning when Joe came up the steps to the terrace at the back of the house he was invited to sit down to share coffee and bread rolls with James. He then began running through a couple of issues involving feedback from a some of the tenant famers arising from the earlier meeting in the big barn. Joe then moved on the say that Tess Clare had called first thing that day and, after apologising for her father's inability to walk the mile or so to the Hall, she had told him that the family very much appreciated the offer made to Jude and that her parents would be very happy if the boy could become a trainee gardener on the estate.

'That's good' said James 'I think the young lad will be an asset and he could be gardening here for the next fifty or more years.'

'Yes, but we need to curb his tendency to pilfer produce.' observed Joe with a smile.

'Well, it seems that this was simply a response to the poverty of his family and I can hardly condemn him.' said James

'Thinking of the Clare family Joe, could you ask Mary if she know anything about the young women Tess.'

Joe looked at James and raised his eyebrows.

'No Joe' said James 'I have no personal interest in the girl in the way that your look suggests. I am at least twice her age, and in any case I am pretty much a confirmed bachelor now. My interest was sparked by the level of literacy that she seems to have achieved, and she has a certain look of intelligence that I wasn't expecting.'

'OK, my own view is that the girl is likely to have been

the victim of the, probably unwanted, attention of her last employer, not uncommon in Manor House settings. The girls are vulnerable, and some masters and their sons treat servants as conveniently usable and easily disposable.

But I will put your query to Mary and no doubt she will seek you out at some point in the next couple of days. In the meantime, can you spare some time to meet up with Christian Greenwood the young man who tenants a 50 acre farm at the farther end of the estate. He came to the estate office last week and it seems that he wants to discuss the possibly of draining a section of his land that is waterlogged for most of the year. I am still feeling my way into farming James and as this looks to be a significant piece of land-work I would value your coming along if you have time.'

'You don't have to ask twice Joe – I have been wary about any possibility of undermining your authority with tenants but if you are offering an invite than I will certainly not refuse. Let's get the horses saddled up right now and get going.'

Within half an hour the pair were trotting steadily along the hedge-lined lane running from the Hall across the farmland. It was on this bright mid-spring day a land with most of the arable fields set in regular lines of shallow furrows ready to receive seeds. In others a farmer or employed worker was following a plough being pulled by a sturdy horse. Over-head gulls and crows circled, ever ready to settle behind the ploughing pair in order to enjoy the worm and insect bounty brought to the surface with the newly turned soil.

From his elevated position James could see how on some farms work was already being undertaken on buildings and on others were newly laid stretches of hedges

'Things are starting to improve Joe.' he said turning to his friend.

'Yes James, I am not saying that all tenants are signed up to our plan but most are coming round. Indeed, one of the gardeners told me that word in the Angel's Arms is that the younger tenants are quite excited by the prospects that are now on offer. It seems that the enthusiasm for modernization has been there, but the necessary capital was lacking. You have now, with a low rent period and the possibility of loans, enabled this to be available. Some of the older tenants, especially those that have enlarged their farms by acquisition of tenancies vacated over the years, are being resistant. With the recent war contributing to higher food prices all farmers have prospered to some extent but the larger farmer have been enjoying proportionately higher incomes and see little reason to change their methods. A number of these have refused even to meet with Arthur Gordon who has travelled down from up country to offer advice. The farmers he has been able to walk their land with and to discuss possible improvements do seem to have valued his input. Mind you, I am not sure that he will be here for long, but I am working on this.'

'Why do you say that Joe, is he unwell.? I was expecting that the three of us would be able to have dinner together after Arthur has had a chance to make an early assessment of the condition of the farming here.'

'If you remember James we were going to settle him into one of the empty farm labourer's cottages. But the state of these is very poor. Most have badly leaking roofs and all with crumbling mud and wattle walls. The whole two rows of twelve cottages were cheaply built and are now showing the more obvious symptoms of this. Some of the men have tried to make repairs but their wages don't run to buying the necessary materials.

It is mainly the larger farmers mentioned just now that these men work for and their wages have been reduced in the last decade from low to very low and most of them are even having to appeal to the parish for support. So having to work from 50 - 70 hours per week depending on the season, and yet still having to apply for relief. I have been putting off mentioning this James until you had properly settled in, I felt that you probably had more than enough to think about what with the house and more generally with the financial business of the estate.'

What Joe is referring to is a scandalous situation brought about with a controversial amendment to the Poor Law known as the Speenhamland System of poor relief. This was began by an act taken by gentleman-magistrates in Speenhamland in Berkshire in 1795. They decided to change the practice of setting a minimum wage paid for by employers and instead they set a quite modest basic level of income and ordered that any shortfall between this level and a worker's actual wage would be made up out of the parish rates. Costly for rate-payers and demeaning for workers. Unfortunately, this only encouraged greedy employers to reduce wage rates knowing that the amount paid by the parish would be increased to cover any shortfall. The practice spread throughout much of rural England during the first decades of the nineteenth century until it was replaced with the new Poor Law of 1834.

Joe continued, 'You may remember that we are due to have our small cottage extended but in the meantime it is quite cramped, so Mary arranged for Arthur to board at the Angel's Arms in the village. But he has had difficulty sleeping due to rowdy behaviour of some beer or cider filled locals and the food is pretty bad.'

'In that case move Arthur into the big house. I know all but my own bedroom and some of the servants' quarters are in the process of being restored and redecorated. But just find an unoccupied one of these and get Arthur moved in. When we get back to the Hall I will ask cook to prepare diner for the four of us for tomorrow evening.'

At this point the pair had reached the farm tenanted by Christian Greenwood and they could see him in the yard energetically cleaning some tools. As they drew their horses to a gentle halt, dismounted, and were tying them to a tethering post, Christian ceased his work and walked towards them. The friendly hellos and easy handshaking were followed by the three of them settling down on a couple of benches set against the sun-warmed south facing side of the modest farmhouse. The farmyard in front of them was dominated on the opposite side by a thatched barn, the sides of which had been coated with a flat-black wood preservative and along the front the pastel-coloured flowers of hollyhocks were contrasted by the dark background. These vertical strips of colour being enhanced by the yellow-flowered cowslips growing in the earth alongside the light green hollyhock stems.

Joe set the focus for their conversation. 'Christian, I understand that you wanted to discuss a more significant aspect of improving your farm.'

'Thanks Joe, I would rather think about my plan as improving my own prospects. But, of course, the specific actions involve the land and the buildings around us. The change which in terms of my lease requires your agreement, would include the draining of Marsh Field. A section of appropriately named meadowland abutting the River Trone at the northern end of the farm. In its current state I can at best only graze cows for about five months of the year because the land becomes waterlogged as soon as the river get swollen with rain water. The water-table is particularly high due to heavy clay from about two feet down.'

'So Christian' said James, 'Three questions: how do you propose draining the meadow? What would you then do with the land? What would be the impact on the flow of the river? On this last point, I assume that your meadow is currently serving as a flood plain for the river, so if you drain the land and raise embankments to prevent it flooding in the future the flow of the river could increase quite markedly, with an impact downstream.'

Christian leaned forward and turned his head from James to Joe as he was speaking, he said.

'I will respond to your questions by covering the first two together before moving on to the third one…..Drainage will be by ditches lined with the type of thick terracotta water-pipes being made at a brickworks over Dorchester way. I calculate two lines of piping set horizontally about two feet down with fine grid-covered vertical piping running down to these from just below soil level. It will take a bit of thinking about but, if strategically well-placed in what is currently the wettest parts of the field, then much of the water could be drained from the land.

For the first year after drainage, I intend using the land for year-round grazing. Then the plan for following years is to use half of the field for hay, and half for beet alternating with green fodder– so this will provide for the animals. I currently have to buy in fodder for part of the year. The drained field should provide sufficient fodder to not only feed my animals all year round but also allow me to increase the size of the herd. So an increased meat and milk production and more income to invest in the farm.'

James was impressed by Christian's intension to re-invest the forecast extra income, this suggesting a longer-term outlook.

'As to the third question about the flow of the river. I would admit that this does need more investigating. There are some flood-plain areas further down river and I think that some of the farmers both up and down-stream would like to draw more water from the river. This would be mostly in the dryer summer period when the river is usually quite low. But there has been talk of farmers digging out reservoirs and so be able to take water from the river during the wetter winter and storing it for use in the dry season. Up to now there has been limits set on the amount of water each of the farms, adjacent to the river from the Trone hills to the sea at Bedmouth, can draw. So any additional flow caused by my drainage plan would allow the limits to be increased.'

'You have obviously thought this plan out Christian' observed Joe 'And I can see that it would a make a useful contribution to your own farm in terms of efficient land management. So, can I suggest that in principle you have the required agreement from the estate but that you just progress the consideration of impact on the river a bit more. Perhaps you might talk to some older people in villages along the downstream, as they would be more familiar with the river's history and so be aware of potential problem areas if the flow was to increase significantly. Best to do this follow up because if it does turn out to increase the risk of flooding down-stream then you will have to reverse the drainage and other flood prevention measures. What do you think James?'

'I think that Christian is taking just the forward-looking approach to improving farming efficiency that we were wanting to see Joe.'

A clearly relieved Christian used this encouraging comment to try out another idea on the pair.

'I have been talking with some other younger farmers and we are thinking of forming what Arthur Gordon called a mechanization cooperative, whereby a group of us commit to taking up the offer you made for a loan from the estate and then use the money to buy mechanical equipment that we can share. The practical operation of the cooperative will need some careful planning as we might all want certain machines at the same time – but the farms of the four of us most keen to progress this idea are quite close so we think that we can share on a pretty much day-to-day basis and so avoid any one of us monopolizing the machinery. Arthur said that he knew of some co-operatives that have formed in the county of Essex have asked a local dignitary to settle any disputes, of which he said there has only been a few. This person can be a local clergyman, a magistrate, or an estate manager. So we were hoping that you Joe might be prepared to fulfil this role.'

James held up his hand.

'Christian, as I said just now about the drainage plan being in line with what we want for the estate's farms, so also is this cooperative idea. But these are the more obvious innovative actions and I had been thinking that soil improvement, plant selection, and animal husbandry would also have a place in modernization. I would also say that the condition for an improvement loan is that no worker will lose their jobs as a result of new machinery.'

Christian was really pleased with the way the conversation was going and now he felt that he had an implicit invitation to talk about an aspect of farming he had put some thought into.

'I wanted to get the drainage and mechanization issues sorted to begin with sir, but I agree with your raising these other important improvement-related aspects of agriculture. And for sure we would not want to antagonise men that we have been working alongside – not just on a personal level but also because we want to avoid having to deal with the type of machine-braking activities that have been taking place in the midlands and further north over the past few years.

'But, as to the other aspect of agriculture you

mentioned….my father was a farm labourer who had taught himself to read and write – he was a tee-total home-based person, I don't think he went into his local public house once in his life. On most Saturday lunchtimes he would finish work about midday, come home, wash, eat some lunch, and then walk the eight miles into Blandford Forum to attend at what he called the workers enlightenment meetings. Anyway, this gave him an opportunity for some education and with it knowledge about agriculture from a more theoretical rather than just practical perspective….'

'Hold on Christian' said James, 'You have sparked my interest, before you come back to farming tell us a bit more about these meetings.'

'Well, if you are interested sir…. The meetings took place in the meeting hall of the Congregational Church in the centre of the town, it involved local artisans and tradesmen, including a few farm labourers, coming together in order to obtain what father called 'enlightenment', hence the previous reference to this idea. The main activity of the group was in following a programme of education – one primarily focused on basic reading, writing, and arithmetic, but which would also include history and politics. From time-to-time speakers from cities such as London, Manchester, or Birmingham, who according to father were touring the county in an attempt to inform workers on the reasons for their poverty and to inspire them to fight for change, would be invited to the meetings. A few of the members had been involved in the radical Corresponding Societies and Hampden Clubs and their campaign for parliamentary reform, so this was another aspect of the group. As a very young man I would sometime be taken along to a meeting, and I do remember the very heated arguments over politics that took place. But agreement was unanimous on the need for working people to have more say in the running of the country and in sharing the profits that their work contributed to making. I think every member had a copy of Tom Paine's pamphlet 'The Rights of Man' in his coat pocket or hidden in a draw at his home. And copies of such newspapers as the Manchester Observer, Cobbett's Political Register, and the Black Dwarf were regularly passed around between members.'

'Thanks for that informative digression Christian' said James 'I am interested in education as an antidote to ignorance and I think England would benefit from having a more educated population. But it seems that too many of the ruling class consider that an ignorant population is easier to control than an educated one would be. Anyway, back to farming.'

'Yes, so you can imagine from what I have said about him that although my father had an antipathy toward mechanization, he did take a close interest in such aspects of agriculture as soil conditions and also plant selection and animal husbandry. This was an interest that he passed on to me. The wonder of taking up a fistful of newly tilled soil and allowing it to run through your fingers. Just imagine the productive potential of something that is often shunned as 'dirt', and yet add seeds, sunlight, and rainfall, and we have the necessary conditions for the sustenance for life....

As they were riding away from Christian's farm Joe turned to James.

'Well James that was rather a surprise.'

'Yes Joe, it was refreshing to hear how articulate and informed Christian is – I think we tapped into a passion for farming that had being building up in Christian's breast for some time. We were treated to a veritable torrent of wonderful ideas on how he can modernise his farm. I think that Christian and his small collective of more forward-thinking young farmers will perhaps lead the way into nineteenth-century agriculture for the estate. And, as such, they might serve as examples to the others.'

'Hopefully that will be the case James, but I don't think that the wind of change is going to blow through some of the larger farms anytime soon – Farmers such as Henry Bedlow seem determined to resist change although they are happy to accept the no-rent/low-rent deal that you have introduced.

I have been looking back at the estate records and what I can see suggests the possibility, no probability, of collusion between the previous land agent and Bedlow and a couple of others. Mysteriously, the details of the changes of tenancy when vacancies occurred in the past ten years seem to have disappeared. Since the old master died, we know that there has been generally very lax management. Not just in terms of the state of the main house, outbuilds, Home Farm, and the tied cottages, that we have learnt more about since taking over, but also concerning certain transactions involving tenancies and indeed over supplies being bought in. There might even be sufficient evidence for us to revisit some of the tenancy contracts if you want to progress this.'

'Let's leave it for now Joe – at least Bedlow and others like him know they are dealing with a different form of management, and I don't want us to get bogged down in a number of protracted legal cases. I will try to make time over the next few months to have a one-to-one chat with Bedlow. I and not happy to keep him on a no-rent/low rent agreement if he is not prepared to at least make some effort to improve the efficiency of his farm. So, my suggestion of an advantageous deal for tenants has only been verbal and I think I said enough to make it pretty obvious that this would be conditional on a positive response from each individual tenant.'

The rest of the ride back was undertaken with each of them reflecting on the recent meeting and the implications of what Christian had suggested. As they rode along they were able to experience a still mild spring as the evening drew in. Nearing the Hall they could smell the newly cut grass mingled with the aroma of one of the cook's roast beef dinners.

'Do you fancy coming to dinner Joe?' asked James.

'I am tempted by the smells coming for the kitchen but my life will be made quite miserable if Mary has already prepared our dinner and I am not there to eat it. Mind you, as I was leaving the cottage earlier today, she said that it would be one of her pork and bacon stews tonight so that will do for me.'

After helping the stable lad to unsaddle the horses the two men parted and having washed and changed into more comfortable evening clothes James sat down to his dinner. A meal that he thought tasted even better than it had smelt. Once finished he thought that he would wander down to the kitchen to thank Jane the cook. On entering the kitchen he could see Jane hunched over a note-pad whilst Susan was washing pots at the large butler sink. On seeing James Jane got to her feet and he could see that she looked rather harassed.

'I just wanted to say how nice that dinner was Jane, but you look in a bit of a state. Sit down and tell me what's wrong.'

'Master I am in a tiss over the kitchen accounts – I just can't make the sums add up – I was never any good at numbers. I did tell master Joe when he took me on. And I am also worried that Susan is being overworked. The poor girl is worn out each night. I know there is only you in the house sir, but the cleaning work never ends. Add the washing, cooking, water heating, and keeping the fires going throughout the day, and we are struggling. I am not wanting to seem ungrateful sir. In many ways I really like working here, but you did ask me what was wrong….perhaps I best start packing.'

Coming to the end of what was, for Jane, a long speech she was quite breathless, and her already watery blue eyes were now filling with tears.

James lifted Jane's hand from the table, gently removed the cloth she had been twisting as she spoke, and said.

'Jane I am pleased that you have spoken up, I realise now that I have taken you and Susan for granted. My London house is tiny compared to the Hall and there I hire agency staff for when I am in residence. When I think about it there is a cook, two under-maids a scullery marid, and a stable-lad who also keeps the fires going. The agency takes over the household management during these periods. I have been focusing on the building work for the Hall and on the farms, but I can see that you and Susan need more help here. Leave it with me Jane and give me those kitchen accounts and I will deal with placing orders and paying bills – you just make a list of what you require. As for leaving, please forget this, I would not blame you if you do decide to leave but I would much prefer you to stay on, and the same goes for you Susan, I can guarantee to you both that additional staff will be taken on as soon as possible.'

The relief spreading across on Jane's chubby face was obvious as she took in what James had said and Susan just looked on in awe of how Jane had spoken to the master and indeed how the master had reacted.

'Wait till I tell mother and father she thought.'

Her mother had commented on how tired she had been looking so she knew that the master's intention to make life easier will be welcome news for her.

Over the following week James asked Joe to progress

hiring more staff for the house and by the end of the month one more under-maid and a scullery maid had joined the staff at the Hall. One of these living in and the other from the village. There was still the need for a house-keeper to take overall charge of running the house, but James had given this some thought and felt that he had already identified someone who might fill this key role. Even if the staff and the candidate herself might be very surprised at his thinking on this.

His idea and an opportunity to progress it came together one day when he was out for his usual walk accompanied by his new red setter. The dog 'Red', was still quite young but it had an abundance of stamina along with an inquisitive nature, and it would run back and forth in front and behind James. Pausing briefly at any scent-made interesting patch of grass verge or slight opening in a hedge where a fox or hedgehog might have passed through. By the time James reached the outskirts of the village he had walked about two miles whereas Red had covered about four!

On this day he was passing alongside the impressive Yew hedge defining the eastern boundary of the churchyard when he heard raised voices. As he rounded the end of the hedge, he saw Alex Cranfield holding his horse's bridle with one hand whilst gesturing toward Tess Clare with the other.

'If you do not agree to come back Tess I will make life for you and your family unbearable. I am quite friendly with your landlord, and I will buy the cottage and then evict you all. To prevent this all you have to do is put the child into the foundling hospital in London, or leave it with your mother, and we can have an enjoyable life at Cranfield. I can take you out of that pig-stye of a cottage and those ragged clothes. Mother has at last died so I have my freedom and we might even share a bedroom.'

Tears were streaming down Tess's face and her body

was stooped over as if cowering from his tirade. She was beside herself with worry about the threat he had made to her family. Thinking that perhaps life at Alex's beck and call was the inevitable fate of a sinner, to be immersed in sin for the rest of her life. She knew that Alex would discard her, and any children that came along, as soon as it suited him but given his threats what choice did she have? Her thoughts were in turmoil.

'Alex please, please, leave me alone and give me time to think – do you really want to live with someone who hates you for what you have done to her?'

For Alex the chance of being able to dominate Tess made her feelings about him even more exciting.

'I am sure that your hatred will turn into willing acceptance once you get to experience life, if not above stairs at Cranfield, then at least life between stairs rather than below them as before.

This is the last chance you have Tess – it's the choice between a comfortable life with me or eviction for you and your family. I will go now, but I will send Jackson for you in two days' time. Be ready to come to Cranfield or be ready for the workhouse.'

During the exchange James had remained unseen in the shadow of the hedge, holding the collar of Red. He felt it best to learn what the situation was rather than directly intervene, although his holding back from emerging and punching Alex on the nose had been difficult.

As Alex rode off at reckless speed through the village James released Red and rounded the corner to stand beside the tearful Tess.

'I heard most of that exchange Tess, and if you think that it would help, I would be happy to get involved'.

Tess looked up:

'How can you help sir, that man has the future of me

and my family in his cruel hands. I am a disgraced women with child – in effect an outcast. The choice is between my being tied to an evil man or of my family having to apply to the work-house. I am sorry sir….I am in despair. Whatever happens I hope that you will keep Jude on.'

'Let walk over to the seat by the lynch-gate Tess so that we can be more comfortable as we talk.'

Once they were seated, with Red lying at his master feet, James lifted Tess's chin with his hand and past her his linen handkerchief.

'Tess tell me to mind my own business if you wish but let me offer my assessment of the situation and I will also mention a possible way forward that could suit us both.'

From being slightly curious as they walked towards the seat Tess's mood sunk back now thinking that she might just be going from one demanding master to another…..why do women suffer so. As mere playthings for powerful men.' she asked herself.

James was immediately aware of what she might be thinking.

'No Tess, I do not want to misuse you as he has. I want to offer you a job, not more pain.'

If still wary, Tess did relax and briefly told James what had happened to her from the time she left home to go into service.

'So here I am sir….. seated here before you is a 'fallen woman.'

'What I see Tess is an intelligent women who has been a victim of circumstances beyond her control. Circumstances that included the poverty of your family. And this now serving as a lever to draw you back under that man's control. What's his name?'

'He is Sir Alex Cranfield of Cranfield Hall.'

'Well, I have a proposition, or rather a job offer, to put

to you Tess, but if you decide to reject my suggestion. I will guarantee that your family will not be homeless – we have a number of cottages used by farm-workers. They are in poor repair just now, but we are soon going to begin a process of restoration using the same builders that will be completing work on the Hall by the end of the month. They will then move on to extending the estate manager's cottage, and the tied cottages. Two of these cottages are currently vacant and if necessary your family can move in. This will need to be into one of the last cottages to be ready for occupation as the current cottagers must come first. But this should not take long, and I think we can make sure that your family are not evicted by their current landlord before a cottage is ready.'

Tess was rather confused – why would such an important person be talking to her like this if he did not want something more than an employer/employee relationship?

'In normal circumstances Tess the estate manager Joe would have approached you. But what happened just now provided an opportunity for me to raise the subject with you. I am sure that Joe won't mind me stepping in. Anyway, the job on offer is that of housekeeper at the Hall….now before you say that you don't have any experience, are too young, have a young child so can't live in etc. I have given this some thought.'

Tess was surprised that James had just run through the very doubts that had immediately crossed her mind. At the same time there was a sense of excitement mingled with the doubts.

'According to Joe, when your Jude has been working in the garden it seems that he never misses an opportunity to brag about your reading, writing, and number skills – but brag in a proud brotherly way. And I think I have learned to be a good judge of people's potential – this was a necessity when we needed to promote the best soldier in the ranks

when commissioned and non-commissioned officers were killed or injured. I accept that this was men, but I can't see how my judgement would differ according to sex. Your intelligence shines out of your eyes Tess. I do understand that it will take time for you to ease into the job, perhaps we can arrange for you to shadow a housekeeper at another estate. As to your child, Thomas I think is the boy's name…..
well we have plenty of rooms at the Hall and I am sure that we can find a couple of rooms for you to share. The boy can grow up between spending time with your parents and time at the Hall where he will have access to the gardens.

I have given you quite a lot to think about Tess, so you probably need time to consider my proposition.'

Tess looked away from James as she took in the green, tree-lined valley sides beyond the village – What a change of fortune in just an hour or so, she was thinking.

'Sir I feel that you have in a way set light to my life. Part of my duties at Cranfield was to read stories to the poorly sighted mistress each evening. One time I began on a book with a main character that would get into various adventures as he sought to right wrongs impacting harshly on the poor and weak. After just a few pages the mistress rejected this book as nonsense, and I was ordered to find something more sensible. But I kept the book in my room and would read it whenever I could. Well sir you remind me of that gallant hero 'Sir Hector of Leeds'.

Now Tess was smiling, even if there were still the fading marks of dried tears on her soft cheeks.

'I think that I will have to keep pinching myself over the next few days just to be convinced that I hadn't just dreamed up your wonderful offer. I do have doubts about my being able to do the job and I would ask that you dismiss me if I do fall short of the required standard'

'Stop Tess.' said James, holding up his hand. 'Even if

the housekeeping job does not work out then I am sure that we can find another place for you at the Hall. You come and see me in three days' time, so Friday, and let me know what you think.'

With that James rose from the seat, beckoned to the eager Red, and continued on his walk. Feeling pleased to have had the opportunity to raise a matter that had been fermenting in his mind since the time when Joe and himself had visited the Clare family cottage to discuss Jude's future.

He left a still dazed Tess endeavouring to clarify her own rather jumbled thoughts – but what already cut through these was the clear sense of relief that Alex Cranfield could now be out of her life forever!

When the following Friday came round a still excited Tess faced her first challenge which was to meet Jackson when he arrived from Cranfield and to turn him away empty handed.

'The master won't like this Tess, but I can understand your decision. You are well out of Cranfield the master is mostly drunk and always abusive. I think that most of the servants would leave if job prospects were not so poor over Brockhampton way. Mind you, the crazy way he rides might mean that he is not long for this world. And fortunately for us, he spends about three weeks every month living at his London club. I wish you all the best for the future Tess.'

Buoyed up with this encounter she skipped as much as walked the mile to the Hall – Her little sister Elsa had taken charge of looking after Thomas. The countryside experienced along the way had clearly fully emerged from winter with hawthorn blossom in the hedgerows, cow-parsley on the grassy verges, and the occasional heavy-bodied bumble bee drifting between bright-coloured wild flowers. But as she climbed the steps to the front door of the Hall she began to feel quite nervous. What if the master has changed his mind? What if she had misunderstood the offer?

Susan answered the door, said that the master was expecting her and led her through the house and out onto the wide terrace where James was enjoying morning coffee while he was looking over the household accounts.

He stood up to greet Tess then directed her the to a woven rattan chair as he asked Susan to bring more coffee.

Unused to such attention, Tess felt uneasy and was somewhat tongue-tied in response to James's small talk about the weather, as he endeavoured to put her at ease. Once the coffee had been served he leant forward and said.

'Well Tess, what do you think about my proposition?'

The time spent on the previous day rehearsing what she would say at this meeting enabled Tess to focus and her nerves slid away as she replied.

'Firstly, I want to say how much I appreciate your offer, even if I do have some doubts about whether I can manage the work. But your generous comments outside the Church this week have given me the confidence to accept.'

She glanced away from him as she sipped her coffee and awaited his reaction.

James smiled broadly.

'I am so pleased that you will be working here Tess, indeed that you will be running the household. So, if you want to think about moving in over the coming weeks. In the meantime, you can begin the process of familiarising yourself with the layout of the building, talk to the other members of staff, and also spend some time with Joe's wife Mary. Mary has been doing some of the housekeeper's work and I think that she has a pretty good understanding of what the job entails. I have the household accounts here covering the two months that I have been living here so these will provide information on the financial aspects of provisioning the Hall. You will be working under Joe's management so for any significant issues to do with the running of the Hall these will need to be discussed with him. The plan is that you will meet him once a month to up-date him and at that time you will hand him a copy of the updated accounts. I do accept that you have a lot to get to grips with Tess. I will advance you a month's pay today and an additional five pounds for you to buy clothes appropriate for a housekeeper.

So, let's walk over to the Home Farm where I think that Joe is overseeing the cleaning out of the winter quarters of the cows. I will hand you over to him to make a start on your working together. Oh, and he will show you the two rooms upstairs that we have identified as quarters for you and Thomas. These will need furnishing, so let Joe know what you require, and he can order this from Dorchester and you might also have a chat with Susan's father, Amos, who is currently working on bookcases for the library. See if there is any furniture or fittings that he can help with. He has a list of carpentry work to do in the house but much of this can wait and your rooms will take priority.'

After leaving Tess with Joe, James walked slowly back to the Hall reflecting that the staffing of the household was now complete. And although Joe had expressed doubts about Tess's youth and lack of specific experience James was confident that with sufficient support and encouragement Tess would grow into the role. To follow up another commitment made to Tess he had already asked Joe to keep one of the two vacant cottages available for the Clare family.

He had a sense that he could now relax for a time and enjoy life in the countryside for a while, a time to nourish his spirt before he returned to consider the progress of his army veterans' campaign.

Chapter Four

And so the weeks passed, with James taking long walks accompanied by an ever enthusiastic Red and taking even longer horseback rides on his own. In these weeks Tess settled into her new working life at the Hall, and with Joe over-seeing the progress being made on the estate's farms. The drive to modernise was somewhat uneven across the estate – the younger famers with less land were uniformly keen on making changes, most of the others were if cautiously, following this lead. But a few of the tenants of larger farms were resolutely uncooperative. After talking with all of the latter group Joe had assessed that Henry Bedlow was at the centre of this group and that if he could be persuaded to modernise the rest would probably follow.

It was during this time that the Hall had a visit from a clergyman, one filled with a sense of his own importance, who was undertaking the annual round of the manor houses and stately homes sited within the five large parishes that he held the livings for. The income generated by these livings allowed this individual to enjoy a very comfortable lifestyle. This man, the Very Reverend Ernest Marks, son of a bishop and grandson of a bishop, also expected ecclesiastical elevation in-line with the family tradition quite soon. After graduating from Oxford University, he then passed the examination on Scripture, Liturgy and Church doctrine, one overseen by the Bishop of Oxford who was fortunately a friend of his father. He was duly ordained and was then able to accumulate the affluent livings that his father's contacts with the peerage and landed gentry of the county had in their gift. The demands of Ernest's spiritual work rested but lightly on his shoulders with poorly paid curates undertaking the more mundane work of each parish. Mundane being almost all the work that would have bought the Anglican Church into contact with the poor of a parish, even if most of those who were not in abject poverty were also expected to contribute to the parish's tithe-based income. The aspects of the role that he did diligently carry out was to attend to the more delicate spiritual life of the aristocrats and gentleman farmers. Some evidence of his diligence in these matters being noted by his expansive waist-line.

The visitor's impressive Landau carriage drew up outside the Hall, with the footman nimbly jumping down from his seat beside the coachman to open the door for his master, then running up the front steps to knock on the main door while the Very Revered Marks lightly dusted down his frock coat as he took in the impressive newly restored facade of the building. He noted with satisfaction the sweeping drive and more general opulence that the Hall and its setting expressed. He was disappointed when the door was opened by a maid rather than a butler or even a footman, but he reasoned that perhaps the new master was still engaged in the protracted task of staffing the Hall.

Having received a letter a week or so earlier James was expecting this visit so when Reverent Marks was shown into the drawing-room he was ready to welcome him. He stood up and holding out his hand said, 'It is a pleasure to receive a visit from you Reverend Marks, I hope that you had a comfortable journey?'

'Passably so' said the Reverend 'But the roads are getting evermore busy.'

'Susan will take you to your room for the night and when you have rested we can have lunch.

The stable lad will attend to your coaching staff and the horses.'

Within an hour the Reverend was sitting with James at a table ladened with newly cured ham and a variety of local cheeses, along with bread still warm from the oven and pickles from the larder.

The talk at table was mostly just concerning the Reverend voicing his critical opinion about local dissenter groups and his praising of the artistic taste, well-presented tables, and the port and claret of a number of local landowners with whom he had been spending time of late.

All the while James's assessment of his guest was sinking from neutral to being unimpressed.

After lunch they retired to the newly restored garden room with an outlook over the walled garden.

'A very pleasant home for a gentleman such as yourself sir.' (This was the companionable 'sir' of social equals addressing each other, not the hierarchical 'sir' proffered by the subordinate)

'Yes', said James 'We are making progress in developing the Hall, and indeed the estate more generally, into a modern agricultural unit.'

'I note that you describe the estate in terms of agriculture sir and of course the practical side of managing an estate is important but have you also considered your social responsibilities? I understand that, as yet, you have not accepted any of the invitations that you have received from other local large landowners.'

'That's true your Revered…. initially this was due to the work required here taking up most of my time. But just recently, when I was ready for at least some level of social activity and had sent out invitations to others, I received polite refusals and no repeat of invitations to events elsewhere.'

'I think that I might know the reason for this sir. It reflects your employing what is frankly a sinner to run your household….Now I know it might seem as a small thing, after she is only a servant, but morality runs deep in a rural community. Let's not make too much of this because now that you are aware of the obstacle to social acceptance, it can I am sure be easily removed.'

James was trying to supress his mounting anger.

'I am surprised that a Christian minister would so be so easily prepared to see the livelihood of a vulnerable member of his flock removed. I wonder who spread the news that Tess Clare, who I presume that you are referring to, who has kindly agreed to work at the Hall, and is quite rapidly proving herself to be able to meet the demands of running the household.'

The Reverend gentleman was taken aback by James's response, but he would be prepared to concede to his own dignity if this would enable him to gain as much information as possible to ensure that he would be the centre of attention for the gossiping that would take place in drawing and dining rooms elsewhere in the coming weeks.

'It was introduced quite by chance as a topic during a post-hunt dinner at Cranfield Hall when the ongoing issue of obtaining reliable staff came up. Sir Alex Cranfield had spoken of a foolish maidservant that had managed to get pregnant and his having to let her go. Judging by the comments of others present this is not an uncommon occurrence. It seems like the heads of young girls get turned, presumably by male servants, when they leave home. As the Bible says: 'He who commit sin is of the devil…John 3 verse 4'

'Yes', said James but I seem to remember that a couple of lines further on it notes that: 'No one born of God commits sin: for God's nature abides in him,… And while we are on the subject of theology can you please tell me why the curate of the village church here has refused to baptise Tess Clare's son.'

The Reverend Ernest was reddening and puffing out his cheeks as he struggled to mentally come to terms with James – an individual specimen of the rare sub-species of human…. a country gentleman with socially liberal notions.

'The curate was only acting as myself as a senior representative of the Church and the likes of Sir Alex Cranfield would expect him to….In fact he was carrying out God's will.'

James looked his guest squarely in the eye and said. 'I have another Biblical quote for you, Jesus said 'Suffer the little children to come to me, and do not hinder them: for such belongs to the Kingdom of Heaven Matthew verse 19.

And, as to Alex Cranfield, you are entirely ignorant of his role it the matter of Tess Clare. If you knew the truth you might hold him in a very different light.'

'Are you comparing the word of a serving maid to that of a knight of the realm?' spluttered the Reverend.

'No' replied James 'I am taking the word of a young women whose innocence has been violated. But I don't think that we will be able to agree on this issue and we clearly would not agree on how to treat Tess. If this costs me a local social life then that's fine, In fact, I would have to thank you for my finding out the unchristian and boorish attitudes of the county's upper classes without having to sit through a series of drawn-out dinner parties to discover this.

I have not been the most assiduous Christian, indeed my experience of warfare has made me question my faith entirely, but as a child I had intensive exposure to Christian teaching both in the local village church and at the grammar school that I attended….If my commitment to the Anglican Church is in doubt I would say that I recognise the eternal truths set out in some sections of the Gospels.'

The Very Reverend stood up and being hardly able to contain his obvious anger within even his substantial body he said: 'I do not think that I can spend a single night under your roof sir – please arrange to have my carriage prepared and I will remain in my room praying for your mortal soul until the carriage , the horses, and my men are ready to leave.'

'Please do not spend this time praying over my soul, I would much rather you use it to consider your own moral outlook as this relates to the teachings of Jesus noted throughout the Gospels.'

'Humph….I can't stand anymore of this.' exclaimed the Very Reverend as he stormed for the room.

'Well, that went well' thought James.

'At least I don't have to spend any more time in the company of that unwholesome individual – but if I do ever run across Alex Cranfield again then I will have some difficulty supressing my anger.'

In the weeks that followed this rather dramatic confrontation the household gradually settled into a regime that seemed to suit both the master and staff. The atmosphere above and below stars was pleasantly warm, partly at least due to the workload being much easier as it was now spread across more hands. The organization and financial management improved at a pace as Tess came to terms with the complex business of running a large country house. And little Thomas revelled in having the run of the garden adjoining the main house.

It was a practice that whenever possible provisions for the Hall would be bought in from some of the estate's farms. And it was on a day in early May that Christian Greenwood was due to deliver some eggs, butter and cheese to the kitchen. By the time he had walked the two miles or so to the Hall, what had been a sunny morning when he had set off had turned to overcast and then to a gathering of dark clouds that soon offered up a veritable deluge of rain. So, when he tumbled through the doorway into the utility room adjacent to the large kitchen Christian was soaked through, his having worn only the lightest of smock.

He shook himself and his clothing as he entered the kitchen, which only enhanced his dishevelled look. The cook and scullery maid looked up at his entrance and could not supress their laughter at his appearance. Tess was seated with the cook at the large well-worn oak-wood table that dominated the centre of the room and she smiled at the sight of the farmer. This was the first time that Tess and Christian had met, and Christian was immediately taken with the housekeeper. They merely exchanged polite hellos and then Tess collected up her papers and left, leaving Christian to gaze somewhat forlornly at her retreating back.

'Close your mouth Christian, stop gawping and sign here for payment for your produce' said the smiling cook – 'The butter looks to be a lovely deep yellow and the cheese tastes as good as we have come to expect.'

Christian hardly noted the cook's praise and was in something of a daze as he slowly walked back to his farm.

'My goodness he thought, that is the women that I want to marry. She had introduced herself as the housekeeper but I had assumed that the housekeeper of the Hall would be cast in the similar imposing mould as those few I have already experienced. That she would be something of sharp-eyed, hard-faced, harridan, not the beautiful slip of a women I have just met. I wonder what her name is. What if she is already married!'

As Christian had not grown up in the local village, he had not seen Tess before today and he was already thinking about how he could arrange for them to meet again.

Our would-be lothario was unaware that all that Tess had retained from their brief meeting in the kitchen was that she had met a pleasant enough looking young man – but nothing more. Bear in mind that the background for Tess's outlook on life was of her being a used woman, a sinner in the eye of the Church, condemned to a life of spinsterhood. The thought of any sort of romantic attachment with anyone was just not an aspect of her outlook.

James's life at this time was quite settled, he felt comfortable with progress on the estate. The restoration work on the Hall had now been completed as had almost all of the redecoration. All but two of the workmen had moved on to the worker's cottages where they were following a plan of repair and refurbishment drawn up by Joe.

It was another fine late spring morning when, to the melodic chirping of a Robin that had settled on the back of a garden chair and the more raucous crowing of a cock nearby, James's was mulling over two matters.

One being the need to tackle the tenant farmers who were proving to be reluctant about modernization. The other was the London gang of army veterans who had been raising funding for their own futures and more so for the co-operative farming project in Devon. He was thinking that six months on the north London based gang had been making well-rewarded progress. Their having gained a considerable amount of funds, primarily made up of gold bullion and gold guineas. But now the forces of authority seemed to be focusing considerable resources on tracking them down. This due partly to the amount of embarrassing publicity the audacious raids were generating. But also due to the fact that most of the guineas were being transported to government offices as tax from the Home counties and all of the gold bullion had been intercepted on the way to regional banks for distribution to jewellery manufacturers and investors, or to the Royal Mint on the north bank of the River Thames near Aldgate.

Earlier in the week James had received a letter from Ezra informing him (using a simple code that they as soldiers had learnt to use for communication in the field of conflict) that one of the gang had been shot during a raid involving a coach traveling along the Great North Road. The coach had two well-armed officers hiding within, as well as an armed postilion astride one of the four horses. And although the four gang members could probably have killed or wounded the defenders, they were aware of James's order to avoid seriously harming anyone and so had fled the scene of the attempted robbery. It was in the process of retreating that one of them was shot, fortunately not seriously.

It seemed to James that the balance of financial gain measured against risk of capture was rapidly tipping towards the latter and it was time to bring the gang's activity to an end. He intended to reply to Ezra's letter later that day and would be advising him and the others to lie low for the time being, think about possible futures for themselves beyond that of highway robbery, and that he would be coming up to London within the next two weeks to meet up with them.

Before making that trip he would ask Joe to set up a meeting up with Farmer Bedlow and themselves in order to gain some understanding of why he was not prepared to introduce modern farming methods and if possible to persuade him to change his mind on this. If the farmer remains implacably against change, then he will be informed that the generous arrangements for tenancy rents that James had offered will not be available to him. James reasoned that if he could persuade Bedlow to cooperate on (if not perhaps embrace) agricultural improvement then the rest of the small group of more reluctant farmers would be more amenable to change.

It was just two days later that Bedlow eased his sturdy horse to a halt at the rear of the Hall and dismounted somewhat awkwardly due to his bulk.

James came lightly down the steps from the terrace to greet him and, taking him gently by the arm, he guided the guest up to the terrace where a table was laid out for a substantial lunch and beside which Joe was seated with a batch of papers and some pamphlets on his knees.

The famer was suspicious about having been asked to come to a meeting – suspicion and caution came naturally to him, his being used to fiercely measuring most encounters in relation to his own financial interests.

James began the conversation. 'Look Henry, I understand that you have been making your opposition to our plan to introduce modern farming methods to the estate very clear to some other farmers, can you say why?'

'The why sir relates to why change what works – my approach to efficient farming is larger farms, removal of hedges and so larger fields, and low rents. That sir is my prescription for success.'

'Yes' said Joe 'Looking back at what tenancy records have not mysteriously disappeared we can see that you have over the past fifteen years significantly increased the size of your farm. And it looks like the estate itself has provided funds to improve your buildings and land-drainage.'

'Yes' interrupted the famer 'This was as investment to improve the estate sir.'

'I can see that the expenditure might be seen in that light Henry, but I don't see that your rent has been increased to enable the estate to gain the benefit of the substantial investment.'

The farmer sat back in his chair and stared sullenly at

what he saw as his adversaries.

'I don't want to rehash the past.' said James, 'But I do think that we need to understand that how some of the tenancies have been managed since the old master died might not have been in the best interests of Downland. But we are where we are Henry, and I want us to draw a line under the past and move forward. Hopefully to the mutual benefit of all parties.'

Joe came in here: 'This mutual benefit will be obtained from your enjoying a period of no and very low rent and then using the freed-up capital to improve your farm and in due course the estate benefiting from higher rents in the longer term. Have a look through this pamphlet Henry it outlines the experience of Sir Edward Coke at Holkham Hall in Norfolk. It sets out the significant benefits that have been gained by Sir Edward as the landlord and the tenants following a series of agricultural improvements.'

'But the soils of Norfolk are light whereas much of our soil here in mid- Dorset is quite heavy.'

'Accepted' said Joe 'But if you change from iron to steel ploughs, use the new mechanical seed drills rather than the traditional broadcast method, and grow turnips and green fodder crops such as alfalfa and clover, then you would be making a good start in terms of efficiency of the land and improved quality of winter food for your animals. Fatter animal equals higher on-the-hoof prices.'

The famer was rapidly re-assessing his situation….his strong sense of survival served as a wider mental context for considering his position. Agree to modernise or possibly face the prospect of forgoing a period of lower rent.

'As part of your consideration of what we have been discussing Henry you also need to be aware that the period of your, and some other tenants of the estates, progressively lowering wages and then expect the parish to take up the shortfall also needs to come to an end. We would expect that all the farm workers will need to be paid at least what you are currently paying them plus any parish relief that is begrudgingly being provided. Whatever you decide about modernisation this is a must. Not to agree will mean that we will not allow you to pass on the tenancy of your farm to your son, who I believe is currently managing most of the day-to-day work.

'But this will increase our expenses quite considerably.' spluttered the farmer.

'This might be the case' said James 'But for too long you have you been taking advantage of a system made possible by the well-intentioned but foolish action of the Speenhamland magistrates to allow farmworkers to gain at least a very minimum living wage. Action which has allowed some landowners and large tenant farmers to choose to exploit the parish rate-payer and to undervalue their workers. In any case, I understand that some members of parliament are becoming aware of the impact on their constituents and are campaigning to have the Act repealed.' *(This would eventually happen in 1834 following a Royal Commission undertaking a review of the system. The Commission report referred to the Act as being '...a universal system of pauperism.')*.

Farmer Bedlow was obviously uneasy, he had expected a difficult meeting, but this had been alarming. He felt that he needed to absorb the implications of what had been put to him. The priority was keeping the tenancy in the family even if this meant some reduction in his own very comfortable lifestyle. Then remembering the pamphlet, he had been given by Joe he was beginning to think that perhaps modernization might just be a way of increasing the farm's income – and perhaps his son Joseph might be the one to take this on.

After the meeting broke up Bedlow rode slowly back to his farm. During the thirty-minute ride his thinking progressed from resentment at what he had just faced, if relief at the idea on drawing a line under his dubious dealings with the previous land-agent, to a gradual realisation that the prospects for the farm, and so his son, might actually be improved if they were to embrace change.

As they watched Farmer Bedlow ride away Joe turned to James and said.

'I think that we have set out our position pretty clearly James. He should not have any misunderstanding of the future he now faces as a tenant farmer on the Downland Park Estate.'

James looked somewhat pensive.

'Time will tell Joe, if our attempt to balance advice and information with an underlying threat will work on the man. I hope so and that within the next week he gets back to you to ask for a meeting with Arthur who, I am pleased to see, seems to have settled into his new quarters in the first of the tied cottages to have been renovated.'

After the pair had worked through the estate's other business James informed Joe that he was going to London for a few weeks, primarily in order to oversee the ending of the north-London gang.

'What do you think they will do then?' asked Joe 'Afterall their skills were military, so quite limited employment prospects.'

'I do have a few ideas, said James 'and they will each have the 5% share of each robbery we have used to buy government bonds.'

Chapter Five

It was a week later that James was standing by a front drawing room window contemplating the scene in Hanover Square, London. The square was in a quieter area of the capital but even so today he could see a number of fashionable dressed residents out taking their late morning stroll around the grassed central area. With a young gentleman enthusiastically riding a wood rimmed hobby-horse type of bicycle down the centre of the recent paved road, dodging this way and that as he endeavoured to avoid the horse-drawn vehicles carrying people and goods about the square. There were also a number of the black and grey suited nannies pushing prams or holding the hands of their young charges. Then there were the servants running various types of errands, and he could see one of the newly uniformed postmen with a heavily ladened bag making his way along the rows of white painted Georgian terraces lining each side of the square. The postman stopped at James's front door and with this being opened in response to his knock, he handed a small batch of letters to the maidservant. He also tried to catch her eye as he smiled and commented on the weather. In return she shyly smiled back and only very slowly closed the door. And so, the seed of a new relationship was planted and in due course the maidservant would be invited out for a Sunday afternoon walk in a park, with this being followed by more of these and the occasional trip to one of the music halls that had recently been added to the popular entertainment on offer in the growing city. In due course this relationship would develop from shy and rather awkward interaction into a more familiar, and so more comfortable, intimacy and on to become a permanent coupling sanctioned by the Church. And in time a long line of children and grandchildren would follow. Such is the romantic mystery that can grow from but chance meetings.

The day's mail was delivered to James by the maid as he was relaxing in a comfortable chair reading the Times newspaper. The letter that drew his immediate interest was one in a cheaper looking envelope which he correctly assumed was from Ezra in response to one he had sent prior to leaving Downland the previous week. Ezra's rough handwriting simply noted his being able to meet with James in the Three Tuns pub by the Seven Dials on the next day, a date that James had suggested.

After an evening spent reading a couple of books on agriculture that he had ordered from the publishers he decided on having an early night.

He awoke refreshed and ready for a longish walk following a circular route taking in west and northern London prior to his lunchtime meeting with Ezra. After breakfast he set off west through Grosvenor Square crossing Park Lane to the expansive tree dotted green area of Hyde Park, stretching out to the west of the city.

It was only a couple of months since he had last visited London but even so he could the changes. What had been markets gardens growing cash crops to feed the urban population as well as the gardens of private houses, were being built upon – making way for offices, shops, and rows of mostly modest houses.

His walk up the west side of Park Lane took him to what had been the village of Tyburn, but which was now part of the expanding capital. The village had gained notoriety because of its long history of providing the location for public executions up until the late 18th century. This gruesome activity had more often been the end of life for those such as pirates, Catholics and highwaymen. But during the 18th century the penalty of death by hanging had grown from being applied to about 60 criminal offences to about 200. And these now included such acts as cutting down a tree, stealing from a rabbit warren or stealing goods to the value of the paltry sum of one shilling.

This legal system 'The Bloody Code', was a result of the reaction of a frightened upper class to a significant increase in crime, this being primarily due to the presence of abject poverty alongside more obvious affluence.

The hangings at Tyburn had become but another form of popular entertainment available for Londoners. Thousands would follow the condemned men and women along their final three-mile journey that took in the length of Oxford Street. Along the route would be pedlars and hawkers selling their various wares as well as many pickpockets dartling nimbly amongst the crowds pressing forward to get a sight of the carts moving slowly along. Pickpockets who themselves could soon be making the same journey in one of the creaky old carts containing those condemned to dance at end of a rope. Carts with some of the felons protesting their innocence, others waving and blowing kisses to the crowd, and a few with their eyes downcast seemingly placidly accepting the inevitability of their fate. This, the 'Tyburn Fair', had become a regular event in the monthly calendar, with as many as twenty felons being executed each time.

After contemplating the dismal history of Tyburn James continued north towards Paddington, a small village some distance up the wide Edgware Road. A village located at the rapidly expanding outer boundary of London, with a canal opened in 1801 serving as a link drawing the village into the city. Paddington was where two major canals – the Grand Union and The Regent – terminated in a wide basin, busy with a continuous movement of horse-drawn canal boats.

James decided to use the towpath of the Regents Canal to circle round the north of the city as it offered more interesting sights and because the air was much clearer here than along the dusty roadways. The canal was a ten mile stretch of waterway running from the London Docks at Limehouse to the basin at Paddington from where goods could be taken to the midlands and further into the north of England. Carrying raw materials for manufacture as well as tea, coffee, sugar, and tobacco for consumption... all drawn from the British colonies. The raw materials being distributed to where manufacturing took place and in-turn manufactured goods could be transported back to the London docks for shipping abroad. The canal system served to convey the material life blood of the developing industrial revolution. It was system designed by clever architects but actually built by hundreds of 'navvies'. The 'navigation' labourers, many of whom had travelled from Ireland for the work. The hard-working, hard-drinking, men were a tough breed. They were relatively well-paid, as much as five shilling a day for some. But much of this would be spent in alehouses, brothels, and on gambling or horse-racing and the bareknuckle fist-fighting that many of them themselves engaged in. Theirs were for most, lives lived hard and fast and lives that were often cut short by accidents or ill-health.

As he walked along the broad towpath he had at times to avoid the muscular horses slowly towing the heavy narrow boats and also to avoid stepping in the unsavoury packages they had deposited on the path. But this inconvenience was a small irritant easily compensated for by the vibrant scene of that he could observe on the canal. The lines of colourful craft passing by, some of these being steered by self-employed boat-men – the 'number ones' – who often travelled with their families on board.

The canal skirted the northern boundary of Regents Park, so named because it had been due to the Prince Regent George's patronage being gained for the development of the land to the north of Marylebone. It was the architect John Nash who led this ambitious project one centred on the construction of luxury houses lining each of the four sides of a landscaped park area to be used by the 'wealthy and the good' as the original plan noted. Access to the park was to be only for the adjacent residents and their companions, and the so called 'carriage folk' who liked to exhibit their social status on regular outings taken in impressive phaeton carriages. In addition, an individual could apply to walk in the park at the cost of a shilling a time.

When he reached the weathered stone footbridge over the canal at Camden Lock, James paused in his walk in order to enjoy a cup of hot chocolate at a canal-side coffee shop. While waiting to be served he took a seat by the low window and reflected on the conversation he was expecting to have with Ezra later that day. These veterans had done really well in terms of money raised and in doing so they managed to avoid injuring those who had been involved in transporting the bullion and coinage that had been accumulated. Due to their work we have been able to purchase another 300 acres of farmland down in Devon, providing up to about 60 new small holdings. In addition, the London agent had organised the passage of ten ex-servicemen to America and another twelve to Australia. All this made possible by Ezra and the others risking their lives. But now it did seem to be best to cease this activity with its ever-increasing risk of being caught. And if caught the near certainty of their being hanged. It was with these sombre thoughts at the forefront of his mind that he continued on his walk....now turning away from the canal heading south towards the more central area of London.

It was about one o'clock when James arrived at the Three Tuns public house by the Seven dials and by the time he had ordered the ales for himself and Ezra his tall friend was stooping slightly as he entered the bar. The pair retreated to the corner of the bar and seated themselves at the same table they had used previously.

James was pleased to note how much better dressed was Ezra than when they had previously met and that the body being clothed had returned to a similar robustness that he had when they served together. Being a bandit clearly suited his old companion.

'So Ezra, what have Tom, Caleb, John, and yourself decided about your futures?'

'Well firstly we are all agreed that we should not push our luck any further here in London. That last attempt to stop a bullion coach shows the authorities are intent on closing our enterprise. It would be best if we do this ourselves and live to fight again. Mind you, colonel, we are wondering if we could perhaps relocate to a northern city and continue the operation. At least two of us like the excitement, as well as our share of the booty, and we are not sure what we would do if living on the right side of the law.'

James held up his hand 'Yes, but that would not work Ezra. Our informant for bullion and taxation cash movements is based at the Bank of England. We do not have any contacts in say Manchester, Birmingham, or Liverpool. In addition, the movement of money in the north would be of only relatively small amounts, and the risk of getting caught would be pretty much the same as now.'

'Yes, we did think that it would be a longshot. It probably sounds odd but being part of this gang and raising funding for your veteran-support project had given us a sense of doing something good. Add the excitement of the actual robberies and it is going to be hard to replace this in our lives.'

'OK Ezra let's leave you and the other one who shares your concerns about the future and think about the two you mentioned in your letter that do want to move on'.

'This would be John and Tom. John is intending to marry a widow-women he has met recently, and they are going to buy a coaching inn in a village called Lyndhurst down in Hampshire. Tom will be returning to the village in Kent where he grew up and will be buying into a carting business where the current owner, one of his uncles, is soon to retire. They both seem keen to start new lives. John's criminal record might mean that he will have a problem with gaining a licence to sell liquor. But he has already thought of this, and he thinks that his new wife Sarah will be able to gain the necessary licence from the local magistrate. And although it will be her name as the licensee over the doorway of the inn, he feels this will help to seal their partnership – theirs is a real mature adult love-match colonel.'

'It's good to learn that John and Tom's futures seem to be sorted. They should have more than enough funds to fulfil their plans.'

Their conversation was interrupted by a cheerful serving maid arriving at their table ladened with their hearty dinner. Both were quite hungry, and the talk lapsed while they concentrated on eating the steaming hot ham pie and potato dinner.

Within about twenty minutes they had both finished their meal and sat back in their chairs.

'Colonel' began Ezra 'Can I ask you a personal question'.

'Sure Ezra, what's on your mind?'

'Well, during the five years that we served together I always found you to be firm but fair. You had more sympathy with men in the ranks than almost all of the other officers who were generally arrogant bastards, excuse my language. You even tried to make living conditions of the mainly female camp-followers as comfortable as possible, or rather as less uncomfortable than it might have been. And I suppose this does go some way to explain your various projects for helping veterans.

But when your service came to an end you seemed to have had the prospects of a very comfortable life – perhaps marriage and children – the easy life of a country gentlemen, mixing with your own class. And yet you have invested so much of your time, and I suspect some of your own money, in helping a group of men that are pretty much the debris of history, cast aside, indeed cast down to the very bottom of the social scale. The phrase 'white knight' comes to mind sir. I am just curious to know why you have set yourself on such a hard road - indeed a road that could end with you on the gallows for complicity in capital crimes.'

James was looking unseeing into the log fire: 'Hm….. my thinking on this has been along these lines Ezra…. each of us has only one life and men like you and I signed up to military service and went to war. Wars began by royalty and politicians who treated the military as but a tool to advance their own interests - I know that they would claim any war is in a nation's interest but when I see the level of poverty in our cities and consider just how costly warring is, I do wonder whose interests are being served. But let's leave that thought and step back.

I was brought up in very comfortable circumstances – loving parents and all my material needs were well catered for. I was able to read widely and I especially enjoyed books about history, travel, and adventure. One book was particularly effective in my thinking about life. This was the novel 'Don Quixote', a tale about an aged knight whose lance was quite blunt and whose mount was a sad-eyed bony horse called Rosinante. This self-style knight travelled about his Spanish homeland invariably misreading the scenes that he encountered and getting himself involved in one difficult situation after another. From each of which his long-serving attendant Sancho Panza had to extricate him. As well as being quite funny, the basic premise of the book was that one should set out each day to help the weak and otherwise to do good. Obviously for Quixote his attempts were misplaced. But for me they were noble in intention. I carried the idea that you should try to do good whenever you encounter injustice, even if you do not fully understand the circumstances, and just like Quixote act on your instinct, and try to make your instinct tend toward the good. When I wrote to the King, the Prime Minister, a number of government ministers, and some leading generals and admirals about the plight of the ex-military I was really disappointed, indeed quite angry, with the response.

At best I received answers that expressed sympathy but no indication at all of any intended action. Action such as a pension based on length of service, or some financial grant to allow veterans to emigrate to lands with better prospects, but nothing. My instinct when I received so many disappointing replies was to challenge the state's obvious disinterest – Just Like Quixote I knew that I might only be embarking on a foolish mission, but I felt that it would at least be noble. And, as I noted when I began Ezra, we only have one life and when we consider our lives as they draw to an end, hopefully in old age, we need to be proud or at least not ashamed of how we have lived.

When I first engaged in conflict in India, I had the belief that fighting for King and Country was something to be proud of. With the East India Company, having a royal charter, so its being but a part of Britain abroad. And of course, an aura of masculine specialness pervading the military also served to boost my ego.

But observing the corruption, self-seeking, and exploitation at times crossing a line to cruelty of the Company, gradually eroded my sense of being involved in a worthwhile enterprise. My conscience was sourced in the childhood playroom, the teachings of Jesus and at boarding school. This experience instilled a sense of justice and fairness in me. These two important concepts Ezra, the content of which were only rarely seen in the Company's dealings with native people. Where most of my officer colleagues saw ignorant, grossly inferior native peoples, I could only see men and women. The poor Indian farmers, if on a smaller scale, were doing work of planting, tending, and harvesting, as well as animal husbandry, just like the workers on my father's farm – indeed just like him when he could get out of the farm office and into the field or the cowshed. Both the average native Indian farmer's and my father's lives were ordered by the seasons, the weather, and the harvest.

On the long sea-borne journey home to England I was intending to resign my commission and follow in my father's muddy footsteps. This plan was disrupted when on landing in Portsmouth I heard news of Napoleon's attempts to aggressively spread his own distorted version of the French revolution across Continental Europe. Even though my patriotism had been diluted from my experience in India, I did feel that the French general had to be stopped. So I joined the British Army and, for a modest payment I was able to retain my rank. Within weeks I had crossed the Channel to the port of Coruña on the north-west coast of Spain. I was commissioned to a regiment in the army of the newly appointed commander Major-General Sir John Moore. I was fortunate to serve under Sir John. Even prior to his deployment in Spain not only was he an excellent administrator, he had also been a pioneer in the training of troops. He had an understanding of the need to maintain troop morale and the necessity of a secure supply train to ensure efficient deployment in the field. He endeavoured to dilute the ridged and carefully modelled division between officers and soldiers of the line. This and some other measures were intended to create a sense of regimental pride – a unity in arms. Unfortunately, the unity did not always hold and the harshness of campaigning in a Spanish winter led some men to drunkenness, thievery and rape when opportunity allowed. To the point where Sir John ordered a few men to be shot as much a warning to others as a punishment. The General's ambitions were inspiring, especially after my experience in India. I wonder what he would have done if he had survived the war, but his life was cut-short during the Battle of Coruña and his body was buried in the ramparts on the outskirts of the town. Even when mortally wounded he still expressed concern about the welfare of his comrades, and he died knowing that the Battle had been won.

A longish poem was written about his end, but I can only remember the final stanza:

'Slowly and sadly we laid him down,
From the field of his fame fresh and gory;
We carved not a line, and we raised not a stone,
But we left him alone with his glory.'

I like to think that in some way I am continuing in the spirt of concern for the welfare of the troops.

General Moore provided the inspiration for this, but a particular incident stayed with me to provide vivid images that added substance to the more abstract inspiration. This happened following a long day's march in the summer of 1810 as we advanced on Burgos – the line of advance had become quite extended as the day's weather went from early morning warmth to late afternoon heat. I rode back down the line in order to gain some general idea of the condition of the whole unit and I came across a group of three troopers siting with heads down at the side of the rough track. I dismounted to talk with them just to sample the morale of the men under my command. I was rather surprised to see that they were all aged about fifty.'

He paused briefly to take a drink and Ezra could see that his old commander had become rather lost in his memories of the peninsular campaign.

James then continued with his story.

'I reflected that when I looked over a line of troops, I tended to see lines of uniforms rather than the bodies of individual men. These three were obviously exhausted. But still the sergeant major who was accompanying me began to shout orders for them to get moving. I quieted him and sat down alongside the men. I offered them water from my own bottle and asked them why at their age they we still serving.

I remember that one of them lifted his head and looked at me as if I was mad. I clearly remember the trooper's articulate answer, it went something like....'

'What else are we supposed to do sir? We three have served in the military since we were children, in fact we were never children in the sense of a having time to play. We survived our childhood by rough types of work when we could get this and thieving when we couldn't. So it was the King's shilling and service from early on for each of us. Between us we have served in Ireland, the West Indies, America, Corsica, India and now here in Spain. We have followed the flag across a number of continents sir. Yes, we are now too old to be on active service – to be honest our best prospects are a musket ball in the head and so a quick death in Battle. No one will mourn us, and our earthly travails will have come to an end.'

'Why can't you return to England and find alternative

work.'

'With respect sir you don't seem to understand what happens to an old solider. We have heard of the possibility of places at a home for long-serving veterans called The Royal Chelsea Hospital down by the River Thames in London. But from what we hear, it is hard to get a place and the inmates have to follow fairly strict rules of behaviour- you are expected to trade your freedom for a place.

Even if there were places the conditions would not suit men like us sir, men used to doing what we please within the confines of miliary discipline. If we went back to England I think we would just be legging it from one town to another, sleeping rough, and no doubt returning to the thievery of our childhoods – at least until we were caught and hanged.

One of the other troopers also spoke up…. 'Yes, it looks like the flag will continue to guide our footsteps for as long as possible sir, and now we are rested we will trudge on until nightfall.'

With that the three men rose stiffly from their resting place, shouldered their muskets and small kitbags, and re-joined the steady flow of camp-followers, supply wagons, carts, and fellow stragglers following in the dusty wake of the main body of the regiment.

This encounter stayed with me through the rest of the Peninsula campaign. From that meeting on, when I looked at a line of soldiers, I saw men not just lines of bright-coloured uniforms, men most of whom would be facing a very difficult time once the military authorities decided they were no longer fit to serve. They, like the three I had met on the road to Burgos, would struggle to survive in towns that did not want them. Men with only a few medals and the nightmares from their bloody experiences to remind them of their younger selves.'

As James came to an end of his story both men held eye contact and knew that between them there was a new level of understanding connected to a shared past.

'I am sorry to go on Ezra – we each have our own past to come to terms with. But I think I needed to say out loud thoughts and feelings that I have only ever kept to myself. I feel somewhat relieved and this has reinforced my view that we are doing something that is justified.'

'I feel honoured to have been able to listen and you have put into words reasons for our work that hits home with me sir.'

'Having got that off my chest, we should now return to the primary subject of this meeting Ezra….We seem to have clarified the future for John and Tom but not for Caleb and yourself. Can I suggest that you tidy up the business in north London, and perhaps take a few weeks to visit your families. Then the pair of you come down to Downland Park and we can billet you there and perhaps between us we can consider a future for you both – and meantime you and Caleb can think about the more obvious options. Which seem to me to be emigration to one of the Britain's colonies or to America, or perhaps settling to some trade or to farming in England – whatever you each decide you will have the money saved from your recent activities to serve as a stake and of course if you opt for emigration then the veterans project will fund the passage and offer a settlement grant to enhance your own savings.'

'Well sir, I can't see Caleb doing anything that does not involve some form of adventure – so I think he might decide for emigration when he has learnt a bit more about prospects in a possible new country.'

The two men left the pub together, walked along to the Seven Dials itself where they parted. With Ezra heading north towards the gang's Highgate base, and James walking south into St Martin's Lane. Where along the way he could observe the dynamics of a city in continuous movement. The movement of people was obvious, with the veritable cacophony of noise generated by the various hawkers, peddles, beggars – gipsies selling heather and other good luck charms, snake-oil salesmen selling miracle medicines, children selling apples and nuts, and prostitutes selling their bodies. This last being mainly due to the vulnerability of women to the economic conditions of the time. When destitution and the workhouse await, all a working-class women without regular income or even the prospect of work would have is marriage or prostitution and sometimes both.

Added to this human mix were all the many wagons and carts hauling goods, and the red-liveried post coaches setting out on, or arriving from, journeys beyond the city. There were stylish phaetons, broughams, and landaus of the wealthy, the single horse draw traps of the young blades, and with the more adventurous of these on the thin-wheeled dandy horse or a running machine. For the man about town there was the cabriolet-type of 'coffin cab' or the hackney coaches, each more easily engaged for short rides. Occasionally he could see a hangover from the last century in the sedan chair with its twin human engines showing the exertion on their faces.

With all these vehicles the means of moving all but the sedan chairs and push-bikes were the horse. On just a few hundred-yard stretch of Piccadilly James could count hundreds of horses – with evidence of their passing being left in the road and the smell of this and their sweating bodies mingling with the many other smells pervading the air – a veritable assault on the senses. If all together providing an unhealthy environment, made even worse by the constantly dust-laden atmosphere.

If unhealthy, it was an invigorating place for James, but

he was aware of how the stimulating 'London effect' can soon become a tiresome experience and prompt a longing to return to the fresh air and luxuriant farmland of Downland Park.

On arriving back at the Hanover Square house, he enjoyed a light super then settled down in a comfortable fireside armchair to plan the rest of the two weeks that he would be spending in London. Weeks that would include his meeting the agent administrating the emigration aspect of the veteran's relocation project as well as the Devon smallholding initiative. He also had to meet with his bankers to discuss some investments. The final 'must do' in his itinerary of the London visit was to buy some pieces of furniture and paintings for the newly restored Downland House. But along with these activities he was free to choose something more intellectually stimulating or more entertaining. For these he had a list that included a Lecture on electricity due to be delivered by Sir Joseph Banks at the Royal Institution, a look round the British Museum to view the various collections of artifacts and documents housed there. And the possibility of a trip down river to Greenwich and a walk from the landing stage up to the Royal Observatory. So, plenty of opportunity for more intellectual nourishment. For more popular entertainment there was the theatre, as well as the music halls and Pleasure Gardens on the south side of the Thames.

The following day he met Daniel Johnson the London agent responsible for organising and more generally overseeing emigration and for purchasing land for the Devon settlement. He was reassured by Daniel's report suggesting that the migration process was working well in terms of organizing the passages and in getting the emigrant's stake money delivered to a bank at their destination, be this New York, Sydney Cove, or Montreal.

'I am sure that you are very busy sir but before you go, I would like you to read this letter received from a veteran Hussar who left for America about a year ago. Its value is that the contents represent a similar story to those told in many of the letters sent to us by emigrants.

James took the letter and as he read he learned about a fairly typical soldier's story of service in Ireland, India, and Spain, how the letter writer had been dismissed from his regiment due to a shoulder-wound that left him unable to ride a horse. He had a wife and three young children living with her parents in a Middlesex village being dependant on his repatriated service pay. When he returned to his family he could not find any regular work, this mainly due to his disability. So he had little means of support other than occasional low-paid labouring work and some grudgingly offered support from the Parish. That it was only a short time before himself and his family would have to accept the Workhouse. He was in despair, on the point of suicide when he was contacted by a fellow veteran who had retired from the Hussars and was heading back to his family farm in Yorkshire. As he would be passing close to the village in Middlesex he arranged to call in and meet up with a fellow ex-Hussar. Over a meagre meal and the sharing of their better memories of service he had admitted his plight to his old companion. The visitor said that he had details of a charitable organization that was endeavouring to support veterans in ways that can help them settle after leaving the military. From his coat pocket he drew out a creased piece of card with Daniel's name and London office address printed on it.

It seems that this man had told the letter-writer that the card had been given to him by the landlord of the Two Brewers public house in Oxford Street. He had a stack of these behind the counter and said that he had been asked to hand them out to anyone who looked like ex-service – According to the letter writer, the landlord had said that the ex-Hussar had what he called a 'service look' about the way he walked. So he took a half dozen of the cards knowing that it was very likely that he would meet up with men from our old regiment who might not be doing so well. He added that such is the parless situation for many ex-servicemen he only had two cards left after having given four away even before leaving London.

The letter writer had paused at this stage of his story and had written that he was sorry to go on at some length but that he wanted Daniel to be reminded of what his situation was when as a ragged, dirty, tired, and desperate man he had stumbled through the office door.

The letter then went on to say that the author – whose name James saw at the bottom of the letter was Matthew Price – walked over five days all the way to London. Sleeping under hedges, eating berries and any potatoes and onions he could steal from fields. When he finally reached the city he went directly to the address on the card. He went on to say how it was such a relief to meet up with the friendly Daniel who immediately put the writer at ease and arranged for lodgings for a week in which he could rest and feed up, prior to his returning home (by coach) to inform his family that they were off to New York and a new life. He expressed appreciation for the funding for initial contacts, arrangements for travel, and the cost of passage to the 'New World'. That day when he met Daniel was one during which a dark cloud had been lifted from his life.

The author went on to describe his settling down in New York, using the money provided by Daniel to set up a small hardware store, and how the business had in but one year gone from strength to strength. To the extent that he had just opened another store in Boston, Massachusetts.

This longish letter ended by expressing the man's sincere gratitude.

James paused to absorb the biographical content of the letter and the sentiments expressed, he then lifted his head and looked across the desk to the agent.

'My Daniel, that is quite a lot to take in. Can you please arrange to have this and a few of the similar letters copied and sent down to me at Downland. I want to share these with at least some of the men who have contributed to raising much of the funding for these 'new beginnings'. Often risking their own lives to do so.'

After a light lunch with Daniel in a Soho Square coffee house, James made his way to the British Museum adjacent to Russell Square. Entrance to the museum at that time was by prior arrangement and limited to trustees and the otherwise well-connected. On arrival he was met by one of the curators who then accompanied him on a guided tour of the various collections. The bulk of which had been past onto the museum by Sir Hans Sloane with his 71,000 curiosities being bequeathed to the museum, conditional on a payment of £20,000 from the government (a fraction of the cost of the amassing the collection by Sloane). James own primary interest was in the library of 40,000 books, some of which were examples of the first books printed in Britain and within the collection were a number of illuminated manuscripts; veritable artworks on velum that were many hundreds of years old.

He was taken to an upstairs gallery holding the Elgin Marbles – the large set of sections of the massive frieze made in the 5th century BCE to embellish the buildings on the Acropolis Hill, Athens. A prize taken by Lord Elgin the 7th Earl from the Parthenon early in the century.

James was in awe at the beauty of this series of

sculptures, the prancing horses, the muscular Greek warriors all frozen in marble elegance.

When he left the museum he caught a Hansom Cab that then ground its way through the heavy vehicle traffic to Hanover Square and for James an evening relaxing and reading a novel. This novel 'Pride and Prejudice' he could see was written by a Jane Austin. He had previously read an earlier book by the same author which he now knew by name. When the earlier book was first published the author was just noted as 'By a Lady'. This was still a time when being a novelist was considered to not be socially acceptable work for a gentlewoman. But, given the success of this earlier book 'Sense and Sensibility', and more liberal attitudes, meant that the later book could be attributed to the female author by name. James found these books rather silly but easily readable. The writing weaved romantic story-lines set in the narrow-minded class sensitivities characteristic of much of the middle and upper classes during the Georgian period.

The writing itself was carefully measured, and for the most part the stories moved along at an engaging pace, made more interesting by descriptions of people and places from the pen of what was clearly an author with an acutely observant eye.

After a restful night's sleep and a light breakfast James settled to read the morning paper. Today there was the report of a Tea Clipper returning on a fast passage from Calcutta and its having been blown off course in a gale and running aground on rocks off the Scilly Islands, located about 80 miles off the south-east coast of Cornwall. It seems that about half the crew of 42 hands had drowned, but the rest had been saved due to some brave Scillonian fishermen undertaking a rescue in very difficult sea conditions. Such a shame thought James that following about twelve months on the passage, those men would end their lives almost within sight of their homeland.

James was aware that the government was in quite a mess following the death of George III in January of that year (1820), and with ambitious individuals already jostling for high ministerial position within any new government. It was in this politically unsettled period that a group of revolutionary radicals sought to take advantage and take control of the country. Even though the action of this group of revolutionary radicals had been ended four months previously in February The Times had continued to follow up the story. Following, further investigations by its reporters more about the background to the subversive plan had been revealed. The story was run under the somewhat dramatic headline of 'The Cato Street Conspiracy'. So called because this was the name of the north-west London street where thirteen members of the group were arrested. The substance of the conspiracy was the planned murder of the Prime Minister Lord Liverpool and most of the prominent government ministers. Of those arrested, five were executed and the rest were transported to Australia. The membership of the group was responding to the more general feeling of unrest in a county experiencing quite difficult times, with high food prices and mostly only low wages. These being significantly due to the still fairly recent war.

A bit later on that day James was enjoying his lunch while seated at a small table set in a bay window overlooking the tree-lined Hanover Square. Meanwhile just a quarter of a mile to the east Alex Cranfield was waking from a troubled sleep in the bedroom at his London club. It had taken him but a few months to spend the fairly modest capital sum left over from his mother's estate and, in addition, he had also run up more gambling debts and was facing the need to either sell land or re-mortgage the estate.

'What a poxy time I am having at the tables' He was thinking 'Surely my luck must change soon, if not I will have to sell land. The land agent down at Cranfield has not been as hard on tenants as he should have been, the rents need to be higher.'

Even someone as self-centred as Alex could see that he would not be able to continue to support the easy-going, hard-drinking, womanizing and gambling life, that had been his experience for much of the past ten years of adult life. And he knew that the rents were about as high as the tenants would stand for and that the possibility of his prospects at the table improving was more about hope over probability.

His weak mind moved on to seek someone to blame for his plight.

'Mind you, if that bastard James O'Connell had not persuaded Tess to work for him I am sure that she would eventually had conceded to my proposal. After all, she would not have seen her family homeless and starving. If I had her at Cranfield I am sure I would have more easily settled to life at the estate and not have been so tempted to indulge myself in the clubs and brothels of London.'

Just then his thinking was distracted by a loud thumping at the door through which he could hear his old friend, Lord Hugh Grenville demanding his attention. Alex opened the door and stepped aside to allow Hugh to stumble through the doorway and throw his rotund body into a well-padded armchair. He then lent back, lifted a leg over an arm of the chair and called loudly for 'Brandy'!

Alex could see that even now in the early afternoon his friend had already sampled sufficient of the spirit, but he opened a small cupboard, took out a bottle of good brandy and two large classes and poured a generous amount in each of them.

'There you go Hugh, don't drink it too quickly or you will be pissed even before we go out this evening. I was wondering when, or even if, you would turn up today, I missed you last night at Whites – where did you end up?'

'I shall be merry not pissed old friend, but I do need a stiffener or three to get over last night's disaster. I managed to lose another thousand pounds at the tables, I then had to take a Hansom to Madame Rose's in Shepard's Market in order to find Selina, my most favourite lady, and to lose myself in her delightfully copious body. Unfortunately this only relived me of more cash and did little to suppress the memory of the losses at the table for more than an hour or so. On waking this morning my financial plight came to the fore. I will not be receiving the next payment of estate rents until two month's time, so I might need to borrow some funds Alex.'

He had now lost his smile and was looking at his friend with an expression that could be viewed as somewhat pleading.

'Well old friend, we seem to be sharing a similar lack of funds. I too have run up debts and will barely manage until I can sell some land. It's looking like I will have to live back on the estate for some time until I can accumulate some funds.'

'God, why is life so unfair' said Hugh.

'I will probably have to do the same. But life in rural Hampshire is so dull. Nothing but heathland and forest. The oh so polite tea parties and very occasional balls, with young women prepared to flirt but determined to keep their legs firmly together until they have found a well-positioned husband. Riding is the only pleasure.'

I suppose we could stay together and alternate between our estates' suggested Alex.

'Suits me' said Hugh

'Right then, before we are consigned to incarceration in the country and hopefully a life brightened just a little with chasing housemaids, let's plan for an evening of merriment – who knows, we might even get lady luck to favour us at the tables.' So these two set off to join their louche friends at White's Club in St.James. Whites, and the Boodles Club that served as Alex's home when he came to town, were notorious gambling haunts. Gentleman of leisure would spend much of their day talking in the lounge or playing more relaxed games such as bridge or billiards. But as the day moved into the evening most would saunter into the gaming rooms to attend to the more serious business of the day.

The gambling room steadily filled as the evening drew on – the noise of laughing winners and of raucous members and their guests exchanging amusing anecdotes and more general gossip. The older men tended to favour the stimulus of snuff sniffed up blue-vein streaked noses or sucking on long-stemmed clay pipes. While the younger members mostly preferred cigars. The noise, the smoke, and smell of bodies warmed as the heat of the room increased, all together created a unique atmospheric miasma that the members found so comforting – confirming and reinforcing their place amongst what they viewed as the gentlemanly tribe at the top of the social hierarchy.

The excited buzz that pervaded interactions, and the competitive nature of some members led some to challenge others to the silliest of bets. Some notable wagers made by members included a bet made the previous year involving Sir Joseph Copley who bet Mr Horace Seymour five guineas that Lord Temple would have an illegitimate child before a Mr Neville. Another bet reported by the politician Horace Walpole was made between two of White's members that a man would be able to survive under water for 12 hours. The poor soul persuaded to undertake this task reported to be a 'desperate fellow' was apparently sunk below the water but was never seen again, the stake was £1,500.

Such extreme bets were apparently not uncommon, but most members played games such as Faro, Whist, Quinze and Hazard. These were games of skill which for success required a level of study and concentration rather beyond the likes of Alex and Hugh. Their experience was a tale of steady loses – interrupted by an occasional widely celebrated big win, even if the money gained for these was soon spent to support their dissolute lifestyles, or soon lost in subsequent card games.

James, although qualified to be a member of these clubs turned down the occasional invitation to join one of them. He preferred membership of the more austere Guards Club, where the only qualification for membership was being or having been an officer in one of the guard's regiments.

He spent his remaining time in London endeavouring to follow up more intellectual pursuits. One of the more notable of these being a lecture by its President, Sir Humphry Davy, at The Royal Institution. This lecture was to be about the natural force called electricity, a rather mysterious force seen only by its effects. James had already read of the French King Louis XV's own fascination with these effects to the extent that he had 700 monks lined up in Paris, each holding hands with the monk next to him and with the individuals at each end of the line in contact with something called a Leyden Jar, which he had read contained a chemical means of generating electricity. With the King and his companions being highly amused at the spontaneous 'dancing' of the electrocuted monks.

The Institution was located in Albemarle Steet, a short walk from Hanover Square and by the time that James arrived the main lecture Hall was already quite full. Although the smokiness of the room was similar to a gentleman's club the conversations here were subdued and much more serious. Here were men of science, for the most part men of leisure with an interest in the natural world and the advancing activity of the sciences. A group who would not gain the label of 'scientists' until about the middle of the century when William Whewell introduced the term, in doing so recognising the rapidly increasing interest in understanding the natural world.

The lecture was an even-paced outline of the history of man's ideas on the phenomenon of electricity. Sir Humphry was a confident speaker, and he began by going as far back into history as the ancient Egyptians circa 2750 b.c. and how they had identified a species of catfish that had electric features this, the 'Thunderer of the Nile', would give a shock to anyone coming into contact with it. A bit later at about 500 b.c. the often called, father of philosophy 'Thales of Miletus', noted the effect of rubbing objects made of certain materials (especially amber) together and how this could create a force that would attract light objects such as feathers. This 'static' form of electricity was much later on in 1600 a.d. studied more extensively by William Gilbert, who termed the general electricity-related phenomena 'electicaus', later changed to 'electricity by Thomas Browne.

Sir Humphry brought the study of electricity up to date by an outline of the more experimental approach taken by Benjamin Franklin in England and Alessandro Volta in Italy. It was Volta who designed the first 'battery', and so a means of storing electricity and making it available in a controlled way.

Following the lecture, James took a brief tour of the Institution's building, with its lecture rooms library and laboratories where the faintly acrid smell of chemicals being used in the experiments was a constant presence and indicator of the type of work being undertaken.

As he walked back to the London house James reflected on the ways in which science had progressed in the past one hundred years. He had been aware of how the killing power of developing munitions and cannon had incorporated the results of experiments made with various explosives and ways of barrelling rifles, as well as the flight efficiency of projectiles. But to learn about the latent power of electricity and some of the ideas he had just be listening to about this energetic power, for lighting or even perhaps driving machinery, had opened his mind. It seems that the secrets of the natural world were being unravelled and 'laws' (regularities) being identify. And this happening on a number of scientific fronts – chemistry, physics, astronomy, geology - being just a few of these.

But common to them all was a similar approach to method. This involved constructing theories produced by informed minds and from these predictive hypotheses that could be subjected to testing, ideally by the use of controlled experiments.

He was thinking that this 'scientific' method was also beginning to be applied to agriculture. With controlled breeding of stock animals and for plant selection. Albeit this type of thoughtful approach had been taken by farmers for millennia, but this was pretty much on a trial and error basis. The use of more controlled experiments was a significant improvement and will progressively inform farmers and so improve the efficiency of their work.

'It feels as if the country is poised on the edge of a revolution in discovery, invention, and improvement.' He thought as he made his way.

'But for now, it's a quiet evening for me with a glass or two of brandy and another chapter of 'Pride and Prejudice'.'

The time James had left in London was taken up with visits to art galleries and furniture showrooms. He was able to buy some of the larger pieces of furniture required for Downland. But now that housemaid Susan's father Amos had proven himself to be a skilled carpenter there was less need to buy in furniture. Skills shown by the impressive range of book-shelves that he had almost completed. Allowing him to soon be available to undertake some cabinet-making. According to Susan, her father had felt that his life had received a real boost.

'With you Sir' said Susan 'Father feels that he is working for a master who appreciates his skills and is prepared to pay a fair wage for the work. He says that for too long his working life has been about bickering with employers who want the best work for the least pay.'

With this in mind James felt comfortable to only purchase the items of furniture that were required more immediately and to wait for Amos to make the rest over the coming years. And this perhaps with a young apprentice or even an adult trainee. His mind was turning towards a possible future for Ezra or Caleb.

His trips to the art galleries, as had the Royal Institution lecture, reminded him that London did have much to offer, but he immediately reflected that this was not sufficient when the more obvious noise and stink of a crowded London was compared to the rural idyll within which Downland Park was set.

He only had time left in London to visit two art galleries. The first had involved a one-hour Hansom Cab trip to the village of Dulwich, ten miles south of the Thames in Southwark. Here he was able to view the impressive series of Old Masters paintings that had been bequeathed to the gallery in 1811 by Sir Francis Bourgeois R.A., himself a capable artist. Whilst James could appreciate the skills of eye and hand coordination, along with the inner eye of imagination of works that painters such as Joshua Reynolds, Rembrandt, and Nicolas Poussin, had produced, he wanted something with more natural settings. And in any case very few of the paintings were for sale and these mostly by lesser skilled painters. The second galley was within walking distance of Hanover Square, and it was a walk made on the final full day of his stay in London. The gallery was situated within the impressive Somerset House in the noisy traffic crammed Strand.

Such was the attraction of the more modern paintings on show here that James spent all of the late morning and most of the afternoon working his way round. Only taking a break for a light lunch in a busy public house in the Aldwych.

He was attracted to quite a few of the paintings on offer but felt that he should restrict himself to buying only about half a dozen of his favourites. These included: 'View on the Thames' by E.Fox to remind him of the impressively broad river winding slowing through the capital – 'A Distant View of Greenwich from Charlton Woods, near Woolwich' by P. Nasmyth, offering a pleasing view towards the distant city, 'Wood Scene' by S.Palmer and 'Kingfisher, Starlings and Woodpecker' by W. Smith so that throughout the year he would be able to view the beauties of floral and faunal nature frozen on canvas. Before he left the gallery he arranged for all of his purchases to be sent down to Downland.

Walking slowly back to Hanover Square he was feeling satisfied with the artworks that he had bought. He might have been tempted to buy more by some of the younger painters if he was prepared to linger in London for a few more weeks in order to take in the Royal Academy of Arts summer exhibition, but he had had enough of the city and Downland was drawing him.

It was early afternoon the following day that James was seated in a stagecoach that was lumbering along towards the hill-top town of Shaftsbury, where his horse had been stabled during his time in London. As he looked out of the unglazed coach window at the passing countryside he was reflecting on his recent stay in the city – The bustling crowds, the constant movement of peoples and of all types of horse drawn vehicles. A heaving, pulsating, body of movement shrouded in the heavy smog each morning and pervaded with oppressive smells throughout the whole day. In terms of movement the street scenes were generally similar to those that would have been seen in the late decades of the previous century. But the built city was undergoing more obvious change. Farmed fields and market gardens were being built on as the city grew. Slum housing cleared, as soon as the residents could be evicted to make way for more substantial villas to house the better-off. The solid buildings housing scientific and artistic institutions – such as Somerset House in the Strand, Burlington House in Piccadilly and the substantially extended British Museum - hailed the advancing sciences as well as the expanding cultural developments taking place in the city. The decorative embellishments on their façades as well as the increasing size of government buildings illustrated the growing size and wealth of the British Empire. Buildings in architectural styles such as Palladian and Neoclassical, designed by architects such as John Nash and William Chambers where built primarily of bricks from Kentish brickworks and stone from Portland Bill.

What had been a more obvious memory of his time in London was the fast pace of change. But within the social process of people making and remaking their lives was the marked contrast between the living conditions of the affluent set against the appalling conditions of the poorest sections of the city's population.

'Do we have to have poverty in the midst of wealth? Can we have a system of taxation that would generate funding for the guarantee of at least some minimum income. And this without the problem of rogue employers taking advantage, as had been the experience of the Speenhamland Act.

Or perhaps a more dignified approach with an Act of Parliament setting out a minimum paid wage with significant penalties for any employer not meeting this.'

He knew that minimum wages were not entirely new, after all, most of the traditional Guilds had set minimum prices for their goods and this would amount to a similar approach in terms of outcomes for workers. The economic system in Britain made it difficult for workers to organize together to enforce a 'living wage' in any trade. This was not only due to practical difficulties in meeting together but also due to the Combination Act of 1799 which basically prohibited any form of collective bargaining. The act was supposed to also apply to combinations of employers, but this aspect of the legislation was rarely if ever enforced. Whereas workers were at ever-present risk of prosecution for involvement in any meeting that suggested an attempt to organize.

On arrival at the busy Half Moon coaching inn on the outskirts of the small town of Shaftsbury, James alighted from the coach and being quite stiff from the uncomfortable journey he decided to take a walk around the town prior to having lunch. He had written to the stables to let them know the day and time he would require his horse, so he was expecting his ride to be there first light the following day. After a night spent at the inn and a good breakfast, he would be ready to set off for what would be a long day in the saddle. Given that it had been a month or so since he had last sat on a horse, he was anticipating a sore rear end by the time he reached Downland. Meanwhile he walked into the Town centre where he could see that it was a market day. The market was set up in the shadow of the medieval St. Peter's Church and after passing the line of stalls he found himself at the top of a very steep cobbled lane and over the roof-tops of the row of small houses lining each side of the narrow street, known as Golden Hill, he was able to enjoy a view across a picturesque expanse of sun-warmed Dorset.

'Why does such a view nourish the mind?' He reflected as he took in the rich green farmland divided by serried lengths of mostly close-trimmed hedges and the occasional copse primarily composed of a mix of oak, beech and elm trees. And within and around the upper branches of each of these he could see and hear raucous groups of crows and the occasional even more raucous pairs of magpies.

He lingered over this scene, breathing deeply to more fully absorb the tingling sense of being in such a beautiful spot on such a lovely day. He then somewhat reluctantly made his way back to the inn via a circular walk round the town. With, he estimated, a population of not much more than a thousand of seemingly prosperous townsfolk. At least two of the town's main products of bread and beer were evidenced by the smells as he walked through the older parts of the town.

When back at the inn he rested in his room until evening then, after a refreshing wash, he made his way down to the wood-panelled dining parlour for what was to be a very full plate of roast beef, potatoes, and carrots, enlivened by a rich beef gravy and horse-radish sauce. This brought to his table by a cheery red-faced serving maid who warned him about the heat of the plate.

An hour later he rose from the table and was intending to drink a glass of two of brandy in the lounge bar before retiring early to his bed.

Having been served his drink and being settled into a comfortable armchair he took in the small groups of other drinkers sharing news and gossip in the bar. The snatches of conversation that came to him through the smoky room was mostly about farming-related subjects, especially the low price for stock animals being sold in the market and the rising cost of their feed. A stout member of a nearby group was railing about gypsies.

'They are liars and thieves. Mark my words if a pie in missing from a windowsill or a shirt from a washing line or an animal from a field, it will be down to one or more of these fellows.

The mark of the culprit is etched on their swarthy faces. There is a band that has camped along the grass verge on the Guilford Road to the north of the town. So be sure you lock your barns, sheds, and houses when you take to your beds this evening, and indeed for as long as their presence is a threat to the King's peace.'

The two others at the table were nodding in agreement. 'Disgraceful' said one,

'Should be cleared off the highways' said the other.

Then all three now bonded by their dislike of traveling people took deep swings of their ales and sat puffing steadily on well-used clay pipes.

Since returning from military service on the Iberian Peninsula, James had become even more aware of how much his own views on many issues tended to differ from those of most of his class and his general approach was to keep a low profile and to endeavour to avoid much of their company. But for some reason he was particularly irritated by the conversation at his neighbouring table.

He turned towards the leading speaker and said.

'Excuse me sir have you any actual proof that this group you mention have been guilty of any of the crimes you have so confidently listed. Two of which I would remind you are capital offences and so those proven to be guilty in a court of law would probably face death by hanging.'

The man peered through the smoke rising from the smokers sat around the table and looking towards James as he puffed out his cheeks exclaimed 'Proof, proof sir, why would I need proof when I have a life-long experience of this tribe.' He then turned to his companions to acknowledge their confirmatory head nodding.

This reinforcing his confidence he continued.

'Tell me sir, what use to respectable society are these people?'

'Well said James 'That is a measure that many of us might not meet if we were to be judged by our value to respectable society – I wonder about you sir, what is your contribution to society?'

'I sir am a supervisor on the local toll-roads, and I make sure that these roads are keep clear of travellers and other such rabble.'

'That is interesting' said James 'I have heard the toll-roads being described as a form of highway robbery and that it is not unknown for supervisors to take informal payment at lower than the full prices and then to pocket this bonus.'

'I will not stand for such insults' said the man, as he rose from his seat and advanced towards James's table with his fists clenched.

James also stood up. 'I am not looking for a fight sir, but if you insist then I will entertain you outside in the courtyard.'

Taking in James's broad physique and a general demeaner that suggested experience of fighting, the assertive drinker decided that perhaps violence was not a sensible option. He turned on his heels with a 'Damn you sir' and with his two companion in his wake he stormed from the bar.

As James sat back down the others in the bar who had paused their own conversations to watch the more interesting confrontation turned back to their drinks. Then the landlord of the Inn came over to clear the vacated table of the drinking jugs.

He looked towards James.

'Thanks for that intervention sir – that character, Amos Green, is not a regular, but when he is in we have to put up with him loudly sharing his opinions. I have been considering the possibility of banning him and your exchange this evening is going to change a possible to a definite, so thank you for this. I myself have some gypsy blood and I am disappointed how easily they are labelled as trouble-makers.'

James smiled at the landlord to acknowledge his comments and having decided that it was time for bed made his way to his room via the candle-lit staircase.

As he lay considering the evening just past, he was thinking about the increasing difficulties being faced by travelling people, especially the gypsies. In the past they would have been able to find a piece of common land on which to set up camp. A place where they could stay for a few weeks or even months with the women and older children collecting medicinal plants for cures and wild flowers to make into posies to be sold in towns and villages. And the men could cut wood and carve walking sticks, crude dolls, or pegs, and the more skilled who have the time would beat copper sheets into pots and pans. But with the increasing enclosure of common land there were fewer places for the gypsies to stay.

'Yes, no doubt' he thought, '…..some were up to mischief on occasion, and you would need to be careful if buying a horse from one, but does this make them so different from any cross section of the non-gypsy population?' He concluded.

He remembered the families of gypsies that used to arrive at his father's Essex farm in late summer to assist during the busy time of harvesting. For the most part they were hard-working individuals who would spend most evening gathered around their crackling, smoky, camp-fires with the old folk telling tales and as the night wore on there would be fiddle-playing, dancing, and singing songs that wove their lives today into the history of the group and all within the rhythms of their traditional musical styles.

He remembered that as a young boy he would hide in the woods by the encampment wide-eyed as he watched this colourful scene. Of making friend with a couple of boys who came on their annual family visits. Their climbing trees for bird eggs and snaring rabbits for food.

With these pleasant thoughts he drifted into sleep.

It was the sound of hoofs clattering on the cobbled courtyard, mixed with the cheerful calling of the ostlers, that awoke him just as day was breaking over the Inn.

Following a decent breakfast of fresh baked bread, ham, cheese, and coffee, he was soon settling his stabling account and was mounted on his horse as he coaxed it along.

'I think that you have gained a few pounds on the girth old fellow' he said leaning toward the horse's ears and patting its neck.

'But twenty hard miles today will make a fair start in reducing this.' The horse pricked up its ears and snorted as if acknowledging his master's comments.

As James's horse trotted easily along in the mid-morning sunshine, Alex Cranfield and Hugh Grenville were just leaving London, heading south in a hired phaeton. They were intending to take turns at driving the pair of sturdy horses that would be driven to the edge of exhaustion by these two young men, both of whom lacked much patience or indeed any concern at all for the well-being of the animals already straining at their leather harnesses.

The two headstrong young men would also be spending a night at the Half Moon Inn when they reached Shaftesbury. And if they were to meet the splenetic toll-booth supervisor whilst in the town they would be at one with him on the opinion of gypsies. Lord Hugh Grenville had inherited his dislike of gypsies from his father, along with the extensive estate. Shaftesbury would be but a waypoint on their long journey down to Hugh's country estate nestled in fertile land at the eastern side of the New Forest. With their creditors becoming more persistent the pair had reluctantly decided to leave the capital and seek the shelter of the countryside. Following a few days at Cranfield and a change of horses they had agreed to spend the rest of the summer at Hugh's home and then the winter at Cranfield. They were hoping during this time to raise sufficient funding to settle their gambling and other debts. Debts that were steadily mounting with the interest being added.

Ever with an eye for their own comforts, they felt that Hampshire for the summer would allow them to visit the increasingly fashionably Bournemouth and enjoy its brothels and gambling haunts. And to do similar by catching the regular ferry across the narrow Southampton Water to reach the fast-growing port of Southampton on the eastern bank. Where they could enjoy balls and card games in the Assembly Rooms. As well, no doubt, also savour the comely goods on offer in the brothels located in the less respectable streets of the town. The winter would see them travelling up to Cranfield where the hunting would be best, and a different social circle could be met. And of course, at both the summer and winter homes they could amuse themselves by chasing the more attractive housemaids and for Hugh also the occasional manservant or stable lad.

An obvious flaw in the financial plan that these two dissolute young men entertained being that most of these activities, especially the intention to continue gambling, suggested that any expectation of balanced books was unlike to come to fruition.

Chapter Six

It was a tired and dust coated rider and horse that clattered into the paved stable yard at Downland with the stableman hurrying to meet them. James alighted, passed him the bridle and thanked him.

'A good feed for Blade this evening please Will, and a restful few days.'

The staff in the Hall had been expecting their master, so a hearty dinner had been prepared and by the time he had washed and changed the meal had been served in the dining room. Tess was standing by the table ready to update the master on the condition of the household.

As he entered the room Tess said.

'I expect that you would want to eat your dinner and rest awhile before we talk sir so I can come back later, or we could delay our meeting until tomorrow?'

'No, its fine Tess, take a seat here at the table and I will ring for Susan to bring some food.'

'I would prefer just to have coffee please sir, and it will be Rose this evening rather than Susan. Rose has joined the Hall staff as a third housemaid, and she covers most evenings now, with Susan and Jennie covering most days. Although of course there is an afternoon overlap when they work together on cleaning and washing – they make a good team sir.'

'That's good, so we have a level of staffing sufficient to manage the house now?'

'Yes sir, well when you are away we are overstaffed, but Jennie father's is a blacksmith and Rose's is a farm labourer so both do have some experience that has proven to be useful on the Home Farm, and they have been quite happy to help out on the farm when work in the Hall has been slack. Myself, I have long taken an interest in gardening – mainly flowers. Jake and Michael have kindly set aside an area of the walled-garden for me to use for growing flowers, and Will the senior stableman has been generous with manure. The resulting blooms have brought some natural colour into the Hall. My younger sister Elsa also likes to spend time helping in our small patch of garden and, according to Jake, she has a real talent for the work. '

James held up his hand. 'My goodness Tess, it does seem that you have been organising staffing very efficiently.'

'I think that if you ask Jennie and Rose sir, they will say that they enjoy the variety of their work. And I even admit to feeling a little guilty for being paid, when housework is light, to undertake such a pleasant gardening task alongside Elsa.'

'That's nice to hear, not that you might feel guilty, but what you have been saying suggests to me that you have settled into life here at Downland.'

Tess smiled modestly and lowered her head to view the notebook in her lap.

'Shall I move on to the provisioning and decoration of the house sir……..and so the evening continued with the fledgling housekeeper outlining progress on decorating the rooms, and showing that the running expenses were in line with estimates made by James when he first moved into the Hall.

By about 8 pm Rose had returned to stoke the fire and she gently laid more logs onto the orange embers of the grate in front of which Red lay, seemingly at ease, but with eyes alert to any movement by his master. In James's absence the dog had become quite attached to the Mrs Goodall, who had ensured Red's affection by the overflowing food bowl that she set down on the tiled scullery floor each evening; along with the more than occasional lamb or beef bone. But if it was a form of appreciative affection that Red had for the rotund cook, it was unabashed subservient love he had for his master. The animal had known the scent of his master as something very special from when it was the first human smell he encountered as a pup, and it was the scent that drew him from his early months of life. This olfactory connection served as the primary mark of recognition of his master, and for James it was the simple love of Red that had welded the two together – dog and master, master and dog.

It was this pair that early the following morning were walking around the boundary of the Home Farm. Red enthusiastically chasing the occasional rabbit that had continued chewing the grass unaware that its companions had immediately scattered at the sight of Red lumbering along with his nose to the ground. Meanwhile James was occupied with observing the changes in both the renovations in buildings and the seasonal crop planting patterns that had taken place in his absence. He paused beside a barred wooden gate serving as the entrance to a wide field of wheat. He leant on the gate and breathed deeply, drawing in the sense-tingling feelings of being alive within the living, breathing, countryside.

It was about an hour later that James, with Red at his feet, was sitting on the terrace as Joe came up the steps from the garden area to join him.

'Take a seat Joe, Susan will be serving coffee quite soon.'

'Thanks Colonel....ops sorry I am still struggling with the more familiar James. Anyway, how was the London trip?'

'As ever Joe, visiting the capital was a mixture of experiences. The positives included the intellectual stimulation of lectures and art galleries, but on the negative side there was the continuous stink, dusty air, and seeing the poverty of so many people, especially the skinny, ragged children. But in relation to sorting out, in effect, dismantling the fund-raising gang of four, this went quite well. There are still the futures for two of the men, Ezra and Caleb, to sort out. But Ezra is due to come down to Downland quite soon and be should be able to let me know if Caleb has decided to go for emigration.'

'It's good to hear that these men have survived the risky business of highway robbery, but will the lack of funding from this source impact on our overall project?'

'Not 'our' project Joe – 'my' project. You must not be in any way associated with the nefarious activities that the project has involved. If anything happens to me, I would want you to take over the running of Downland. In line with my will, all but the Home Farm will be put into a trust, with the surplus income being donated to the settlement of ex-servicemen. So continuing the project in my absence. We can't afford to have both of us arrested Joe. If questioned, you must deny any knowledge of what has been going on. Oh, and the Home Farm will be left to Mary and yourself as freeholders.'

'That is very generous James.'

'No Joe it is what you deserve for your years of service, years inadequately recognised by the government.'

Susan arrived at the table with coffee and biscuits and the pair turned to discussing the business of the estate.

'It has spread slowly but all tenants do now seem to understand the value of modernisation. I think that after the meeting in the big barn a significant minority of the tenants were suspicion about your motives. The no-rent, low-rent, years on offer seemed to be just too good to be true. But Christian Greenwood, and the group of younger farmers that have formed into a cooperative have led by example and the ripple effect of their work, added to informed advice provided for each tenant by Arthur, is progressively transforming farming at Downland. But the hard test for the tenants will be the size of this year's harvest and the prices gained for stock animals when taken to market.'

'That's all very encouraging Joe.'

'I would also add James that Tess has really impressed both Mary and myself in the way she has taken over the running of the Hall. She has a lovely way of praising a member of staff at the same time as suggesting how their work on this or that job can be improved. It has been nice to see her grow into the role of housekeeper, let's hope we can retain her for a few years at least.'

'Why do you say this Joe? Has she shown any sign of wanting to leave for employment elsewhere?'

'No, no, not that but she is still young so marriage is a possibility – mind you the obvious unfortunate experience she has had would deter most suiters in such a narrow-minded community as in Cerne Parva and its locality. But Mary has drawn my attention to the fact that Christian Greenwood does seem to have increased his visits to deliver produce to the kitchen and his appearance has improved, from old and dirty smock of a typical farm worker to more young man on the lookout for a wife! And she has found him on a number of occasions in the walled-garden talking to Tess, and this would not have been on a direct path between his farm and the Hall.'

'Hmm, I don't suppose we should stand in the way of young love. Even if it might present a challenge for us at some point – perhaps running the Hall from a farm might just be possible, at least until children come along.'

After dealing with a few more administrative tasks the two men enjoyed a slow walk around the Home Farm and parted when they came to Joe's cottage. With Joe off to enjoy his supper and James returning to the Hall and to dinner followed by an evening reading Jane Austin beside the log-crackling fire, with Red asleep at his feet.

Christian Greenwood's life had become complicated of late, if in an exciting way. The more he saw of Tess the deeper his love became. At times when ploughing his imagination would drift into creating a possible future. One in which in his mind's eye he could see Tess leaning on the doorway of their farm cottage with a baby on her hip. This image being further embellished with Thomas and two more small children playing amongst some chickens wandering about in the dusty farmyard. As the horse pulling the plough felt the ploughmen's lack of concentration he strayed from the intended line with the furrow assuming an increasing bend away from the straight. Feeling the slight movement in direction Christian snapped out of his daydream and tightened the reins to get the horse back in a straight line.

'Well, I can at least dream.' He thought, as he looked forward to the next visit to the Hall and another chance to 'accidentally' encounter the object of his adoration.

It was a week later that Jenni came to see him just as he was preparing the horse for the day ahead. She was a little breathless from the walk, but she held a list out to him that the cook had given to her, not trusting that the somewhat absent-minded girl would remember a spoken list of the sundry goods required for the kitchen.

'Thank you Jennie, tell Mrs Goodall that I shall bring these over early this afternoon. Would you like a drink of lemonade or cider before you walk back?'

Now that she had completed the 'official' purpose of her errand Jennie was keen to start back, so she politely refused the offer of a drink and started walking. On her return taking a slight detour to allow her to pass close to the farmyard of one of Christian neighbours. This being another young farmer and one with whom Jennie had been progressing from shy smiles to friendly waves and hellos and more recently to a couple of Sunday afternoon walks. Jennie and her intended suitor, Eli Cooper, were moving inextricable towards a lifetime partnership by taking the traditional, almost timeless, steps in rural courtship towards the marital bond. Their thoughts were becoming ever-more entwinned as also would their bodies in the not-too-distant future. This happy pairing was a contrast to the relationship between Christian and Tess – for these two young people there was an as yet unspoken rift. A fault-line of social expectation to be overcome or not.

Eli, Jennie's lover and Christian's closest friend had grown up in Cerne Parva and he did know something of Tess's past, including the reason (as spread and embellished by village gossips) for her having a child. But not being given to gossip Eli had never seen a reason to talk to Christian about Tess as something other than the new housekeeper at the Hall. Christian himself had assumed that she must have been married and that her husband would have died (not uncommon in early nineteenth century England) – after-all she was a respectable housekeeper, a valued position in a rural setting. 'Why should I not marry a widow' he thought. 'If I had been married but then died, I would have wanted my wife to marry again if someone worthy of her came along, so there should be a chance for us to marry.'

Such was Christian's thinking when the next afternoon after delivering eggs. milk, cheese, and potatoes to the kitchen of the Hall, he tied his horse to a tree by the heavy wooden door to the walled-garden and strolled in as if just taking a general interest in the garden. When, as we know, he was hoping that he would find Tess there tending to the small area that had been set aside for her. His wish was fulfilled when he saw her working her way down a row of Foxgloves using a hoe to tease out the weeds.

They had met in a similar 'accidental' way on a number of occasions over the past month or so and they were fairly comfortable in each other's company.

'Hello Tess, what a fine day, those flowers look lovely.'

Tess glanced up from her work and smiling at Christion said. 'Thank you Christian. Please pick a bunch if you want to brighten up your cottage.'

Christian was thinking that Tess's own presence would brighten up his cottage considerably more than some flowers, however pretty they might be.

When riding to the Hall earlier that day he had been practicing how he might phrase an invitation to Tess to accompany him for a walk this coming Sunday. He tried various ways of phrasing how best he might put this. But after trying these out on his disinterested horse, he could not decide on one of them, so he thought that he would just say what came to mind when the time came. Afterall, if she did have some feeling of budding affection for him the phrasing should not matter. But now he was actually in Tess's presence his resolve to put the question had rather weakened. She had returned to her hoeing, and he stepped in front of her.

'Tess, would you like to go for a walk this Sunday afternoon.' he said in a rush.

There was an extended silence as Tess looked at him with an expression that mixed surprise with confusion.

She took in the almost pleading look in Christian's face and the implications of what he said slowly dawned on her.

'No No! It can't be…. It can never be.' She said, dropping her hoe and walking away from him.

As she had taken in the look on Christian's face, she could see that what she had assumed to be a simple friendship was clearly not what he thought in terms of how the friendship might develop.

'But Tess......what's wrong?' he asked.

But she was now passing through heavy door from the garden and was almost running towards the Hall.

Christian's head drooped and his demeaner alone showed his disappointment, indeed confusion.

'Why was she so adamant?' he thought she might just have declined his offer 'But why the dramatic reaction and such certainty in her refusal?'

'It can never be...' were the words ringing in his head as he made his dejected way back to his horse.

Meanwhile Tess had hurriedly sought the privacy of the self-contained set of three rooms in the west wing that James had set aside for her and Thomas. Far better accommodation than would normally be allocated to a housekeeper. But then James was hardy a normal master.

Tess slammed the door behind her and as she leant back on it she was trying to re-run in her mind what had just happened.

'Why had I not seen how Christian was wanting us to become more than just friends. But then again he only suggested an afternoon's walk so hardly a romance. But it was more the way he had looked at me when he made the suggestion rather than the relatively innocent activity being proposed. Does he know that little Thomas is mine? Does he know what befell me?'

Then she remembered that he was an outsider to the village and so....

'Perhaps he thinks that I might have been married and deserted by a husband or that he had died.'

I will have to speak frankly with him.'

But what had just taken place in the garden, and her subsequent reflection on this, led over the following few days to her feelings towards Christian beginning to undergo a subtle change. She knew that she was drawn to him as a friend, his easy-going nature was attractive, and he was more than just pleasant looking. But the obvious barrier between them formed by her past had for her meant friendship would be the emotional limit of their relationship. But now to realize that, for Christian, there did not seem to be any barrier, caused her to briefly imagine something beyond friendship –

'But no' she said to herself 'He must be unaware of my past, I need to explain my situation. In a few days' time, when my emotions are under the control of my good sense, I will write him a letter to explain the reason for my reaction to his invitation. Doing this by letter will mean that he does not have to suffer the embarrassment of learning the truth when facing me.'

So it was in a letter Tess wrote two days later that set out the story of her traveling to Cranfield to become a maidservant and her being ill-used by the master of the house. She did not feel the need to go into much detail or to offer any convincing defence. Afterall, she thought hers was a not an uncommon story. Many young girls when away from home became prone to temptation with male servants or fell victim to the persuasive tongue or the physical force of a predatory master. Immediately Christian read of her downfall he would easily understand why they could not go further than friendship. It would be unlikely that any man would want a disgraced woman for a wife, whatever circumstances had brought this about.

On completing the letter, and having sealed the envelope, she sought out Jennie and asked her to deliver the letter to Christian's cottage. Tess herself did not want to come face to face with him and she was aware of Jennie's romantic feelings toward Eli Cooper and so would not mind another opportunity to call in to see him on the return trip. With the letter sent on the journey to enlighten Christian, Tess turned to her day's regular work, intending to let a focus on her duties help take her thoughts from the reaction to what she had just set in motion.

On arriving at the cottage, Jennie was as usual quite puffed out, this due to her wanting to spend as much time with Eli as possible, even if it would just be the pair leaning on a farmyard gate during a pause in the young farmer's fieldwork. She briskly used the heavy brass knocker on the cottage front door and as there was no answer she called Christian's name, but still no response. She took a quick look round the yard, into the hay barn then the dairy, but it was clear to her that the farmer must be out working in the fields. Impatient to leave, she slipped the letter under the front door. A simple act, understandable given the young woman's thoughts, but one that would impact on Christian's and Tess's lives for much of the summer. Jennie would not have been aware that the letter she had pushed under the door then went under the doormat on the floor just behind it. Jennie skipped off to Eli's, her mind set on their future together.

And so we leave this stifled romance, with Tess thinking that Christian now knew the sad truth about her past, and Christian with the 'It can never be' coming into his mind whenever his thoughts turned to Tess. Both convinced that even their previous innocent friendship was now at an end.

It was still early summer when Ezra and Caleb arrived at Downland. Caleb had not been able to come to a decision on emigration so thought that he would put the decision off until later in the year and meanwhile he decided to accompany Ezra to Downland. Both of them were financially quite well set up, having benefited from the interest paid on the government bonds bought with their share of the bullion raids. He knew that he could support himself for some time and so could defer making a more definite decision on his future.

When this dust-coated pair arrived at the Hall they were welcomed with enthusiasm by James and Joe.

'You look just as I remember you at the end of hard day's march on the road to Burgos.' said Joe

'That is not a complement – I mean that you look just as disreputable as you ever did.'

The potentially embarrassing gap since their last meeting was easily overcome by the comradely foundations of their initial friendship.

During the following weeks Ezra would spend most mornings initially just watching but then assisting Amos with his carpentry, and so was able to observe and learn from a master craftsman at work. Then in the afternoons he would usually be working on a cruder type of woodwork to restore a carriage that he had found in one of the storage sheds adjacent to the stables. The carriage must have stood unused for years, if not decades, and once he had pushed it out into the stable yard and had washed it down with copious amounts of soapy water, he had been able to assess the poor condition of this once fine vehicle. He looked forward to returning it to its former glory.

Caleb meanwhile took long walks through the local countryside, mostly following the boundary of Downland Park. On the warmer days, he would strip off all but his trousers and take to the river.

'Such freedom' He thought, as he enjoyed the stimulating physicality of swimming against the current in the deeper centre of the river.

Some of the bloodier aspects of his past military services had recently returned to haunt his dreams. The gang's activities, being both exciting and financially rewarding, had distracted his thoughts for a time. But since the gang has been disbanded, he now more often awoke sweating and fearful during the nights. But the walking and occasional swimming was helping. He was pleased that Ezra had become taken up with the carpentry and the carriage renovation, but neither this nor work on the land held much interest for him.

'I will just have to accept the devils in my head as the price to be paid for years of service and hope that time itself will ease their impact. And possibly spending the future in a new county such as America or Australia, with new opportunities, will make this more likely. Meanwhile I do find my experience here a deal better than an alternative life in London where I would now be on my own.'

Most evenings Caleb and Ezra would make their way down to the village to enjoy the pub's best bitter beer, its rural company, and where they would usually lose at good natured games of skittles with the regular drinkers.

About four weeks after the pair had first arrived at Downland James sent Susan to ask them to meet him and Joe on the terrace after lunch. So, in due course these four, plus Arthur Gordon, were seated around a wrought iron table on which was set out a map of south-west England.

Following friendly hellos, and with coffee and lemonade having been served, James began.

'Thanks for coming, Arthur and I are going on a trip to visit the ex-servicemen's relocation project that has now been running in Devon for about five years. Although I have been receiving regular up-dates via the London agent, I felt that it would be useful for me to take a first-hand look. Arthur's work here has more or less finished now as all the tenants, at least to some extent, are working to a modernization plan that each one of them has drawn up, as informed by Arthur's advice and with Joe's agreement.'

He flattened the map onto the table and pointed to a small area that he had marked out.

'This is where the 1000 acres that we have brought into the cooperative so far – thanks to your efforts Caleb and Ezra we are in also in the process of negotiating for 300 more. We have 200 veterans and their families with 5 acres each – these are not farms but smallholding. The intention being that 5 acres would enable each tenant to become self-sufficient and should also allow a small surplus available for sale.

We have also made available two carts and two horses, and these are now owned by the co-operative. This to be used by any member of the group to send their surplus products to market in Honiton or, if a more substantial load, then further afield to Exeter. Arthur has agreed to come with us to see if he can offer advice to the tenants on possible ways of making their land more productive. I was thinking that you two might also like to come along. You can meet up with some old comrades and perhaps consider if you might see your future as tenant smallholders.'

'That sounds good to me.' said Ezra.

'I am enjoying the carpentry and carriage restoration, but the idea of being self-sufficient in the longer term does sound attractive, and perhaps I can also do carpentry for some additional income.'

Caleb was looking more reflective and said.

'I just can't see me taking to any form of farming. But I would want to come along as the trip sounds rather like a holiday.'

'Right' said James 'I will see if I can hire a carriage for the journey.'

'No need for that colonel' said Ezra 'If we can delay

setting off for say three days, we will have a carriage fully renovated and ready to go, we also have four strong young horses in the stabling, so we already have the means of comfortable transport.'

And so, by the end of the week the carriage had been loaded up with provisions for the journey – including a cold cooked joint from Mrs Goodall and pies from Mary.

They were planning on taking it easy on the horses and were expecting to take two days to cover the 65 mile journey.

There was something of a sense of excitement when early on the day of departure the four men set off heading west. With Ezra taking the first spell at the reins in recognition of his role in returning the carriage to a useable state.

They had expected an uncomfortable journey given their awareness of the condition of most highways. And in general, this was an expectation fulfilled. The road was hardy more than a muddy track in the winter, being dust-blown and deeply rutted in the hot summer months.

They were pleasantly surprised with the occasional stretches of newly tarmacadamed road along which they would have been able to make good progress if it were not for the amount of traffic jostling for position on the highway.

The stream of heavy wagons pulled by sedately moving oxen, the crowded passenger coaches, most with cheaper ticketed individuals clinging to the various trunks and cases strapped to the tops. Then the fastest of all were the bright red mail-coaches speeding this way and that, as their haughty coachmen made liberal use of their whips and their tongues. These last carrying letters between businesses, families, and no doubt also separated lovers. Then there were very occasional light buggies on a local errand, having to give way to almost all of the other traffic and doing so by mounting as far up the grass verges at they could get.

The further to the west the carriage carrying James and his companions travelled, the more the traffic thinned out so allowing them to make better time. In the late afternoon their carriage rattled over the cobbles into the stable yard of the white painted King Arms in the centre of Dorchester.

All four of the travellers were quite stiff after the eight hours spent in the carriage, with only a short lunch break to eat some of the comestibles that had been packed to sustain them on the journey. They alighted from the carriage and stamped about the yard to:

'Get the blood flowing' as Caleb put it.

The portly landlord came out to meet them aware that James had written to pre-book two rooms for them to sleep in and the private dinning room for their dinner. Once the ostler had been instructed, and generously paid to rub the horses down and to provide them with a good feed, the four went to their rooms to wash and refresh themselves.

Within the hour they were seated round a substantial oak table enjoying a dinner of oxtail soup, followed by roast pheasant and vegetables washed down with a couple of bottles of a somewhat heavy red wine. Finishing the meal by picking at a shared platter of almonds, cob nuts, cheese and apples, completed with a glass of a surprisingly decent port.

Where to spend the rest of the evening was easy for Ezra and Caleb, they would be ensconced in the Inn's main bar recuperating from the day's journey. A decision influenced at least to some extent by their having seen the comely youngish women who cheerfully tended at the bar. But James and Arthur were determined on a visit to the old Roman Hill Fort sited at Poundbury, an area at the southern boundary of the town.

It only took James and Arthur about thirty minutes walking for them to be looking across a fairly extensive

142

elevated area of grassland. In their minds eyes they could imagine the oval wall composed of thick wooden stakes that would have enclosed a campsite of huts, campfires, and animal compounds, belonging to the Roman soldiers and their families stationed in the fort as well as the tribal peoples that the wooden barriers would have also protected. They could each also imagine the people who for generations, thousands of years ago, had wandered to and fro across the campsite. The children playing on the dusty ground, the women cooking, and mainly the younger men who if soldiers perhaps returning from a day on patrol of for the tribesmen a day spent in the fields. Or perhaps soldier and tribesmen returning from the occasional boar or deer hunting trip. With the older men sitting around, no doubt talking over exploits from their younger days, whilst they engaged in making such items as shoes, weapons and even perhaps religious artifacts.

If they had more time, they would have liked to walk the further mile and a half to also view the even more impressive Maiden Castle, the Iron-age fort providing evidence of human occupation (and indeed conflict) in the area long before the Roman legions had arrived. But with the sun now beginning to dip below the horizon the pair turned to walk back to the town.

It was early the next day, following a substantial breakfast, with a cheery wave to the landlord, and after passing a generous tip to the ostler, that the four set off on the second and final day of their journey west. The carriage rumbled out of the yard turning right to head up the High Street, soon passing the bleak-looking Dorchester Prison at the top of the hill. The prison was the location of the gruesome hangings that were a regular aspect of its business. This was a time when crimes for which capital punishment served as a penalty were steadily increasing. This primarily in response to political pressures from the likes of the Duke of Wellington and his reactionary Tory 'King and Country' colleagues in parliament. A group of men concerned about the rise of radicalism amongst the working classes and determined to halt its progress.

Looking back, the three passengers not driving the carriage could enjoy a panoramic view over the settlement of neat modest cottages. As well as the civic buildings, churches, inns, and the stone-built homes of more affluent citizens offering an architectural tracery of a more conventional idea of the material substance of the town. Leaving Dorchester behind they soon found that the state of the highway was as bad as that experienced on the previous day. But the traffic was much lighter, allowing the travellers to make good progress as they enjoyed the scents of the fertile countryside being carried to them on a fresh breeze.

If we leave these four to enjoy each other's company on the day's journeying, we can turn to consider Alex and Hugh, the dissolute pair who had sought shelter from their creditors at Hugh's country estate. A 2,500-acre manor set on the eastern side of the New Forest in Hampshire. An estate that had prospered up until the time when the 7th Earl of Budleigh, Hugh's late father, had inherited the estate. The behaviour of the 7th Earl and his son would be strong evidence to support the view of human nature's being inherited. This father and son pair shared a very strong propensity to squeeze as much enjoyment as possible out of every single day. Even if this came at the cost of personal relationships, the well-being of servants, and the neglect of the land they had inherited. If a master does not have the interest or ability to ensure that an estate produced a profit, then the least he could do was appoint an able estate manager. Unfortunately the 7th Earl and his scion could not even do this and instead the estate had been managed by a series of incompetent individuals. One result being that it was now heavily mortgaged and, as we already know, added to this were mounting gambling debts. Hugh's friend Alex was in a similar position and their expectation that distance from their London creditors would make life easier had proven to be founded on a false hope. Or rather on ignorance of how much the postal service had improved. It was an almost weekly experience for these two to find official-looking manila envelopes laid out on a silver tray positioned alongside their breakfast dishes, if this meal was more often being taken at lunch time.

They had been spending much of the time since their arrival at the Manor house out hunting during the days and in the evenings morosely sat in the drawing room playing card games for tokens and drinking their way through the contents of the wine-cellar of the house.

At least twice a week they would drive or ride to nearby Lymington to frequent a gambling club prior to going on to a brothel. The fact that their losses here were relatively small compared with those of London did little to remove the fear for their financial futures which as far as they were concerned was their whole future – to lose their property would mean disgrace, which they could probably live with, but also poverty, that they could not.

To introduce at least some variety into their lives, they occasionally took the ferry across Southampton Water and would visit pubs and clubs in the town. They tended to favour a somewhat run down pub, the Moor's Head, in Bridge Street and on recent visits they had joined the company of a number of pretty shady characters, one of whom was a George Higgins. George had been a well set up young man and sometime before he had been a college friend of Hugh. But due to a series of poor financial decisions, caused at least to some extent by addiction to opium, he had now turned to crime to support himself.

As the renewed friendship became warmer, Alex and Hugh shared their difficult circumstances with George and he in turn told them something of his involvement in the smuggling of contraband goods into the country. Over the weeks following their meeting up, Alex was beginning to see the possibility of a solution to his own and Hugh's plight. He thought that George's fairly modest endeavours in progressing the evasion of customs duties could be developed quite considerably. If smugglers could afford a fast cutter able to carry much bigger cargoes, and with a turn of speed sufficient to outrun the boats of the customs officers when necessary, then substantial sums could be made. He calculated that sailing across to France or Spain and purchasing spirts, tea, tobacco, in bulk, along with modest amounts of more valuable goods such as gold and silver, could provide a significant return on capital invested. The cost of a cutter would be shared half and half with Hugh, or they might form a group of funders made up of some of the more disreputable men they knew from London. If these might not all need the money, Alex felt that they might well like the excitement of being involved in a nefarious activity.

All Hugh and himself needed to do was to sell the, as yet unmortgage, land remaining on each of their estates and the capital for opening up a new stream of income would be available. And if they managed the activity with care, and used George as a go-between for themselves and the men who would engage in the actual smuggling, then the risk of being convicted of smuggling would be low.

The more Alex considered this enterprise the more obvious it seemed to be a way to restore their finances.

'What have we got to lose? If we don't do something very soon then we will lose our estates. When at best if we can avoid bankruptcy and debtor's prison, then we might be left with a miserable Home Farm each and having to live in some hovel and eke out a living on the land - ugh not for me!'

When he put this plan to Hugh it was taken up with some enthusiasm - if rather like a drowning man grasping for driftwood - as being the only means by which he could maintain his standard of living.

When a couple of days later these two met up with George in the Moor's Head they put their idea to him. His reaction being that 'It is as if you two had read my mind.'

He had already been thinking of ways to turn the trickle of illicitly gained income into a more substantial stream, but he lacked the funds and the contacts to be able to raise sufficient capital to pay the cost of building a boat.

Alex and Hugh came away from this meeting buoyed up about the enterprise they were about to embark on. They immediate each sent letters to their solicitors instructing them to progress the sale of land. And they also conferred on how they would put their plan to the two London friends that they had identified as possible joint investors.

'You take the overnight stagecoach to London and I will ride down to the boat builders at Bucklers Hard to see if they can build a fast cutter – I think that we also need to fit two small cannon, just to deter chasing customs officers and any privateers intent on competing with us for the cross channel trade.'

'Yes, and George said that he would be sailing to France to meet up with his contacts and to broach the possibility of substantially increasing the amount, and if possible, the value, of goods.'

Over the next week, the plan had move on quite well. The senior boatbuilder at the Buckler's Hard Boatyard had replied to Alex's initial letter and said that the yard happened to have designs for a fast cutter already drawn up, one used on a previous build of a craft to be used in Falmouth for the race to get from shore out to the ocean-going sailing ships that would need to be towed into port. The work and so the fee going to the first boat to draw alongside. Alex arranged to ride to Buckler's Hard in the coming days in order to discuss this project in more detail. Hugh had returned from London with the good news of their having two more investors in their dubious consortium.

The new boat would be paid for on a monthly basis as the work progressed, so with the new investors and the probability of an early sale of each of their lands, Alex and Hugh felt that they could relax and focus more intensely on their hunting and fishing lifestyle.

At about this time, after a long day spent on horseback with the Beaulieu Hunt and its pack of hounds, all together seeking the elusive fox, the pair returned to the Manor House in something of a temper.

'Those bloody gypsies' said Hugh 'They have taken so many rabbits that any foxes that were around Beaulieu have themselves been off hunting elsewhere.

'But I had assumed gypsies to be mobile.' said Alex. 'So moving on.'

'Not this bloody tribe, some of them do come and go, but they also maintain a permanent settlement on common land near Lyndhurst.'

'So, why haven't those commons been enclosed as has happened across much of the county now.' asked Alex.

'As you probably know Alex, any motion to enclose requires a specific act of parliament – if this is pretty much an automatic process. But it needs landowners with property adjacent to the commons to petition for enclosure. As yet, the two landowners in a position to do this are happy to leave the gypsy encampment. The amount of land involved is quite small, so they take the view that it's not worth the trouble to annex this using the enclosure legislation. '

Following a pause during which Hugh was pulling off his boots his friend was looking thoughtfully out of the bay window, Alex turned and said.

'Well in that case, we must make it our job to convince those fellows to favour enclosure and rid the place of the rabbit killing bunch.'

'Not only rabbit Alex, but deer when they can get them and trout from my river throughout the damned year, they are a blight to the huntsman.'

'It seems to me that we now have a potentially enjoyable task here Hugh one with which we can entertain ourselves while we wait for our new boat, and with it our new enterprise, to be launched.'

Hugh looked up at his friend. 'I am not sure that much can be done to remove the encampment Alex, what are your thoughts.'

'I haven't yet formulated a plan old fellow but I am thinking that if we can expose the gypsies as wood, sheep, cattle or even horse thieves, or perhaps identify them as responsible for some form of criminal damage, the good people of Lyndhurst and the local landowners might be turned against them.'

'The problem with this Alex is that our gypsies are poachers rather than outright thieves and unfortunately the commoners in the New Forest are sympathetic towards those taking the rabbits and trout belonging to their social betters, a view motivated I suspect by envy.'

'The size of the challenge can only add interest to this amusing task my friend.' said Alex

Who were this, up to now anonymous, tribe of gypsies that the two friends were conspiring against?

Family rather than tribe would better describe the group as they were all related by blood or by marriage and were proud to share the family name of Pearson. It might risk distracting the reader and be of but little interest to learn the names of all of the thirty-eight adults and eighteen children making up the whole group, so I will mostly just highlight those who come to play at least some if more general role in our story. The most revered elders were Pa and Ma Pearson. Revered as much for more for their longevity, their being in their eighth decade, as for any wisdom gained during long lives. Longevity being unusual for these peoples whose living conditions were generally unhealthy, whose sources of food were unreliable and with both sexes smoking and drinking too much. Few Pearson's managed to see out five decades of life, so the elder Pearson's stood out more simply due to their tenacity for survival.

The ancestors of this group, tribe, family, or whatever collective term you wish to apply has as history of occupying this camp for generations. Along with Pa and Ma there were the four surviving children of this old couple. These being, John, Francis, Nancy, and Beth, and five surviving children of Pa's two now deceased brothers, Harry, Mark, Lizzie, Wicker, Merlin. There were also the three children of the one surviving sister Sue, Louise, Nic, and Woody, the four children Ned, Lois, Matt, and Ringer of the one surviving brother Tom. This bringing us to the next generation, who were various offspring of the ten just introduced. These last, now aged between eighteen and thirty-two, numbered sixteen individuals and rather than list all of them, I would only highlight – John junior, Mark junior, young Beth, young Louise, young Sue, along with Mick, Maggie, and Estell. I highlight each of these due to some of them featuring more prominently as our story unfolds. The eighteen younger children can remain anonymous as individuals, but as a group in our story they do provide noise, distraction, and mouths to feed as they mixed within the general life of the encampment.

The encampment enclosing this close family group is composed of half a dozen mobile caravans (vardos) and another half a dozen static dwellings, a similar number of small tents and the more substantial benders. The static homes being a rather motley collection of quite impressive two and three 'roomed' benders, a repurposed shepherd's hut, and a few of what were once usable caravans now being wheel-less and so immobile. In some places between more sturdy trees wood-framed, canvas covered, structures had been erected to serve as open air kitchens. These becoming sleeping shelters for some of the older children during the warmer summer nights. Some lurcher and smaller whippet-like dogs, along with chickens, roamed throughout the site and tethered on its margins were two donkeys and a number of ponies. The camp covered an area of a clearing within a hollow folded easily into a gently sloping area of woodland – the circle of trees providing a sense of safety and privacy for the group.

The gypsies made a living by such activities as peg, matt, basket, and walking-stick, making. Some of the men travelled round the local villages and farms, walking alongside a small cart pulled by a pony in which was a grinding-stone used to sharpen knifes, axes and other tools. In summer most of the younger men and some women, would leave in vardos for an extended tour of Hampshire and Wiltshire, calling at farms that had welcomed their fathers and their father's fathers before them. On this annual round they would earn cash income from work bringing in the various harvests, including – potatoes, corn, barley and hops. Then in early autumn it would be fruit picking before arriving back home with sufficient income to enable the group to get through the harsh winter months when food was short and work scarce.

There was also an amount of poaching to supplement the hedgehogs and squirrels encased in clay and cooked on open fires, along with any foodstuffs that they could afford to buy from the stalls and shops of Lyndhurst.

And of course, there were a number of quite inventive ways of producing alcoholic spirits when the smuggled alternatives could not be afforded, and there was always the well-practiced brewing of weaker beer to sustain adults and children alike.

Life for this group was generally difficult, but there was the occasional celebration for weddings, births, religious holidays, and when nature had been kindly and so food surpluses being available. Then the central area of the camp would be cleared to allow room for dancing – a couple of fiddles would be tuned up and a paddle-drum and a bassoon would be deployed to provide much needed musical ballast to the thinner-toned but melodic stringed instruments. The women would put on the best dresses with bright-banded hats and colourful scarfs, with the men dressing in their best, if for most it was well-worn suits, some with paisley-patterned silken waistcoats, topped off with the trade-mark gypsy neckerchief, always being made of red cloth.

Then, usually around midday, the party would start – excited children would be chasing each other between the smoky campfires and the smaller groups of adults standing around talking. With some more mischievous children seeking to try any unattended glass of beer or spirits. At the early stage of the day the men would be set on lining their stomachs with food and supping the mostly home-brewed ales and cider. Whilst the women would be focused on cooking pots suspended from aged-burnished metal tripods or balanced on similarly aged metal trivets, and in keeping the fires going. Pots of stew, joints of meat (usually poached venison), the heaps of pre-cooked pies and the many loaves of crusty bread were added to the fare on offer. These comestibles would soon be swooped on by individuals whose appetites had been stimulated by the aroma of cooking meat that had been drifting across the camp since early morning. This initial stage of satisfying hunger and thirst would progress slowly but inevitably towards the time when the musicians would produce their instruments, take up a prominent position, and begin to play. The music would be the signal for the mood of the whole group to brighten even further and for some of the adults, and a few of the older children, to take to the central area cleared for dancing. The dancers at this stage would mostly be younger women and perhaps just a couple of the younger men further into the drinking than their companions.

At this point the sober observer of this activity would note how the movement of the dancers was becoming more vigorous, with arms shaking about, torsos twisting, heads turning this way and that, and with feet stamping the dusty ground. Now more men had joined the dancers and some of the unmarried men and women have drawn much closer together. By now most of the children have disappeared into the woods to play games such as tag and hide and seek, and also to dare each other to climb the tallest trees or to attempt to jump across the widest parts of the nearby river.

As the sun went down the party would be in full joyous swing. If with the occasional break for the musicians to rest, and for more food to be consumed. With some of the older individuals then seeking comfortable places to settle and to drift off into gently snoring naps.

But a closer attention to the assembly would allow one individual to rather stand out. She tended towards the fringe of the party, wandering around mostly smiling, but at times, especially when she looked at the children playing, her face would assume a more concerned appearance. This woman, Luca (Lucerne), was now in her early thirties and still unmarried, a rare conjunction of gender, age, and social status in the gypsy community.

This woman stood out not only because of the time she would be on her own – and this not just at community events, but also for the many days she would spend alone tramping through the forest collecting various medicinal plants. This last been an indicator of her important role within the group. She had accumulated a knowledge of how to recognise the plants to be found in woodland and heathland useful for alleviating, and sometimes even curing, various ailments. These including headaches, period pains, constipation, insomnia, and indigestion. She would also assist the matriarchal gypsy midwife during the more difficult births. Luca was one of a long line of gypsies who used raw plants and various potions as treatments. But Luca was going further than tradition. She was unusual within the gypsy community in that she had learned to read and write. This due partly to her attendance at Sunday school, and also from the teaching of her own mother who was a non-gypsy by birth and had herself learned at least the basic skills of numeracy and literacy in her childhood.

But in addition to these opportunities Luca was a women determined to apply her intelligence to her experience. As a child she had read and re-read the Bible, but she had a sense that there was more to learn beyond religion. Her first step towards extending her reading material was to apply to the small lending library in Lyndhurst had been frustrated by her family background, with her being held in suspicion by the middle-aged women who oversaw the lending arrangements. But her determination to learn motivated her to keep trying and after a few attempts the hard-hearted 'librarian' relented and at least allowed the young Luca to read books in the library reading room itself, if not to take them out. After a few weeks during which the initial social barriers were eroded by regular association, the relationship between these two developed, with Luca being granted lending rights. Luca's reading, although still restricted by the limited stock of a village library, helped to significantly advance her knowledge of the wider world. One well-worn book was of particular interest. This was an English translation from the Latin of, 'The New Organon' ('Novum Organum') written in the seventeenth century by the scientist Francis Bacon who advocated a particular method of investigating the natural world. This, the use of experimentation, was to some extent only formalising practices that had been going on for centuries, but for Luca this method of gaining more secure knowledge beyond opinions and tradition, was a revelation.

It was a method that she was endeavouring to apply to her understanding of the medicinal potential of plants and wider dietary practices to improve health. There was phrase from Bacon's book that she often thought about, that 'Knowledge is power'. This became a sort of internal mantra urging her to continue learning.

An aspect of this learning and the reason for her frowning at times when wandering around the camp on this day of celebrations, was an awareness that the social space for the gypsy community was being eroded by an increasing antipathy toward traveling folk and the relentless enclosure of common and waste land. The very places where they would traditionally camp both when traveling and when more settled. We will come back to Luca as our story develops, but for now let's return to the party and a group unaware, so unconcerned, about any future threat to their collective well-being.

As the day's celebrations moved towards midnight the

children would be curled into tired sleep. Some in tents and others anywhere comfortable they could find near to their mother's skirts. The musicians by now had ceased playing, having decided that it was their right to catch up with the eating and drinking. The older men were all now awake and, as they anticipated a more prominent role in the day's proceedings, would have manoeuvred themselves onto the best seats. Most of the dancers were now exhausted and they also moved to join the circle gathering around the largest campfire. Although a few couples had slipped off into the privacy of the night-dark forest and the comfort of each other's arms.

This was the time for the older men to illustrate one of the reasons for their being respected within the group. It was time for story-telling. The history of the tribe was stored in the memories of three grizzled patriarchs. Aware of the importance of his role the first speaker, Pa Pearson, nosily cleared his throat, took a sip of brandy, and waited for the chatter passing through the assembled tribe to cease.

Then, with a deep but quiet voice, he set off on a detailed and elongated narrative of times past, of the roles of hallowed individuals, of the importance of the countryside that had sustained them throughout the seasons of each year. He spoke of past dangers being overcome by the tenacity and bravery of their ancestors. The voice raised in volume and deepened in tone in order to impart dramatic impact and so to instil awe amongst the always attentive audience. This first speaker would follow the traditionally prescribed pattern of outlining the earliest times of the tribe – Of its origins in the barren hills of the northern Indian sub-continent. Of traveling across north-western Asia into eastern Europe and then for generation on generation the tribe travelling west through country after country until settling in England. And for the more immediate ancestors of this group to have blessed the extensive 'Nevi Wesh' (New Forest) with their presence. This first speaker would have outlined a fairly factual narrative – if more often some of the finer details were liable to changes and heroic achievements exaggerated for each performance. Then the two speakers that followed would offer more imaginative tales involving villains and heroes entangled in various dramatic scenarios sprinkled with magical occurrences and introducing some mythical beasts.

As seemingly innocent as these stories might seem – they were implicitly intended to serve as both entertainment and as a means of highlighting a form of the tribe's identity and to secure imaginative connections between its past and its present. Within the various tales would be a narrative thread emphasising forms of morality, so allowing tribal norms to be past down the generations. Norms that would be unconsciously inveigled into the everyday interaction of adults and more specifically children as they absorbed the cultural complexity and moral standards of their tribe.

These times of the whole group being gathered together around the crackling logs as they became glowing orange embers in the campfire, overarched by a woodland canopy through which a star-clustered sky could be glimpsed would be events long retained in the memories of each member. It was in the misty darkness of such evening assemblies that an enduring tribal identity was reinforced.

Once the stories had been told, the drink and food finished and the fire damped down, the gipsies would seek the comfort of their straw-stuffed bedding.

And so, we can leave this relatively innocent group, with all but Luca being unaware of the dark cloud moving towards them. And with Luca herself only knowing the threat as a generality not as specific. The specific would be instigated by Alex and Hugh as something akin to entertainment for

157

them, intended to bring interest to the weeks in which they waited for their boat to be ready.

Their friend George had persuaded the small gang of ruffians that he had already been sponsoring for a modest level of the smuggling of contraband goods, to commit to the more ambitious plans of Alex and Hugh. He had also travelled to France and had been able to expand his shady contacts and so establish a supply line of goods that was about twenty times the volume he had previously been smuggling and he arranged to make two trips per month rather than one. This would be smuggling on a near industrial scale and would require customs officers to be bribed to ensure that they will be patrolling away from the new group's landing site.

Within a few days of Hugh having returned from his success in obtaining London-based investors he and Alex rode the five miles south-west to Bucklers Hard, where a busy boatyard took up about a quarter-mile stretch of the west bank of the River Beaulieu. This yard had already had a 70 year record of constructing men-of-war for the Royal Navy. Most notably ships such as HMS Euryalus, HMS Swiftsure and the largest of them all the 64 gun HMS Agamemnon, all three of which fought at the Battle of Trafalgar in 1805.

The pair dismounted, tied their horses to a convenient post and strolled towards the yard office. They could not but notice the number of craft drawn up on the shore in an obvious state of neglect and that only one of the three slipways had a craft being worked on. Once they had informed the yard manager of the nature of their business, he led them out of the office and pointed at a craft tied to a swing mooring in the river and bobbing gently in the current.

'That boat is due to be sold off to pay the yard fees of

an owner who has been unwell and has been unable to pay for repairs that we have carried out after it run aground off the Isle of Wight. I can sell her to you for a good price and she would form a good base for the boat you say that you are looking for. She was designed as a cutter working out of Falmouth and is in very good sea-worthy condition. If you want to make her even faster we can fit a taller main-mast to enable her to carry about 25% more sail area. To balance this we can increase the weight of the keel and add a bit more ballast. And of course, if you do intend to drive her hard, then you will need all of the standing and running rigging renewed and the securing brackets strengthened. Doing this work will make her a very fast boat.'

The manager spread his arm out to point towards the mostly empty slipways.

'As you can see, we are short of work, this being due to the war coming to an end. But our bad fortune could be your good, as we can get the work done on that boat within about three weeks. I assume that you young men are part of the new generation taking to sailing as a pastime.'

'Yes, that's the idea' said Alex, lying came easily to him.

'Some of our friends in a couple of London clubs are going to start sail-boat racing in the Solent – an exciting way to spend our weekends.'

The manager's working life had been spent making warships of various ratings as well as different types of working boat. But he reasoned that this new form of sailing could be where the future work might lie. Given this, he felt able to offer Alex and Hugh a good price for the boat and the work required. He also committed to a delivery date in just three weeks' time.

So pleased were the two friends with the outcome of their boatyard visit and the deal done, that they only rode as far as the inn at Beaulieu village before they began the day's drinking.

Chapter Seven

At the end of their day's journey from Dorchester James, Ezra, Caleb and Arthur, arrived at a small village close to the collection of small-holdings which were the primary purpose of their visit.

They were not surprised to find that there was a substantial inn located at the centre of the small village of Calstock, about eight miles east of the town of Honiton. The reason for this being obvious in that the main road to the south-west coast past through the village. And so with the daily passage of stage-coaches, post-coaches, goods wagons and more general traffic, the inn was quite busy. With coachmen, postilion riders, passengers as well as horse riders, all requiring both liquid and solid refreshment and for some an overnight stay.

The four men settled into their rooms and after washing and changing they decided on a walk around the village, party at least in order to stretch their legs after a day spent siting in the carriage. They were not due to meet with the two representatives of the smallholders until dinner time back at the inn, so they had a couple of hours spare.

The village of Calstock was fairly typical for east Devon. Mostly a collection of modest in size white- washed and thatched roofed cottages lining the main roadway, with a few narrow lanes leading from this. Wandering down one of the lanes they could see the small gardens, most with bright coloured patches in which flowers such a sweet-pea, stocks, and hollyhocks, were in bloom. Further on were a section of allotments, each being used by cottagers to grow vegetables for their own tables.

Returning to the main highway, they soon came up to the church, one surprisingly large given that the village itself could only have a population of a few hundred. The group were not to know that the church had been built three centuries earlier, just before the time in 1536 when Henry VIII enacted the Dissolution of the Monasteries. A move progressed for the vain king to raise funding for his military ambitions and for self-aggrandisement as expressed in building projects. The size of the church reflected the affluence of the locality at that time. There were two monasteries within a thirty-mile radius of the village and the fertile land of each allowed for: sheep to produce wool, cows to produce milk, bees to produce honey, and the skill of some of the monks to produce excellent wines and ciders. In addition to the abbots of each monastery wishing to enhance the Christian sense of the village, the village itself at that time had a larger population, this being due mainly to the work available on monastic lands. and for the transport to market of the goods produced.

Once the religious institutions had been closed down, with the land passing to the Crown, Henry's agents sold the land to favoured noblemen at what were knock-down prices, and for some even just being gifted. Many of these new landlords were not much interested in farming and preferred to let it return to the wilder conditions suitable for hunting. As the land became unproductive, with less need for farm labourers, many of the villagers had to move on to nearby towns or other locations where work was available. Now only the substantial church remained as an indicator of a more prosperous past.

As the companions were passing the church they could hear a regular metallic ringing which was lacking the more melodic ring of church bells and which they immediately recognised as the sound of a blacksmith at work. Arriving at the smithy, they could see an obviously strong man, broad shouldered and with sun-browned forearm's folded with muscles. His thick leather apron offering protection from the waist to the knees being scarred in many places with burn marks. This to such an extent that it was mainly black with burns, having very little of the original light brown leather showing through. The condition of this apron indicating two decades of hard work undertaken at a spark inducing anvil.

After the blacksmith and his visitors had acknowledged each other's presence, if with just nods and grunts, the four men stood and watched this artisan skilfully beating out a lump of metal that would be slowly formed into the head of an axe. Alternating between using elongated tongs to thrust the metal lump deep into the glowing bed of cinders coating the bellow-blown forge, and then holding it on an anvil to continue shaping the axe-head.

Looking round the smoky shed they could see a series of hooks along one of the solid wooden beams on which pre-made horseshoes of various sizes were ready to be fitted. On some broad shelves beneath these were a couple of frying pans, some sets of fork tines, and a few spade blades. Some with shallow blades for lifting turf, wider ones for general digging, and ones with sets of long sharp-forked tines for digging heavy soils and others with flattened sets of tines designed for such tasks as lifting turnips and potatoes. The variety of this production reflecting the craftsman's skill as well as the needs of his customer-base.

As the inert lump of metal was progressing in stages to become an axe-blade the watching group were mesmerised with the way in which heat and percussion could be applied to transform an inert metal object into a valuable metal tool. Once the blacksmith was satisfied with his work he lifted the axe-blade and held it hissing and steaming in a large bucket of water. The final act being to place the dripping blade on a nearby shelf alongside the other products of the man's labours.

After exchanging some small talk and thanking the blacksmith for the chance to view him at work, the four made their way back to the inn.

The first part of the plan for their stay in Calstock was to have dinner that evening with two of the original veterans who has taken up the chance to be part of the smallholding initiative. James himself had been happy to leave the administration of the site to the London agent and for him to liaise with representatives of the community when necessary. They also intended to meet with all of the military veterans who had become smallholders, and any members of their families that wished to come along. This meeting would take place in a large communal barn built adjacent to the highway to serve as both a communal meeting place and also as a store for surplus goods before these were transported to a local market.

Once these meetings had taken place James's intention was to leave Arthur to work with small groups of smallholders and offer them advice on how they might improve the productivity of their holdings. He also intended to leave Caleb and Ezra with the veteran-based community, partly for them to spend time with a number of the men that they had served alongside but also to given them the opportunity to experience agricultural work at first hand. With the possibility of their taking to small-scale farming on land that their highway robbery had enabled the agent to purchase recently.

Over diner that evening they were joined by David and Alun, both being originally from Wales and having volunteered into the same regiment in which Ezra had served for a time. At first it was only with some difficulty that James and Arthur were able get these three to focus on the main business for discussion, which was agricultural rather than anecdotes from their time in military service. But once it sunk in that Ezra and Caleb would be staying at the inn in Calstock for the next two weeks, the companions did at least try not to get distracted as new memories came to mind.

David covered an overview of the 200 plots of land that had been settled so far.

'The harvests of the two years of 1818/19 since Alun and myself first came here have been quite poor but we have managed to get through and for this year so far the weather has been kind and the range of vegetable crops are looking good.'

'Yes, I agree with David' said Alun 'And, as with most of the group who are new to farming, I have also been surprised how satisfying working on the land can be. But two families so far, and another two possibles, are thinking of leaving. They haven't quite taken to a farming life and are missing their families in Manchester and the bustle of the city itself.'

'Well two, possibly four, families out of fifty does not seem too bad.' said James 'And of course, we will help any family that wants to leave to resettle elsewhere, and the emigration option remains open.'

The evening continued, with the condition of the veteran community being considered in more detail. Unsurprisingly, some of the veterans had been suffering from the affects of awful experiences of conflict that were difficult to assimilate or forget. But working in the open air and living in a more emotionally sustaining natural environment had at least helped with the healing process.

The preparatory meeting at the inn enabled James to be

informed and so better prepared for the next day's meeting in the large barn. This later meeting, more a gathering, was much busier, with most of the wives and lots of children also attending. After failing to get the children to quieten down these were all led outside and ordered to play together well away from the barn.

As the meeting progressed James listened carefully to the comments and was encouraged to learn that almost all of the community was very happy to be settled here in Devon. More than one man stood up to say how much he and his family's prospects had been improved by becoming a smallholder, and whenever this happened an echo of agreement rumbled around the barn.

The meeting drew to an end with James making a short speech noting how pleased he was to learn of the overall success of the enterprise. He told the gathering that in their hard work they had clearly proven the viability of smallholding within a wider farming project based on co-operative endeavour. This being in relation to sharing equipment, a marketing strategy for surplus goods, and a willingness to support each other. He congratulated the assembly for showing the viability of this approach, especially in relation to ex-military personnel. That they were in the vanguard of what he hoped would be similar settlements across the country as well as a further expansion of this one.

The following morning over a shared breakfast in the dining room of the inn, James informed the others that he was going to make a visit to the coastal town of Lyme Regis and would be there for about a week. In the meantime, the other three would be accommodated at the inn, with Arthur undertaking a series of meetings with the smallholders and the other two spending time with old companions and helping them in the fields as a short exposure to this type of work. As already noted, the idea of this being to see if Caleb and Ezra felt that they could settle to a life in the Calstock based small-holding community.

Although they were curious why James would wish to travel to the coastal town, they respected him enough to not push him to explain. As their breakfast was coming to an end James said that he had something for Arthur and from a small leather bag at his feet he produced a smallish but expensive-looking silver tin. On its lid was engraved a sentence thanking Arthur Gordon for his work with the farmers of Downland Park and with the ex-servicemen of the Calstock community cooperative. Beneath this was engraved the date of 1820.

'I feel rather overwhelmed but honoured by this gift James – I have been well-paid for my work and I do so much enjoy sharing what knowledge I have with a new generation of agriculture workers.'

'Open the tin please Arthur, I want to explain its contents' said James.

'What on earth have we here' said a smiling Arthur as he opened the tin, while Caleb and Ezra had each assumed rather bemused expressions.

James lent forward, removed two small packages, placed them carefully on the table, then opened each one.

'You can see that in this package there is some soil that is sandy and pale whilst in the other package there is soil that is finer, more fibrous and of a much darker hue. To repeat a comment that you just made Arthur….'What we have here….is an illustration of the fruit of your work.

It was about six months ago when, in response to a query from me, you sent a letter by return in which you offered a range of more general advice on how to improve the condition of various types of soils. Then, following your accepting my invitation to act on a consultancy basis at Downland itself, you have for the past two months been providing more specific advice to each of the tenants and also for Joe and our Home Farm.

What we have before us are two soil samples both taken from the same corner of the same Home Farm field. One was taken prior to using your advice and the other six months after your initial contact by when the soil has already been improved due to your input. The difference between the samples is stark and I wanted show you how much Downland has benefited.'

Glancing up at Arthur he could see that tears were forming in the corners of this tough old farmer's eyes. Who, shaking his head and drawing a large handkerchief from his trouser pocket loudly blew his bulbus nose, wiped his eyes, and in a somewhat broken voice thanked James for such a meaningful gift, adding that he would treasure the tin and its contents for the rest of his life.

'By the time I return from my trip, you will have left Calstock Arthur, but I to want to say that if you ever feel the need to spend time in Dorset you will always be welcomed at Downland.'

And so the party broke up. The future for Arthur being his spending a week or so working with the smallholders and then traveling back to the large farm in the Midlands, now being managed by his son.

For Caleb and Ezra it was off for the first day of renewing old friendships and experiencing fieldwork – they both looked forward to the former but shared doubts about the latter.

Within the hour James had packed a pair of saddle bags that he had brought with him for this trip, hired a horse from the inn's stable, and was on the highway heading south-east towards the coast. He felt relaxed to be alone and seated in the comfortably creaking saddle. His elevated position allowed him to view more of the countryside beyond the lane. A lane comfortably enclosed within hawthorn bushes trimmed into hedging, interspersed with the occasional beech, elm, or oak tree, this being further enhanced by dog-roses trailing over sections of the foliage. At the edges of the lane a variety of grasses and some wild- flowers grew in profusion. The more prominent being the various types of cream-flowered cow-parsley. And it was the scent of these infusing the more general organic temper of the air that highlighted the rural prospects set out before him. He was happy to be once again on the broad back of a horse. If, by the late afternoon as he was approaching the coastal town of Lyme Regis, he was looking forward to easing his now quite stiff rear end out of the saddle.

He was reflecting on the reason for his coming to the town and his thoughts took him back to the lecture he had attended at the Royal Institute a couple of months earlier during his recent visit to London. In the ten minutes or so when the lecture hall had been slowly filling with attendees, James had overheard some of a conversation between two members of the audience seated in the row in front of his. Although the lecture was due to be on electricity, these two were engaged in a quite animated conversation about geology and the controversy over the age of the earth. One of them, being of a more dogmatic Christian outlook, said that he was firmly committed to assuming that heaven and earth had been created by God on the very specific 23rd October 4004 b.c. This had been the date suggested in the previous century by James Ussher the Archbishop of Armagh, who had calculated the age of the earth by following the biblical genealogy from Adam onwards, as set out in the early Books of the Old Testament. The archbishop then supplementing this by a study of the calendar-related information drawn from some early Greek and Egyptian texts. This seemingly fact-based date ('God's Truth'), having the substance of statistical calculation, had both a spiritual and mathematical authority, and so was considered by most educated men of the time as sound. But more recently this date was being challenged by men of science who studied the fossil remains of long dead animals and the geological condition that these were found in. Such objects had long been commented on by some ancient Greek philosophers such as Aristotle who, being of a curious and observant mind combined an interest in the natural world with the analytic skills of a philosopher. What was of particular interest to these ancient individuals was the unexpected finding of fossilized marine creatures in rocks hundreds of miles from any coast. Inevitably, the Christian Father's explanation sought to align this seeming anomaly with biblical text, and so gave the floods as set out in the story of Noah's Ark, during which the seas were said to have covered all of the land, as the reason for the location of the remains of marine creatures.

But some individuals working within the newly termed sciences of Geology and Biology were directed by the actual evidence of such fossils being found deep into many layers of sedimentary rocks which they knew would have taken much more than a few thousand years for the deposit of fine layers of sediment to become solid rock. Aligned to the geological evidence, there was a growing interest in the large number of fossils being found of species of organisms that were no longer alive. Whereas the Bible suggested that species are eternal (immutable). Being claimed to be survivors of the creatures that were taken two-by-two on board Noah's Ark and so saved from the floods. This controversy was based on advancing knowledge - both discovery and theory - of geology and biology. It was a controversy that would come to a head later in the century with the publication of Charles

Darwin's book 'On the Origin of Species'. But would be made more public at the historic meeting in Oxford where The Christian defender of the Bible, William Wilberforce, clashed with the biologist Thomas Huxley ('Darwin's Bulldog') from when the theory of evolution was developed and would progressively displace the Biblical ideas, at least for the more open-minded individuals prepared to consider the evidence rather than being wedded to ideas written about 2,000 years in the past. James, as an interested reader, had been aware of the new ideas, so he was only half listening to these two heatedly exchanging their differing views.

But when he heard the more modern-minded of the two men in front of him challenge the quite dogmatic Christian with the evidence of a fossilized sea- creature found by a woman named Mary Anning he took more interest.

The Christian suggested that. 'I can only assume that the young women has made some model from the bones of such animals as chickens, pigs, and various bones from very large fish or sharks, and is passing it off as some creature from times past. She has fooled the more gullible people such as yourself sir into believing her....and no doubt to pay guineas to buy the skeleton of some marine-freak'.

'I think that you are merely trying to find a reason to ignore evidence sir.' said the challenger.

Going on the suggest that. 'I just think it is a shame that Miss Anning is not getting the full credit for her finds and more especially for the knowledge she has gained about fossils more generally. She has even been shunned by such institutions as the Geological Society who would not even allow her to enter their London offices – disgraceful treatment sir I would say.'

These two each shook their heads in unison and turned away from each other to allow tempers to cool before the lecture on electricity began.

His witnessing this heated argument had stimulated James to find out more about the latest advances in geology and biology and he was intrigued as to why a young woman, who he later discovered was from quite a poor family, was so interested in fossils. But for now, his focus returned to the immediacy of his progress towards her hometown of Lyme Regis.

Looking up he could see that he had turned a bend in the lane and set out before him was the broad span of Lyme Bay. Where a light blue sky met the darker blue of the sea at a misty distant horizon. He could see a few small in-shore fishing boats going about their business and further out some larger sailing ships making steady progress towards ports further along the coast. From his elevated position at the top of the steep hill leading into the town he could see that the settlement was loosely contained within the lower slopes of a steep-sided valley, through the centre of which flowed the fast-running River Lyme, to end its journey in the sea below.

The town itself was a collection of small cottagers, stuccoed villas, and some more substantial stone buildings in a style that would come to be called Georgian.

He was leaning back in the saddle as he rode down towards the town and he could begin to smell the evening meals being cooked and this stimulated his appetite, as well seemingly that of the raucously squawking gulls circling above the houses. On finding the inn that he had arranged to stay in and, having passed the reins of his horse to the ostler, he was able to satisfy his hunger with the enthusiastic consumption of a generously portioned roast beef dinner. By about 8 o'clock he had rested and so decided to take a walk along the seafront towards the west. He knew the best fossil hunting ground lay to the east, between Lyme and the small coastal village of Charmouth about five miles along the coast. But he wanted to leave this until the following day when he hoped to meet up with Mary. He had written to her to say that he was very interested in her discoveries and would like to meet up. Mary had replied in a short letter written in a spidery hand stating that she would be out fossil-hunting early in the day but if he called at her family shop in the afternoon she would be there and would be happy to receive him.

Mary's life had been quite difficult. Having been born in Lyme in 1799 to parents Richard and Mary ('Molly'). Richard had been a poorly paid cabinet-maker and was, like Mary, a collector of the fossils that could be found in abundance in the rocks along the coast. It was when accompanying her father on his regular fossil-hunting trips that Mary's interest in these was established. For Richard there was a general interest in the stone-entombed organisms but of more practical relevance was their value. When cleaned and polished, they could be sold to some of the increasing number of tourists visiting the town.

Early in the previous century the town's primary mean of gaining a living had been the use of its port by large fishing trawlers and by merchant boats, involved in exporting the production of the west-county wool industry. The shallowness of the port and the increasing size of the merchant boats, along with a significant reduction in the local wool trade, meant that merchants moved their business away. Similarly, the increasing size of the off-shore fishing boats also caused these to find deeper ports and ones with more extensive boat-building and repair facilities than the small units at Lyme. But the reduction of the more commercial operations made the town more attractive for the increasing number of the middle-class who favoured being by the sea and with the leisure time to progress this. They were influenced by the medical advice of the benefits of sea-bathing and of breathing in the fresh sea air. By the early nineteenth century the town had become a popular tourist location. With the newly built Assembly Rooms being a cultural centre, offering popular dances (for some more aspirational residents these being elevated to the status of 'balls' on occasion) as well as more serious forms of entertainment.

Given such attractions the town was becoming popular with tourists and on any warm summer's day the smooth-sanded beach would be lined with wheeled bathing huts. With a number of similar huts having been pulled by donkeys or horses into the sea to allow their female occupants to slip with modesty intact into the water.

James's post-prandial walk that first evening in Lyme saw him heading west along the narrow Marine Parade. This was a pleasant walk with the day's high winds having eased to become a gentle on shore sea-breeze, allowing James to feel nicely relaxed as he came to the harbour area of the town. This smallish harbour was protected from strong winds and heavy tides by the solid structure known as the Cobb. A protective wall, initially built during the reign of Edward I by driving massive oak piles into the seabed and filling the spaces between this with large boulders. Such was the strength of the relentless force of nature that this harbour wall was swept away one winter night following a series of wild storms. The rebuilding sought a more substantial form of defence, so much of the new harbour wall was built using large blocks of Portland Stone arranged in a cleverly rounded design that helped to deflect at least some of the strength of the enormous waves that the sea would cast against it.

James climbed a set of stone steps set in the wall and walked along a section of the wide top. As he strolled along, he reflected on the calmness of the water beyond the solidity of the Cobb, with the evening's swell lapping at the seaward side rather than the more common experience of heavy waves rolling in from the west before crashing into the wall and casting fountain-like plumes of spray high into the air. The eternal regularity of the sea's movement – co-ordinated by the pale moon's diurnal passing over the planet – was for James one of nature's wonders.

He enjoyed the walk back to the inn and later in the evening as soon as had washed, climbed into the clean-sheeted bed and closed his eyes, he drifted easily into a sound sleep.

As James awoke the following morning the sunny weather was warming the town into life, with quite a few tradesmen, labourers, and others already up and about their day's business. Following a light breakfast, he walked the three hundred cobbled yards to the Anning family's shop.

It was noted earlier that this was a poor family, but we should now add that the status of poor but managing was now reduced to poverty and just surviving. The reason for the change in living conditions being the untimely death of Mary's father, Richard. If in dying the man's spirit was considered by the religious Anning family members who had survived their husband and father to be joining the spirts of those eight of his ten children who had preceded him to heaven.

The mortal coil that Richard had shaken of was now more firmly tied about the family he had left behind. Mary's older brother Joseph had just been apprenticed to an upholsterer, but such an apprenticeship was seen by the working classes as a privilege leading in due course to remunerative work as a craftsman. But for the training period the very low pay was seen as a token of the apprenticeship bond than anything more.

This meant that the principal income to support the family needed to come from the sale of fossils collected by Mary. The favoured fossils being the imprints of ferns and other plant leaves on rocks that, once washed, polished, and Mary discovered when brightened up with a thin coat of varnish, were quite popular with tourists. Even more collectable were the fossilized shells of various species of ammonite and belemite that were commonly to be found in landslip material of the cliffs composed of Blue Lias rocks adjacent to the town. Quite a number of tourists came to the shop to view the exhibits on show but just a few would make a purchase to add to collections of objects that were filling the cabinets of curiosities being adding to the bourgeoise furnishing of some middle-class suburban villas. As well as to the more genteel furnishing of some grander upper-class houses.

But it was a much more dramatic find that had brought Mary's name to the attention of individuals with an interest in the long dead specimens that brought geology and biology together. It was Mary's brother Joseph that actually found the fossil partly protruding from of the cliff face one morning after a stormy night. But it was an eleven-year-old Mary who had the patience and determination to undertake the time-consuming work of carefully removing the fragile skeleton of the specimen from its rocky grave. This creature would come to be named the 'ichthyosaurus' (fish lizard). In life it would have been a fast-swimming porpoise-like creature. In death, once removed from the cliff and laid out on a large wooden table in the Anning family shop, it still presented as an impressive object. As the news of the find spread it did not initially create much interest from the scientific community. Most members of this group with any interest in fossils dismissing the find (most without even viewing it) as but a specimen of crocodile rather than of an unknown sea creature. But as the years past, and Mary's local reputation as a fossil collector grew, a couple of influential gentlemen - Lieut. Col, Thomas Birch and the physician Everard Home - did come to take a more serious interest in the ichthyosaurus fossil as well as some of Mary's other finds, and it was Home who wrote a scientific paper on the creature that, when published, did begin to increase interest more widely. Partly through material need, but also through a keen interest in fossils, Mary persevered with her fossil hunting, and also took advantage of any opportunity to improve her knowledge of geology and anatomy.

It was a twenty-one year old fresh-faced Mary who greeted James. Then, following her showing him round the small shop and its stock of fossil remains, she guided him across the main road and on to the sea-shore on the eastern side of the town. As they walked along the shore towards the stretch of higher cliffs, the conversation between them was quite easy. James's attitude came as something of a pleasant surprise to her. Usually, any gentlemen visitors would assume a level of knowledge suggesting a grasp of the subject that was not manifested in their actual understanding. But they were rarely if ever conscious of the knowledge they lacked but of which Mary had an abundance. Mary herself stoically bore the patronising attitude of these visitors and adopted a diplomatic means of engaging with them – suppressing her wish to correct errors and hoping that the visit would at least end with a transaction of benefit to her family. With James she found a modest individual keen to learn rather than to pretend to knowledge.

In the short time it took them to reach the length of cliff that they we going to focus on, Mary had realised that this visitor was prepared to allow her to take the lead in the conversation about fossil hunting. She began by explaining that the cliff was primarily composed of a material known as Blue Lias, a form of rock made up of alternating layers of limestone and shales that, due to their granular composition, were liable to absorb water and so, following days of heavy rain, the cliff face would be vulnerable to landslides. This, whilst being potentially risky for the collector, was also a natural mechanism for exposing new fossil materials.

'Some years ago, my brother Joseph and myself found the ichthyosaur after a stormy night. At first we only saw a small section of the skeleton had been revealed but what we subsequently dug out taught us that any part of a bone however seemingly insignificant should not be easily passed over and might just be an indicator of a whole specimen still hidden within the cliff face.'

They spent the afternoon working their way along the cliff face towards Charmouth, with James noting what a lovely workplace this was, at least on a fine day such as this. He could see the shore offering a wide arc leading to Charmouth, and beyond this to the cliff-top feature known locally as 'Golden Gap'. This name being due to its exposed rock reflecting sunlight in a way that seemed to make it shine.

They only found a few specimen's – a couple of ammonites, a belemnite, some stones washed up on the beach with images of ferns, and a gnarled coprolite. But for James this was an unexpected bounty. These organic curiosities stimulated him to reflect that these now extinct creatures had once roamed the earth, swum in the seas, and that the fossilized plants had once grown upon the land. It was as if our past is written in stone, in some organic form of hieroglyphics with patterns of bones operating as patterns of letters.

'My goodness' he thought. 'I am getting a bit too imaginative now. This comparison can only be stretched so far. But both the fossil legacy and the hieroglyphic alphabets are forms of communication. In the case of fossils the information is about the secret history of the earth entombed in stone. And Mary is at the leading edge of revealing the mysteries of this long dead past.'

Over the next few days James and Mary went on three more hunting trips, with the final one following a stormy night. Just the preconditions suitable for successful hunting and it was a day that saw a bounteous return for their endeavours. One sufficient to make a useful contribution to the stock of the Anning fossil shop.

On the last afternoon of his fossil hunting week, the couple enjoyed coffee and cake in a small hotel adjacent to the beach with Mary and James rounding off the week by acknowledging that their original meeting as strangers had in a short time developed into a friendship that they felt would continue into the coming years. A friendship expressed in regular correspondence and occasional visits by James to Lyme. They parted company, with James walking back to the inn and Mary with a large muslin bag containing that day's finds heading to the Anning fossil shop

Early on the following day James mounted on his horse was making his way slowly up the long hill leading up and out of the Town. He retained an image of Mary in his mind's eye. Of her being of average hight, with a fresh, open, young face, smooth skin, if it's being lightly tanned as one would expect given her main pastime. A face blessed with even features more often framed within a loose-fitted bonnet having its untied red ribbons hanging down over her coat. He was still thinking of the unfairness of Mary's being in effect shunned by the patriarchal and somewhat insular scientific community of early nineteenth-century Britain.

At that time, he wasn't to know that during the following two decades Mary's work would come to receive at least some respect from more enlightened practitioners within geology and palaeontology. There was a succession of such scientists who visited her and quite a number of these accompanied her on fossil hunting trips. As Mary steadily added to her list of significant discoveries, including a noted plesiosaur, her fame gradually spread across Britain, Europe and beyond. One more notable visitor was King Frederick Augustus II of Saxony. Mary also maintained an ongoing correspondence with the well-known scientists Louis Agassiz of France and Charles Lyell of England. The American curator of the New York 'Lyceum of Natural History', George Featherstonehaugh, came to the shop to purchase items that would be exhibited in the Lyceum.

Although never financially secure, the Anning family prospects did improve quite markedly, especially when, in 1826, Mary was able to open a new shop 'the 'Anning Fossil Department'. A venue that became pretty much a favoured place to visit on the Lyme tourist agenda. Perhaps the most enduring legacy would appear 200 hundred years later, with the setting up of a bronze statue of Mary in a prominent site on Lyme Regis seafront. The figure has what looks like a fossil trilobite in one hand and a geologist's hammer in the other. With a model of her pet dog Tray at her side. The statue is positioned as if gazing towards the long stretch of cliff-face running round to Charmouth. But for now James could only regret the ignorance of the early 19th century scientific community.

It took him until early evening before he arrived back at the inn in Calstock where he found that Gordon had left that same day on the journey back to his home.

Over the following week James called at each of the fifty smallholdings just to have a talk with the veterans on a one-to-one basis. As he walked between the holdings, he was encouraged to see how productive the land has been made.

When speaking with those responsible for this productivity this encouragement was reinforced by the comments of the smallholders who littered their conversions with implicit and explicit references to the communal nature of the whole enterprise. Two more recent settlers emphasised the help their neighbours had been in terms of specific agricultural and marketing advice, but also how welcoming they had been to new families.

'I think the knowing that we all share the experience of military service was an important bond in ensuring the success of cooperative working' said one smallholder, and this served as quite representative of the other conversations.

On the final evening in Calstock the three friends shared their impressions of the community that they had all made a contribution to supporting.

'I have enjoyed our two weeks here' said Caleb 'Especially being able to meet up with some old comrades, and to see them doing so well. But if I were to be honest colonel, I just can't see myself taking up your offer to join the community here. Digging, planting, cropping, and such work is just not for me. I need the excitement of a city or at least of a large town. I miss the buzz and I know it sounds daft but I even miss the smells! The countryside is fine to travel through or visit and much of it is does look pretty, but it is also pretty dull for me. I think it will be emigration for me. I am thinking of Sydney Cove, Australia. I understand that that faraway land was initially settled with criminals so, given my own highwaymen's past, a move there would be appropriate.'

'Goodness Caleb' said Ezra 'I think that was probably the longest speech that I have ever heard you make. But I do think a person would need to be very committed if they were to take up a new life here in the countryside.'

'I can also understand your decision Caleb' said James

'Even if we will miss your cheery company. What about you Ezra have you come to a decision about your future.?'

Ezra looked thoughtful as he rubbed his rough-bearded chin.

'Well, this trip had also helped me to come to a view about how best to spend the rest of my life colonel. In a word it is 'wood'! My working with Amos at Downland Park has introduced me to a natural material that is satisfying to handle, is pleasing to look at with its creased bark, fine grain and knots, and has practical elegance in what it can be made into – be this a chair, stool, table, shelving, etc. Amos's own obvious love of the material has infected me. Where I used to see anonymous trees I now see oaks, ash, birch, willow, larch, and similar, each one being especially suitable for this or that product. With these products being created by applying the skills of carpentry. Even with my still very basic skills I can find making something of good design and practical use to be rewarding. Amos is the most physically skilled man that I have ever met, a man whose abilities I very much respect. I have been working with him for four weeks now and he says that I have a natural affinity with wood and that there are real signs that the skills of carpentry will yes need hard work, but which should come quite easily to me. So, my intention is to use some of the money saved from my previous life outside of the law, to buy a good set of tools and in due course to seek work somewhere near the village of Cerne Parva. If you agree colonel, I would like to find a lodging in the village and come to the Hall each day to work alongside Amos without pay. This until I have developed the skills and the confidence to set up on my own. '

James looked from one to the other of his friends 'Mm, well, this journey has proven to be very useful for you two in terms of thinking through the issue of each of your futures. I agree with you Caleb that it would be difficult for you to contain your natural restlessness within the confines of a smallholding, and a new start in Australia does seem to be a realistic alternative. If it does not work out, and you decide to return to England, you do know that you will be welcome back to Downland Park.

As to your proposal Ezra, I think we can do a bit better with this. What if you progress the plan of working alongside Amos but instead of lodging in the village you stay in the newly renovated workers cottage that Arthur Gordon has just vacated. I have some quite ambitious plans for The Hall. Starting with having a large Orangery constructed on the south-facing side. And there is a significant amount of work to be done inside the worker's cottages. Susan has told me that her father has been finding the more physical aspects of his work increasingly difficult. So, I propose that you work with Amos to learn the skills of carpentry but also support him so that he can continue working for as long as possible, or at least for as long as he wants to. You and Amos can together become the renovation stroke maintenance team for the Hall. What do you think?'

'I think that such work would suit me very well colonel.' said Ezra

'And having my own billet would be perfect – no-one will be disturbed by my snoring and occasional noisy nightmares. Although I do have doubts about my cooking skills'

'You will have to find a wife' said Caleb laughing as he pointed at Ezra

'I think that Mary will provide as much advice as you will need in the cooking area.' said James.

'Just bear in mind how good Joe looks on her cooking – probably the best beef and onion pies in Dorset.'

'Finding a wife might well be an aspect of my taking to a more settled life.' said Eza 'I do have a comely widow currently working as a barmaid in the Cerne Parva village pub as a possible candidate.'

Now that the main business of Caleb and Ezra's futures had been decided, the rest of the evening was spent in their talking about some aspects of their shared past and of their possible futures.

Over breakfast the following day James proposed that rather than taking a direct route back to Downland Park they should divert to the New Forest village of Lyndhurst to see how John and his wife Sarah have adjusted to life as innkeepers. The other two were pleased with this suggestion, thinking that it would be good to meet up with their old friend in military service as well as in crime.

We will leave these three to a night's rest before they embark of the journey to Lyndhurst and ourselves move our attention to the New Forest to consider how Alex and Hugh are progressing their fundraising enterprise of smuggling and their intention to find entertainment in harassing gypsies.

We find the two dissolutes in the rear drawing room of Hugh's impressive mansion. Hugh is stretched out on a chaise lounge and Alex is standing by the wide window looking thoughtfully into middle distance.

The pair were relaxing after lunch and each of them has a glass of claret within easy reach.

In the time since we last considered Alex and Hugh they have made progress is their latest business endeavour and in their more entertaining interests.

A central part of the entertainment being their pursuing an intention to clear the Lyndhurst gypsies from the Forest so that their hunting and fishing activity would be made more rewarding without the depredations caused by poaching for which they wrongly held the gypsies solely responsible. But for them the simple fun of harassing a vulnerable group had drawn their interest even more.

This project had received additional motivation for Alex due to an encounter he had when out for a ride in the Forest with Hugh. As they came to a small lake known as Hatchet's Pond, he saw Luca on one of her medicinal plant hunting expeditions.

Taken with her looks, Alex dismounted and complimented the gypsy woman on her beauty and asked if she needed help and wanted some company.

Luca took in the leering expression on Alex's face and the amused look in Hugh's.

'No thank you I am fine on my own.'

Alex moved towards her and reached out to touch her arm.

'Come girl.' He said. 'I don't mind paying for your company – I am sure you would not charge much.'

He did not even see the hand that slapped him hard across the face. His vison was blurred as he stepped back slipped and fell.

This caused Hugh to burst out laughing at his friend's plight - for Alex coating anger with embarrassment.

Luca walked off and, as Alex rose with an intention to attack her with his riding crop, he saw a wagon with a number of the Verderers (a form of New Forest 'police force') passing by.

He remounted his horse with a 'Damn you girl…. you and the rest of your dirty tribe will soon be cleared from this land and you might then regret being so offensive.'

Luca walked off over a marshy section of heathland aware that men on horseback would find it difficult to ride over. But Alex's words about their being 'cleared from the land' added to her concerns about the future of her family group.

This incident had reinforced Alex's determination to progress the action to have the wasteland that the gypsies were camped on enclosed. Over the past few weeks, he and Hugh had been engaged in a strategy of flattering the two yeomen farmers whose land abutted the gypsy encampment and whose agreement would be required for enclosure. They had invited these aspiring gentlemen to join their fox hunting parties and to attend the receptions in the Hall following the day's hunt. Even prior to receiving the friendly advances from Alex and Hugh, the two farmers had been viewing themselves as moving up in the world, as their farms were becoming financially more successful. Benefiting from the progressive introduction of modern methods of agriculture. But for them to receive the attention of the local aristocracy (as in Lord Hugh, Sir Alex, and their social circle) was more than they could ever have expected. It is easy to be flattered into thinking that previously beyond reach social recognition was in fact an earned entitlement. This view was reinforced by the way in which their wives took to the unexpected social elevation of their families. This, not just in enjoying the expectation of parading themselves and their marriageable children at the balls that they were now looking forward to receiving invitations too, but also in the satisfying conversation they could have with neighbours. They would now pepper their comments on life with phrases such as 'As Lord Grenville was saying to my husband' or 'Lord or Lady this or that was so funny when he/she said....'. Along with other such indicators of the company they now keep. The elevated social status would also be reflected in the haughty demeaner they would now assume when walking along Lyndhurst High Street or when attending the Sunday service in St Michaels and All Angels parish church.

It only took a few meetings to persuade the two farmers

to agree to cooperate in the move to enclose and for their being willing to add the common land to their own. They were reluctant at first given their previously fairly amicable relationship with their gypsy neighbours and the lack of much value in the land being considered. But the hinted at, if not openly stated, suggestion that they might not be so welcome within Hugh's social circle was a more convincing argument for cooperation than holding to their previous views.

Hugh's family had long been friendly with the family of Sir John Wentworth Lemming an individual who had been elected to parliament as a Tory at the 1820 general election. This supposed representative of the people was in fact elected by a mere fraction of those living in the constituency. If this was somewhat more 'democratic' than the representational scandal that was Old Sarum, the nearby Hampshire parliamentary constituency with two MPs. One of which had only 43 people who met the income qualification necessary to vote. The other MP having a tiny constituency area absurdly covering just one farm and some fields grazed over by a few hundred sheep! This was time when the 400,000 strong population of the city of Manchester had no parliamentary representation at all.

The project for enclosure would be considerably assisted if Sir John could be persuaded to support the petition for enclosure to be laid before parliament. Then to follow this up with representations to the commissioners who would be appointed to assess the validity of the proposed change of land ownership. Hugh's initial approach to the M.P. was even easier than he had expected. Over a sumptuous dinner Hugh casually began the conversation by asking Sir John for his views of gypsies.

'Absolute bloody pests.... poachers, thieves, and conmen.' was Sir John's 'thoughtfully considered' response.

Hugh, hearing how closely Sir John's view aligned with that of his and Alex's own, then put the proposal to clear the Lyndhurst site to his guest.

'Yes, that seems to be a bloody good idea, get a lawyer to draw up the petition as soon as you can.'

It seems that the MP's enthusiasm for the plan was at least as strong as theirs. So buoyed up by this reaction they engaged a Southampton based lawyer with a reputation for dubious undertakings and a willingness to carry out pretty much any instruction if the remuneration was sufficiently generous.'

If we return to the cosy scene of Alex and Hugh's post lunch rest in the drawing room, we can see that Alex has moved to sit at a writing desk on which are spread some sheets of papers covered in figures. Looking up from these Alex turned towards Hugh.

'Since we began our venture into smuggling, or rather our enterprising trade with the continent, we have been able to make two payments to our bank creditors Hugh. Hopefully, they will view this as a sign that we will be able to both service the interest on the debts and progressively play down the outstanding capital amounts. But we do need to increase the value of the contraband goods we are importing in order to pay some of the interest owing to the old skinflint moneylender Erasmus Blackstock.'

It had been nearly two weeks since they had taken delivery of their newly restored sailing ship from the boatyard at Buckler's Hard and had already managed two very profitable trips. They had engaged as captain an individual who had been cashiered from the Royal Navy for negligence, resulting in serious damage to a ship of the line. This, Captain Robert Jenkins, had been recommenced to them by George who suggested that Jenkins had already been engaged in some small-scale freelance smuggling even while in service. They had also rented a large, newly built, warehouse on the west bank of the River Beaulieu not far from Lymington. Where according to the sign over the door 'Agricultural Wholesalers' plied their trade. A fictional trade that served to provide cover for the storage and distribution of the more general contraband goods such as strong spirts, wine, tobacco, snuff, and some sought after spices. While the more high-value goods such as gold and sliver ingots, uncut diamonds, and some satin-lined boxes in which nestled pairs of French or Italian made dualling or sporting pistols, where hidden in cellar beneath the floor of an extravagant if now neglected folly in the grounds of Hugh's estate. It was with these more valued goods where the serious money was made. They had their own more respectable London contacts, some quite wealthy individuals always looking to lower their liquor and smoking bills. And George had enlarged his own contacts in the business world where much of the gold, silver and diamonds, could be sold and so be profitably absorbed into the jewellery trade.

'I think that we are moving, or rather perhaps sailing, along in the right direction Hugh.' said Alex 'Agreed' said Hugh 'When is the next trip? I understand that George has negotiated a very full load. With a couple more of such trips and we will be able to satisfy all of our creditors at least to the extent that we will be able to return to our London haunts without the fear of the debtor's court hanging over us.'

'The next full Moon is two weeks from tomorrow and so should be good to cross the channel and unload the goods during that night.'

Chapter Eight

It was late afternoon on the day that the carriage carried James, Caleb and Ezra along the gently sloping hill down which ran Lyndhurst High Street. The rain had been falling steadily for much of the day and by the time the carriage had drawn to a halt in the courtyard of the Bulfinch Inn, the broad backs of its pair of horses were steaming as the rain ran off their warm bodies. The animals stood patiently, just occasionally stamping hoofs on the cobbled ground, whilst the hosteler and his young stable lad came forward and began the practiced process of unhitching the animals from the carriage and striping the reins and other equine accoutrements from their bodies.

As the visitors approached the rear entrance of the inn the burly figure of John came charging out of the door.

'It is so good you see you again' he said.

'You Caleb and Ezra look pretty good - the country air and summer sun has been kind to your looks. You are still ugly, but perhaps not quite as bad as before.'

John then turned to offer his hand to James 'It's so good so see you colonel – you can now see how you helped to turn my life around. This time last year I was sitting in a dank, dark, prison cell, but look at me now.'

As he said this, he spread his arms to take in the substantial building of the main house of the inn.

'Me and Sarah are so happy here and you will notice when you see her that she is now carrying our first child. Mind you, I am concerned about her giving birth at her age. But she just dismisses my worries, and I would say that being with child really does suit her.'

Three of the friends tumbled into the inn, arms round each other's shoulders. They were closely followed by a smiling James thinking to himself.

'I expect that there are going to be more than a few glasses of strong ale downed this evening. And no doubt some tall tales told.'

It was later that evening that the four men enjoyed a venison and boiled bacon dinner cooked by Sarah who then, after supervising the serving of the meal, joined them at their table.

During the meal James took the opportunity to make it clear to John and Sarah that they would be paying in full for their board and lodging during the week or so that they intended staying. It did take some arguing and James's insistence, and for him to make the pretend threat to leave the next day, before the couple reluctantly accepted the arrangement. Once the dinner table had been cleared and foaming jugs of ale were being lined up, Sarah and James took leave from the others. Sarah to supervise the washing up and the general running of a busy inn and James to take a walk around the large village of Lyndhurst.

As he emerged out into the main street the heavy rain of earlier had eased to a gentle drizzle. He made his way slowly to the top of the street, where two of the village's principal buildings were to be found. Here on one side of the road was the substantial St Michael and All Angels, set within a neatly kept graveyard. A place of eternal rest for generations who had lived and died in the village. On the opposite side of the road was the imposing King's House. owned by the Crown and often used to accommodate royal visitors to the forest. Much of the forest itself being in effect preserved for the benefit of the Crown. It was William the Conqueror who first established the New Forest as a royal hunting ground and from the eleventh century the Forest had been a preserve for the leisure activities of Kings, Queens, Princes, and Princesses, along with various types of hangers on. Whilst those who lived within the woodland were allowed only limited rights of access.

Attached to the King's House was the somewhat austere Verderers Hall within which the Verderers Court was located. A court initially established in the medieval period to serve as part of a system charged with administering forest laws. It was the Verderers who were the main means of enforcing these laws. With issues such as the poaching of deer and the illegal taking of wood using up much of their time.

James crossed the road to the Hall and, peering through the leaded glass windows, he could see a large wood-panelled room with substantial wooden furnishings and walls lined with the heads of what had been magnificent stags. These were set in shield-shaped frames, with their antlers intact. The décor of the Hall expressed only certain aspects of the forest – the authority of the Crown and its means of control and exhibits reflecting the hunting interests of the aristocrats who spent leisure time in the area. James thought how much more there is to a forest than this. In terms of both the natural faunal and floral environment as well as the activities of the many people who live and work within its boundary.

By the next morning the weather had brightened, and the day ahead looked promising. For James sufficiently so for him to look forward to taking a long walk in the forest. He was particularly interested in species of tree that he might see. This due to an idea that had been forming in his mind of planting an area of the Home Farm of Downland with trees. Traveling through the countryside during the past weeks had made him think about how much of the ancient woodland of southern England has disappeared, with the needs of agriculture and the construction of ships for the navy having taken precedence.

He was thinking that.... 'It would be nice to leave a legacy to future generations living at Downland, with a woodland composed of a variety of native species along with the many different types of bird, small mammal and insect life that this would attract, to be an enduring gift to the future.'

Over breakfast he was able to talk with Sarah after she had finished supervising the cooking and serving of his and the other guests meals. Sarah's enthusiasm for her new life with John in Lyndhurst reinforced James's view that military veterans need, indeed deserve, help to settle into useful post-service lives.

The reason he was breakfasting alone was due to the three friends he had left drinking and in exuberant conversation together the last evening were still sleeping off the effects of the strong ale. But Sarah did assure him that John had best be up very soon 'or else' she said with hands on hips and a look on her face suggesting the 'or else' was to be avoided and might just involve a bucket of very cold water.

Having packed a small canvas shoulder-bag with a notebook and pencil, along with some food and drink that Sarah had prepared for him, James set off on his walk. A walk that took him in a wide circle taking in an area of dense woodland that at times gave way to open heathland. Heathland dotted with the occasional wind-bent tree and large clumps of gorse with its bright yellow flowers being the most obvious spots of colour within the predominantly green palette of nature's brush.

He felt good at experiencing the emotionally nourishing intermixing of sounds, sights, and smells of the terrain he was passing through. At one time as he approached a clearing in the woods he froze at the sight of a small herd of fallow deer. The elegant animals, mainly does and their spindle-legged fawns, were spread out but with most keeping to the clearing's edge as they gently chewed the leaves of some low-branched trees with some bending to eat the acorns and beech mast that had fallen to the woodland floor. As he looked on, a large imperious looking hind raised his head as if scenting the breeze and it seemed to James that this majestic animal was looking directly at him. As he shifted his feet to get more comfortable, he snaped a twig and the stag immediately set off, which was clearly a signal for the excited herd to follow. Without realising it James had been suppressing his breathing whilst soaking up the man to deer experience, and now he breathed deeply, exhaled and turned to continue on his walk.

By lunchtime he was ready for a rest and fortunately he had arrived at the village of Brockenhurst about five miles south of Lyndhurst. Here was a picturesque settlement, with a number of thatched or slate roofed cottages clustered about the village centre where, apart from the church, the 'Rose and Crown' was the most prominent building. With the blacksmith's shop just across the way from the alehouse, this was the busiest part of the village.

James walked slowly through the village to a feature known locally as the water-splash, a section of roadway across which ran a stream of the clearest of water. This being a tributary feeding into the more substantial River Lymington. He sat on a grass verge beside the stream and set about having his lunch. As he ate he reflected on his life. The veteran relocation projected was going well, if there was a potential issue with gaining funding for further expansion. At Downland the renovation of the buildings and the modernisation of agriculture was progressing in line with his plans. So, all generally good….and yet there seemed to be something missing from his life.

'I was thirty-eight on my last birthday and no prospects of finding a wife, so there will not be any children to inherit the estate, which seems a shame. But this is rather selfish as I could always convert the ownership into a Trust and then combine it with the current Trust of the Devon tenancies and lawyers can be made responsible for selecting an overall manager – but which of course would be a role filled by Joe until he dies or retires.'

It seemed that he had a plan for the future but he could not shake off the disappointing lack of an intimate companion and of any children.

Just then he was surprised by an iridescent blue flash skimming over the stream. When this streak of colour settled on the low branch of a nearby tree he could see that it was Kingfisher.

'That small bird seems unnatural in its colouration.' he thought 'But how beautiful.'

His sighting of the bird had shaken him out of his ruminations about life and he realised that the day was moving on and if he wanted to get back in time for a rest and a wash before dinner then he needed to get moving. He did have a crudely drawn map that Sarah had put in his bag but, after a couple of hours walking, he had lost his bearings – the position of the Sun told him that he was generally heading in the right direction but the density of the forest at this point caused him to be unsure.

As he came out into an area of open grassland, he saw a woman's body lying face down amongst some long grass, seemingly unconscious. He rushed forward, knelt down, and tried to turn the body over. The seemingly inert body came alive, and the angry face of a young woman confronted him.

'Get your dirty hands off me you oaf.' she said as she shoved him away.

She was on her feet in seconds, and he could see that she

had balled her fists and her aggressive look suggested she was about to launch herself at him.

He held out his hand palms towards her in an attempt to placate the wild beast.

'Whoa…. I am sorry I thought that you were injured.'

'Don't you whoa me – do your think I am a bloody horse! You idiot'

She said, as she turned away and she, for it was Luca, had soon disappeared into the woodland.

But she thought that she had at least been able to pick some wild garlic plants before the idiot had tried to manhandle her.

'Bloody gorger men!' She said under her breath. 'Why can't they leave a women to go about her business unmolested.'

Luca had left a somewhat dazed James standing in the clearing as he tried to process what had just happened. He felt ill-used, given that his intervention was at least an attempt to come to someone's aid. He bent to pick up the shoulder bag that had fallen to the ground and walked slowly in what he felt was towards Lyndhurst. Fortunately, within a few hundred yards he could see the village's church tower in the distance. Now more relaxed about getting back to the inn in time for dinner he was thinking about the young bundle of anger that he had just been confronted with – 'Angry yes, she certainly was, but what an attractive face!'

He shook his head thinking that it was a shame that they had not been introduced to each other in more benign circumstances.

The inn was quite busy that evening, with the three friends having eaten another satisfying dinner they were relaxing in the public bar. Being joined from time to time by John when Sarah was occupied elsewhere. When asked about his day in the forest James only gave a brief outline of the woodland and heathland he had passed though. He decided that he would keep the encounter with the wild young women to himself. It felt odd, but he wanted to retain this encounter in his mind as something special for himself rather than for it to become but an amusing tale told to others. As Caleb was just returning from the bar with another round of drinks the bar door burst open and a young man rushed over to John.

'John we badly need your help said the agitated young man holding out a creased piece of paper. I can't read but our Luca read it and she says it is a marker of a serious problem for us, and that we might be cleared from our campsite.'

The man was one of the Lyndhurst gypsies, and the paper he held out had been torn by Luca from the Church door as she was passing on her way back to the camp from the day's plant hunting. Her natural curiosity had caused her to walk down the short path from the roadway to the Church to see what the piece of paper pined to the door was about.

The young gypsy, Wicker, his brother Merlin, and their cousins had become regulars since John and Sarah had been running the inn. These two had no prejudices against gypsies – indeed one night John had told him that he had fought alongside gypsies in Spain. If somewhat lacking in discipline, he said they were top fighters and probably the best forward scouts in the regiment.

Most of the citizens of Lyndhurst were indifferent to the group living by village. So the warm reception from John and Sarah was valued by the menfolk of the camp.

John had taken the paper from the Wicker, who looked on intensely as he tried to interpret John's expression while he read and took in the import of the message.

'This looks to be an official document, it says at the top that the petitioners are acting with the authority of the 1773 Enclosure Act. I think that the colonel might understand what this means more than I do.'

James, having been listening to the heated conversation, walked over to the bar and took the offered paper from John's hand.

'Hm…this does look quite serious and legalistic – I do know something about enclosure and I had thought that the first step should have been the calling of a public meeting to consider presenting a petition to Parliament under the Act. Has there been any such meeting here recently?'

'Not to my knowledge.' said John 'And presumably we, as prominent village innkeepers would have been invited to any such meeting'.

'Yes, I suspect some deviousness at play here' said James 'I have read of arrogant landowners abusing the system and avoiding the public meeting stage – and given the local influence this class wields as county Sheriffs, Magistrates, and with MPs, they have been known to get away with this in effect illegal action.'

Wicker slumped into a chair and held his head in his hands.

'So, it looks like we are to be cleared off land that our families have camped on for generations. What will we do – our type are being oppressed just for being different.'

Now Caleb and Ezra had joined the group at the bar and these two, as well as John, were looking at James, hoping, perhaps even expecting, he might suggest some action.

He looked around the group then bent down and took Wicker's hands away from his face.

'I cannot guarantee what the outcome will be young man, but I do want to see if there is any way we can prevent this action – I so dislike the powerful misusing their power. But this is a legal matter and I think that we need specialist advice from an honest lawyer – not any in Lyndhurst or the neighbourhood as these can be more likely to cooperate with the large local landowners who would be the source of their most rewarding fees.'

Wicker was looking at James, now with just a glimmer of hope in his sun-creased face. But then his head dropped, and he exclaimed that.

'We don't have the money for any fancy legal men sir, so I guess we are done for.'

'Let's not worry about the legal costs, I will cover these - we are only seeking advice at this stage.'

'Wicker jumped from his chair and grabbed James in a body-encompassing bear-hug.'

When Wicker had let him go and he had regained his breath and his more general composure, he said.

'We must not get our hopes up.... let's just see what an honest lawyer advises. I think we might well be able to find a decent legal practice down in the port of Lymington.'

So it was at daybreak the following morning that James and Erza had led two strong horses between the shafts of the carriage and adjusted the harnesses and tied on the reins. They then loaded food for the beasts in a wide trunk at the rear of carriage and alongside this the large canvas bag (more a sack) containing fresh-baked crusty bread, a block of local cheese, joint of cold lamb, and a brown stone flagon of cider. They then made their way to the cross-roads at the edge of the village where they had arranged to meet the two gypsies that were coming with them to Lymington.

Just as Ezra eased the carriage to a halt, two gypsies emerged from the nearby woods. James stared hard at this pair one being Wicker the other Luca.

'Can this be the women I met just yesterday?' He thought.

He stepped down from the carriage and with a smile said.

'We meet again, can I help you into the carriage madam?'

'I am not a madam and no, I can manage myself.' She said, pushing his offered hand away as she swept up into the carriage, took a seat on the forward-facing rear bench and looked straight ahead. She was as surprised to meet James as him to meet her.

'Now I am confused.' She thought 'This was the oaf who accosted me yesterday, but he also seems to be one of the gorgers trying to help us.'

The conclusion she came too was to keep herself to herself as much as possible, to be polite, but to retain a sense of suspicion on what might be the motives of these two men.

During the journey James did try a couple of friendly advances towards Luca, but her cool responses led him to just sit back and join in the much easier conversation with Wicker and Ezra. The gypsy was a rich source of anecdotes about whatever part of the forest they were traveling through 'Under that tree a magnificent red deer stag with a record for the county of a 26 point set of antlers'…. 'In that pond a monster pike was caught'…. 'On that village green a famous bare-knuckle fist fight had taken place between two gypsy champion pugilists fighting to settle a long-standing feud between two New Forest families. A fight that took place over two hours, alternating between furious bouts of punching and time spent with each man on his knees trying to recover their breath, rubbing bruised areas of their upper-bodies and wiping sweat and blood from eyes, noses, and mouths. The fighters had fought to a bloody standstill when the referee called time and declared a draw. The men then embraced and all present agreed that the feud was now settled to the honour of both families.'

At lunchtime they stopped at a small village in the centre of which was a massive oak tree. Around the base of this tree some skilled villager had erected a circular slated wooden seat. Nailed to the trunk above the chair was a small wooden plaque on which was carved the invitation to those passing by to: 'Please rest awhile from the day's work.'

Luca had brought food for Wicker and herself but when offered the finer fare that Sarah had prepared, he declined Luca's less appealing offer. She refused to share in the men's food and instead opened a folded kerchief, took out a hunk of hard bread, a piece of cheese, and an apple, and after eating these she walked towards the woodland, always looking to find some medically useful plant, leaf, or fungi.

Within half an hour they had satisfied their hunger and were making their way back to the carriage.

James looked up at the tree that had provided the shade within which they enjoyed their meal.

'That is a substantial tree' observed James.' Perhaps the largest living thing in the whole of Hampshire

Wicker followed his glance and said.

'There is a belief that an oak tree takes 300 years to grow from a fallen acorn to full sized tree, then it thrives for 300 more years, and then it takes a final 300 years for it to slowly die.'

'If so, just consider what a mature oak such as this one has seen during its long life.' said Ezra

'This one might even had seen mounted knights passing by on their way to take ship for France and heading east on the Crusades.'

'Well, if it had then it would now be about 100 years into its dying phase.' said James.

The four travelled on to Lymington, with the three men continuing their conversation about the parts of the forest they passed through, and with Luca seemingly quiet and uninterested but at the same time she had been surreptitiously studying James.

'He does seem to be quite modest, his features are not that bad, and if he is rather an oaf perhaps we will at least be able to get along for the time of this trip. It does look like he and his friend are trying to help us.'

But her experience of non-gypsies still made her cautious about possible motives. Rarely if ever does a gorger help her people and then only when they are seeking something for themselves.

It was late afternoon where their carriage rolled down Lymington High Street, passing the newly built grey-stone prison, and on passed St Thomas's Church, before driving under the wide arch of the whitewashed King's Head Inn. Stepping down from the carriage, Luca and Wicker hefted their bags onto their shoulders and started to walk towards the exit – 'Hey' said James 'Where are you two going?'

'We are off to find a camping place on the outskirts of the town, somewhere along the river where we can pitch our lightweight benders and cook dinner. We will meet you here tomorrow morning.' said Wicker.

'No, no. the plan is that you will spend the four nights in which we will be staying in Lymington here at the inn with us. I have booked four bedrooms, and I am paying the bill.'

Wicker immediately turned around and walked back towards James and Ezra with a beaming smile on his face.

'Suits me sir.' he said.

Luca put down her bags and with one hand on her hip and the other gesturing toward James.

'Thanks, but I do not want to be in your debt mister. I would rather sleep in a hedge and wash in the river.' With that she strode off down the High Street.

'Best leave her' said Whicker 'She has her own peculiar ways and is not to be crossed – she is more of an over-proud man in a woman's body – god's mistake.'

James shook his head – 'Well I suppose if that's what she wants' he said.

But he was concerned about her safety, here in a port town. He could see that she was an attractive woman, one who could easily draw the attention of ruffians out for mischief or worse.

When they met up earlier in the day, he had assumed that she would be Wicker's woman. But according to Ezra who had questioned Wicker during a short walk into the woods that these two had taken to relive themselves during the lunch-stop, Luca was single and this from choice.

And he had told Ezra that if he knew her, he would understand more about this unusual gypsy woman.

'The family has just grown to accept her as being different – we think she must have fallen from the sky into our camp.' He laughed slapping Ezra on the back as the two made their way back to the carriage.

In fact, Luca's being single was not due to a lack of potential suiters, of which there were initially quite a number, these being deterred by Lucas's tendency to forensically examine each of them about how they viewed marriage. Unlike all of these somewhat confused young men, she favoured a more equal partnership than a gypsy women would normally expect. As the principle years for marriage - late teens to mid-twenties - progressed into the late twenties and early thirties, her spinsterhood became rather just taken for granted. And her valued medical skills ensured that occasional comments about her unmarried state were only quietly made behind hands raised to mouths. Her spinsterhood became accepted and, given her reading and writing skills and her obvious ability to understand issues, she was more often than not chosen to represent the group when contact with the non-gypsy society was required. But, as with the matter at hand, she would always be accompanied by a male gypsy during such matters.

As to the woman's physical features, Luca was tall for a woman with a slim, if rather angular, body. Her hair was dark chestnut brown and her face broad with high cheekbones and a proportionally sized nose above which were set grey-flecked brown eyes. And it was in the keenly focused eyes that an observant person could see the intelligence. At no time in her life could she have been described as beautiful, unlike some of her raven-haired, green-eyed peers. All now married with youngsters clinging to their skirts and babies at their breasts. Girls whose beauty would be gradually fading as their waistlines would be expanding.

If not beautiful then certainly handsome would serve to describe Luca, and the general handsomeness combined with the high cheek bones of her features would ensure that progressively maturing versions of this would endure well into middle age and perhaps beyond.

James had a restless night, waking at times with Luca on his mind – yes the night was mild but he felt that no women should be spending the night entirely alone on a riverbank.

He decided to get up as soon as the sun began to rise, hastily washed and dressed, and whilst the inn still slumbered, he slipped out of the rear entrance and made this way towards the river where he thought Luca might have made camp the previous evening. When he arrived at the river-bank there wasn't any sign of a bender but, after following the river for about half a mile, he saw a wisp of smoke rising from behind a clump of bushes just a yard or so from the water's edge.

As he came round the side of the bushes, he saw Luca kneeing by the river and topless as she bent her head into the water to wash her hair, face, and upper body. He was unable to move, being mesmerised by the sight of the smooth white skin of her shapely back. As she turned, with water dripping from her head, her eyes closed and a smile on her face, his eyes were drawn to the erotic curve of firm breasts.

'What the hell!' She shouted on seeing him.

'One time you assault me and now you are spying on me

– are you a peeping Tom? Can't a woman get any privacy?'

'I am really sorry, I was worried about you being here all alone. I did not mean to surprise you.'

Luca had pulled her shirt to her chest and waved her hand dismissively.

'Well just clear off and leave a body to enjoy their breakfast'.

'Look I do understand that we have not gotten off to a very good start, I am thoughtless and clumsy, but please forgive me and at least come and have breakfast with us at the inn.'

Luca thought about this….such a fulsome apology from a man for anything was a nice surprise and she was beginning to think that he was perhaps more daft than dangerous.

'As I can see that my oats have now dried hard in the cooking pot while you have been ruining my morning, I think that I deserve a decent meal on you sir. But just keep your distance.'

As she poured water on the small fire, took down the rather makeshift shelter, and packed her belongings away. She also felt rather pleased that James was sufficiently concerned about her well-being to come out looking for her.

Back at the inn and having been joined by Ezra and Wicker the four enjoyed a substantial breakfast during which the conversation flowed quite well. Luca was less lively than the others and James was as times distracted by the memory of Luca turning from the river with strands of wet hair sticking to her lovely face and water dripping down her body.

'Something is happening to me, as I am looking across the table at this wild woman I am experiencing such feelings that I have never had before.'

After the meal, and still early in the day, they made their way down the High Street looking for the offices of 'Priestly and Gosling' a firm of lawyers that John had suggested. As an innkeeper he often overheard customers talking in the bar, an aspect of this conversational harvest being that he could now recommend a skilled blacksmith or carpenter and an honest butcher, baker, tailor, or candlestick maker who would offer quality service or products at reasonable prices. Value for money and where to obtain it was a regular topic for the regulars who frequented the public bar of the Bullfinch. And the legal practice of Priestly and Gosling, although practicing 20 miles south of Lyndhurst, came as recommended.

They found the double fronted bay-windowed offices about half-way down the broad High Street, nestled between the Old Town Hall and the Market House. It seemed that they had arrived on a quiet day, and they found both partners seated in the outer reception area enjoying coffee served by a young woman assistant. The younger man stood up and held out his hand to James.

'Hello, I am Simon Gosling, what can we do for you.'

James took the lead 'Well' he said. 'We are seeking advice about resisting an attempt to enclose a piece of land.'

'That sounds familiar, that particular Act of Parliament has caused misery to many farm labourers, the products of whose thin strip of a field that had for centuries been held in common was for many all that had stood between their families and poverty. Please step into my office.'

He pointed at Ezra and Wicker.

'If you can bring those two chairs in with you I think that my office will comfortably accommodate all five of us.'

James was encouraged that the lawyer had without any prompting taken such a negative – or rather fair – view of enclosure.

Once they were all seated in the lawyer's office, he told them that enclosure was not that much of an issue in the

New Forest as most of it was Crown land. So, although there were certain rights held by the commoners such as: pannage, dead wood collecting, and some grazing on the heathland areas, there was very little common land.

As he handed it across to Simon, James explained that they had discovered the note pined to the Lyndhurst Church door and although they were aware that it must be an indication of trouble for the group of gypsies who had for generations lived on the site, they did not have any knowledge of what the process of enclosure entailed or if there was any way of preventing it. The lawyer took the paper and sat back in his chair to consider its contents.

He looked up and around at this small group.

'Well, the process itself is fairly simple, once a group of landowners want to petition parliament under the said Act to have a piece of common or waste land enclosed, they would need to call a public meeting in order to gain local views on the proposal. If the local public were overwhelmingly opposed, then enclosure could not be successful pursued. If no significant local opposition, then the petition could be presented to Parliament. A standing committee in Westminster would then consider the detail of any petition referred to it, and also consider any representations made against it. If the committee decided that the petition has merit, they would then order that the enclosure could progress. The next step would be that the petitioners would have to attach a notice such as the one you have here to the local parish church door on three consecutive Sundays in August or September.

The final stage would be a visit by parliamentary commissioners, who would then distribute the land to landowners, usually to those whose farms abutted the now enclosed land.'

The four listened in silence as they took in the import of

what they had just heard.

Luca was the first to speak.

'But there hasn't been any public meeting, at least as far as we know.'

'That does not surprise me.' said the lawyer 'It is quite common for landowners to hold a barely publicized meeting at a location and a time difficult for most local working people to get to, but which does just about meet the basic requirement of the Act. If we can find out the circumstances of any meeting related to this petition, then it could help with a representation to the committee.'

'I presume the primary petitioners would be the farmers Williams and Casey whose land is adjacent to our campsite.' said Luca

'But we have always gotten on well with these two, we even help with their harvest every year.'

'Do you have any influential individuals who might dislike gypsies more generally?' asked the lawyer.

The two gypsies exchanged looks and Luca said,

'Not really, but of course we do get the blame for all of the poaching and any theft that takes place in the whole of the neighbourhood.'

The lawyer stood up. 'Look, leave this with me, we have legal connections and a couple of our own agents in most of the of the large towns across southern Hampshire. Give me a few days and I will see if I can find out more about the background to the petition and I will write to you.'

So that was as much as they could do for now, and James suggested that the lawyer address the letter to Luca and Wicker care of the Bullfinch Inn.

When they left the lawyer's office it was raining quite heavily, and Luca agree to take dinner with the other three. Over the meal James tried to persuade her to occupy the room he had keep on for her.

'Look it is still pouring with rain and the wind has picked up. The water level of the river might well be in high by the morning and the bank where you were camping last night could be flooded. And even worse, I would not be able to sleep if I have to worry about you being washed away and out to sea!' he said with a broad smile.

'Oh well of course sir we can't have that can we....' Luca was also smiling.

'I will stay here but I am not sure I will get much sleep lying on the sort of soft lumpy mattress you folks prefer.'

The group split up for the evening with Ezra and Wicker heading down to the Town Quay to an alehouse where Ezra was expecting to meet an old service friend who he had that morning sent a message via a willing King's Head stable-lad to let him know he was in town.

This was a friendship had began in naval service. Ezra had started his military career as a Marine on board Royal Navy ship HMS Samson (a third-rater, so one of the largest class of ships of the line at that time, these having 74 guns). The Marine's primary task was to ensure that the badly treated sailors did not mutiny. His friend, Dick Mostin, had been a young cadet. The Samson had a particularly hard master and when pushed to the limit of endurance the crew took the cadet hostage and demanded improved rations and better treatment more generally. Whilst Ezra and some of his fellow Marines sympathised with the sailors their strong sense of duty caused them to confront the men and, being better trained and armed, they soon put down what was a fairly modest attempt at mutiny – more just a cry for some compassion from an obdurate captain - and Dick was released unharmed. The young cadet had been convinced that the captain would not give in to the men's demands, however justified, and that his life might be ended in a mad burst of the frustrated men's anger. So, from that day Dick had seen Ezra as the person who had saved his life.

Even though Dick had risen steadily through the ranks to become the youngest first mate in the British Navy, the two had remained good friends.

Incidentally, the leaders of the would-be mutineers were court marshalled and after hearing the testimony of the men before them, and that of couple of the Marines and junior officers, the Naval Board showed compassion and just ordered that each of the culprits be flogged with two dozen strokes of the infamous, blood drawing, cat-of-nine tails.

If only a few years older, Ezra felt rather fatherly toward Dick and although he had enough of life at sea and had moved on to join James's regiment in Spain, the two had kept in touch via an occasional letter. This is how Ezra knew that his old friend lived in Lymington after having been pensioned off some 10 years earlier, still a young man, after being seriously wounded at the Battle of the Nile in 1798.

While Ezra and Wicker made their way to the bustling Town Quay, Luca had unpacked her small sacking bag in the first-floor room overlooking the High Street. She then took up a sketch pad and some pencils and made her way back down the main staircase to settle within the brighter light of the larger candles in the guest's lounge. Where she was not unhappy to see that James was already seated in a comfortable high winged armchair reading.

He rose up at she came into the room. 'Hello Luca, can I order you some coffee or something stronger?'

'No thank you sir.' said Luca, as she smoothed the top sheet of the sketch pad in her lap and began to draw.

As James's looked at Luca he began to realise that the strange feelings he had been experiencing were what novelist such as the one he had been reading call 'love'. The strangest of human emotions and one that can come unexpected and unbidden as it had for James.

He was thinking that 'Our backgrounds are very different and yet I am so drawn towards this woman'.

Luca looked up and he glanced away pretending to take close interest in the book that was open on his knees.

Luca's feelings towards James had also been changing and some magical unseen unbidden emotions were now seeping into the short space between them. A form of quietly crackling erotic energy that could only be seen by its effects on the pair. Much of this being an internal experience for each of them. But a perceptive observer would also note the softening of Luca's glances towards James and his somewhat more yearning looks towards her. With the glances and the looks taking place more often as the evening wore on.

Let's leave these two with the god of attraction, desire and erotic love, hovering unseen above them, his bowstring taunt, his arrow aimed.

On entering the alehouse set back from the Town Quay Ezra immediately recognised his old friend as he rose from a bar stool and came toward him arms outstretched.

'It's so good to see you Ezra, and your companion…. what would you like to drink?'

Ezra took in his old friend's rather shabby clothes, and he thought back to his being in similar clothing when he had first renewed his friendship with James back at the Seven Dials in London.

'Let me get the drinks in Dick' said Ezra 'This is Wicker, you two go and sit down at that table by the fire.'

Once settled, Ezra briefly explained that the reason for Wicker and himself being in the town had been to seek legal advice about a petition to enclose a piece of land, he then prompted Dick to bring him up-to-day with his own situation.

'Well Ezra, I can't say life has been all that good of late. I am not complaining….goodness, I know full well how hard the conditions are for many people in the district. – Farm labours, fishermen, boat builders, and almost anyone in service, are seeing prices going up and wages frozen or even being reduced. Of course, it's worse if they have a family. I am at least spared this responsibility, and I am not at risk of the workhouse just yet.'

His friend paused to take a drink and Ezra said: 'But I thought that you naval officers did quite well out of being in service.'

'I left the Navy with a reasonable amount of prize money, but I was persuaded to invest this in company of merchants trading in the Far East and it turned out that the principle of the company was a crook. He bought the cheapest of ships – forging purchase bills for twice what he paid and siphoning off the difference for himself. The ships were pretty rotten below the waterline and so unfit for the long voyage east. Two of the largest ships sunk with uninsured cargos and the company was put into liquidation. When the financial dust had settled there was nothing of any value left and the principle could not be traced. I have since heard that he has started a new life in the Americas.'

'What a bastard!' said Wicker who had been listening wide-eyed to Dick's story.

'I am pleased us gypsies only deal in cash and only with people we know that we can trust – spit into a palm and a hand shake seals a deal for us.'

'Go on.' said Ezra 'So how are you managing?'

'I do have a small naval pension and I had the good fortune to have inherited a tiny cottage from my fisherman father. I occasionally get to crew on one of the boats carrying a cargo of salt – which you probably know is the primary product of this town - up to London when a regular sailor is sick, But that is not very often and I do miss the sea. I can't go back because there are times when my old wounds play up and I am laid up for a week or more. No shipping company wants a master or even mate who can't be relied upon to make the tide when required. Anyway, that's enough of me what have you been up too Ezra apart from helping Wicker here and his tribe, you look quite smart for a military veteran.'

'You had best not know the details Dick, I have spent some time on the wrong side of the law. I have been working for one of my old officers, a singular man, who has been on a mission to help ex-servicemen. He might be able to offer you something Dick – have you ever thought of working on the land or even of emigrating.'

'I am too old to start a new life in an unknown land and I would hate working on the land. No, all the time I can manage I will be living within sight of the sea – but thanks for the thought Ezra…. Let's leave my circumstances to one side now and spend the rest of the evening enjoying each other's company, along with the ale served here. We might even try some of the contraband brandy that has found its way past the customs officers.'

It was about three hours later that Ezra and Wicker were endeavouring to support each other as they made their way up the short length of cobbled, hill leading up from the Quay and back down the now night-dark High Street, arriving back at the inn at a time when most of its occupants were already in their beds.

Chapter Nine

The following morning it was under a grey overcast sky when the four visitors to the town got back into their carriage. Two of them looked rather pale and unsteady on their legs and they slumped down onto the cushioned rear seat and tried the double task of sleeping whilst also retaining their breakfast in their stomachs, as the carriage rumbled over the mostly uneven surface of the roadway. This left James to take the reins with Luca sitting alongside him.

'The demon drink has done for those two.' observed James, shaking his head. 'I expect that they will be of little use for the rest of today.'

Luca looked back at the two.

'I do have a herbal liquor that will help them, but I think they deserve to suffer, at least until lunchtime she said smiling.'

Even with the terrible thought of the dark cloud of enclosure hanging over her family, she was on this early August morning quite happy, and James's close proximity had made its own contribution to her mood.

The journey back to Lyndhurst went quite easily. With Ezra and Wicker recovering only slowly from their evening of excess until, during their lunch stop when Luca administered a dose of a 'cure-all' herbal concoction, from when the two soon returned to their normal sociable state.

On their arriving in Lyndhurst in the late afternoon, Wicker and Luca stepped down from the carriage and as they began to walk toward their camp James jumped from the driver's seat, caught up with them and took Luca to one side.

'Luca I would you like to show me more of the of forest, perhaps we can ride out tomorrow, but only if this suits you.'

Luca's faced lit up – 'That would be nice. But if I do dismount to pick some medicinal plants, I do not want you to rescue me, please?'

James laughed at the reminder of their first meeting.

'No, I promise that I will only be there to assist if necessary.'

It was early the next day when the pair met up again at the same cross-roads. James on a chestnut mare borrowed from the inn's stable and with Luca mounted on one of the wild ponies that roam free in the forest. Some of which the gypsies would capture and then tame for their own use, and occasionally to sell on.

James was seated on a soft leather saddle, his boots in stirrups nicely adjusted for his leg-length. Luca was seated on a coarse blanket tied onto her pony's body with a canvas strap, and with her seated astride the animal's back, with skirt pulled up to allow her tanned legs to hang free. But this difference was more cultural rather than one style being more comfortable than the other, at least for the relatively short day's ride they were setting out on.

With Luca mostly taking the lead, they made for a denser part of the woodland. She was heading towards a location in the forest where the dense woodland gave way to wide, open, heathland beyond which, on a clear day, the hills and high cliffs of the Isle of Wight could just about be glimpsed. She had always experienced this point of transition from dense woodland to open heathland as uplifting and wanted to see if James's reaction matched her own. As the morning wore on and they became more at ease with each other the erotic tension that had been building between them over the past few days was becoming more palpable, even the horses could sense it and were at times quite skittish, requiring firm handling from the riders.

They emerged from the woodland onto the heathland and a clear, blue-skied day that allowed the Isle of Wight to be seen in the distance. James, let out a sigh.

'I so much like those boundaries where water meets land and where landscapes change as we see here – and the distant view is just an unexpected bonus.'

After a pause to take in the surroundings he suggested.

'Shall we have lunch here….the ponies and deer have chewed the grass low and there is a patch over there that is more moss than grass and looks to offer a comfortable place for us.'

They were both on their knees as James began unpacking the canvas bag that Sarah had packed with their lunch. As he passed Luca a cup of cider their eyes met and held, what had been a possibility when they rode away from Lyndhurst, they now each knew was a definite - it was as if a spark had been struck and the dry tinder of their emotional condition was about to burst into fire – now holding hands they stood and came together with the urgency of accumulated passion. Clothes were cast off and their naked bodies were blended together in a miasma of moistly vibrant rhythmic unity – a sensual unity in a form that had characterized humanity from the earliest of times. It was the emotional hunger of these two sexually unpractised individuals that needed to be satisfied.

A while later, with the food still untouched, and the clothes cast about, the pair were lying side by side, each feeling a mixture of confusion about what happens next but crazily happy at what had just occurred. A line had been crossed, an entanglement had been formed, not only by the physical act but also by the emotion of love that had infused it. But their lives were so different.

Luca assumed that now that James's passion had been spent he, as a seemingly wealthy landowner, would move on, leaving a brief liaison with a gypsy girl in his past – but she knew that she would nurse thoughts of this, her first intimate experience, within a tiny space in her heart for as long as possible.

James as the reader, having gotten to know the character of the man would probably suspect, was not contemplating moving on, at least not without Luca by his side. Any social distance between them was for him irrelevant. For the first time in his life, he was emotionally bound to a women who was not his mother.

'Luca will you marry me?'

She could not speak at first….she sat up and just looked in his face. Then she stood up and picking up her shirt she walked a little way off and then turned towards him.

'Are you mad - how can we marry? Socially, you are a thoroughbred horse, and I am but a donkey, we can come together as just now, but we are entirely different animals.'

'Look Luca, don't make any decision just yet and when we have sorted out the matter of enclosure at least come with me on a visit to Downland….I have never said these words to a woman but I do know that I have fallen deeply in love with you.'

The time taken for the pair's return ride to Lyndhurst was mostly passed in silence, but they did occasionally exchanged smiles. Each now had a sense that something more than a brief affair might just be possible.

Over the following days, these two would meet to slip off into the woodland and repeat their intimate coming together and, rather than dissipate their passion, this only served to make the initial bond even stronger.

Two days after the trip to Lymington a letter from Simon

Gosling was delivered to the inn. James insisted that they would have to wait for Pa Pearson, Luca and Wicker to be present before the letter could be opened and that after breakfast he intended walking to the gypsy camp to enable this.

So, it was about an hour later that James, Ezra, and Caleb, made their way to the camp where they were welcomed and invited to sit by a central campfire while almost all the adult gypsies and some more curious children from the camp gathered round their visitors.

James handed the unopened letter to Pa Pearson his being the leader of the group. He held it up to the light, sniffed it, and with a bland look on his face called Luca forward and put the letter in her hand with a nod. Luca opened the letter and then slowly read the message from the lawyer out loud.

The letter stated that following the lawyer's investigations…. 'We now know that the principle sponsors of the petitions are the two local farmers and a substantial local landowner Lord Hugh Grenville (8th Earl of Budleigh) – the constituency M.P also supports the petition and there seems to be a shadowy figure named Sir Alex Cranfield who is to friend of Lord Grenville and is currently resident at Grenville Hall.'

The letter went on say that there was a record of a public meeting, but that this took place at Lord Grenville's home and, as far as can be determined, the proper public announcements were not made. It was this obvious attempt to circumvent the required procedure that the lawyer felt could have been the grounds for a challenge. But that he could not say that such a challenge would be successful as he assumed that if an M.P. and substantial landowners are include in a petition, then a 'blind eye' might be turned at the committee stage. And in any case, the petitioners have already made the first posting on the parish church door, so he thought that they should assume that the committee stage has been passed. And that even if a challenge had been possible, the opportunity to make a representation has now been missed. The solicitor ended the letter by noting that he was waiting for confirmation on this because there seems to be some more minor aspects of the required procedure that have also not been properly carried out. But, taken overall, he was not optimistic that the enclosure could be prevented.

As Luca finished her reading of the letter James could see that some of the older women were wiping tears from their eyes, and some of the younger men were angry – The young gypsy named Ned stepped forward.

'We will not stand for this, let's go and smash these bastards.'

'Hold on' said James 'I don't want to interfere with what you all decide to do – the proposal is vindictive, especially given the lack of much if any agricultural value to this land. It makes me think that here is something more behind this petition. But if you Ned start to threaten any of the petitioners you would just bring the law down on you and you could be in prison just when the group needs you most – I can easily understand your frustration but please at least wait until the lawyer has completed his investigations into the procedure taken by these people.'

Pa Pearson held up his hand to quieten the now noisy group as they excitedly attempted to share their views with each other.

''This is a very serious business....some more mischief that the gorgers are up too. Their leaders in that parliament make the laws to suit themselves – This enclosure thing might be law, but it is not justice. They have the power and we, being powerless, are liable to suffer when they turn against us. We might have to fight, but for now I say we wait for the lawyer-man's next letter.'

Pa's authority and the obvious sense of his comments did quieten the mood of the group which now slowly dispersed back to their benders, tents, and vans.

Back at the inn on the following morning, Ezra was quite surprised to receive a letter from his old friend in Lymington. On opening the letter and taking in its content, he decided to share it with the others as soon as possible. It was at breakfast when he had the first opportunity, and rather than read it out himself, he past it to James. The reason for this letter was directly related to Ezra's Lymington friend Dick's experience over the previous two days.

It seems that Dick had been paid to take a fishing boat round to the boatyard at Buckler's Hard for repairs to the hull after it had been damaged by an underwater rock at low tide. As it was an overnight stay Dick intended to sleep on the boat and he decided to use the 'Master Builder's' alehouse adjacent to the yard for the evening. While there, he could hardly avoid overhearing a loudmouth individual boasting of how his master and friend were going to rid the forest of gypsies. The man was the land agent for the Grenville Estate, and he had obviously been enjoying the beer on offer for some time that day. More for conversation than much interest the landlord asked him why they wanted to remove the gypsies. The man had taken a deep swig of his ale and then as best as Dick could remember said.

'They are all poachers and bloody thieves which is reason enough, but for the masters it is also entertainment during a quiet summer. They have been flattering two local farmers and have the MP in their pocket – so ridding the forest of pests has been a distraction for them whilst they develop another more profitable business.' As he made this last comment, he had raised his head and made an exaggerated wink of one eye.

For Dick this last comment and arched gesture was an

indicator of some dubious activity and along the north coast of the Solent the most likely such activity was smuggling. Although why two aristocrats would be risking their necks by being involved in such activity, he was unsure.

After he had moored up the newly repaired boat in Lymington Harbour the following day, he decided to make a few enquiries of some fishermen he knew who on occasion topped up their uncertain fishing income with some modest level of smuggling. What he found out was that a quite well- known local gang of smugglers had recently stepped up from low-level activities to a much more substantial level of trading. It seems that they had moved from liaising with a French, Spanish, or Dutch boat a few miles offshore to themselves operating a large fast cutter and importing their contraband goods by direct contact with the continent. The fishermen he spoke to were quite resentful of the unfair competition and they asserted that the gang itself would not have had the means to buy and fit out such a cutter and then fill the hold with high value goods. That they must have well-healed backers behind them.

He knew that this sort of arrangement was rumoured to be involved with smuggling gangs operating further up the coast in Kent – as a type of 'dark company' - when a number of well-off individuals form an arrangement where they do not get involved in the actual smuggling but fund the activity and so gain a more substantial part of the considerable profits that can be made.

It did not take Dick long to make a connection between the Grenville Estate's loose mouthed agent's talk, and what he had heard from the fishermen, to think that the individuals behind large-scale smuggling could be the same individuals who were involved in the enclosure action to remove the gypsies.

Dick did not put all of this level of detail into his letter, but he did make it clear that the same pair that were behind the enclosure petition also appeared be involved in a substantial smuggling operation.

When James had finished reading the letter to the others, Ezra stood up with his hands balled into fists.

'The let me get my hands on them, I'll stuff the aristocratic bastards.'

'I'm with you Ezra, they are just playing a game and our new gypsy friends will pay the cost of their fun.' said Caleb.

James gestured for them to sit down.

'Hold on, you two. Yes, there is something seriously amiss here. But remember what we had to say to Ned yesterday. There is no point in our just charging in and threatening these two. We need to out manoeuvre them. Let's think about some tactics for doing this. I suppose that if the lawyer can find a point where the procedure was not followed correctly and a realistic challenge to the enclosure can be possible, then whatever our feeling toward this unsavoury pair this would be the best way forward.'

If grinding their teeth, Caleb and Ezra bowed to what they realised was probably best for now.

Later that day James had met up with Luca a little way out of Lyndhurst as they were endeavouring to keep their more intimate relationship if not secret, at least not too obvious. Their efforts with this were entirely pointless given that whatever female, whether Sarah or a gypsy, who saw them together could tell by their glances towards each other that the pair were more than just friends.

He handed Luca Dick's letter and sat down on the trunk of a recently fallen tree while she it read through.

'It does look like we are being ill-used by these two but what would a Lord and his friend have against us. We have never harmed them.' She said as she hitched up her skirt and took a seat beside James.

'I think the reason that you can't understand the motivation of these two Luca is that their way of thinking is so different from your own. For men like this, other people, especially those not of their class, are just objects to be used played with and discarded. Their experience is of an overindulged childhood, gilded youth, and leisured adulthood. Not all aristocrats are like this of course, but too many are. By coincidence, I do know something of this Alex Cranfield – he and I have met before.' James was remembering the incident outside the church in Cerne Parma and the details of Tess's sad experience at Alex's hands.

He then outlined the situation with Tess, including Alex's initial cruelty to her and his later threats to her family when he could not get his own way.

'This man seems to be a pretty nasty character.' said Luca 'And if the lawyer can't help us, I am not sure what we might do.'

James had been giving the possibility of a lack of a legal route to stop the enclose some thought, and he recalled that farmland of the Cranfield Estate had been coming up for sale at auctions over the last year or so. Learning about the smuggling business was providing him with an idea that might be worth pursuing if bad news did come from the lawyer. This was the seed of an alternative that turned out to be necessary when the next morning a letter was received at the inn and the three friends again took it unopened to the gypsy camp.

The scene at the camp was similar to two days previously when the first letter from the lawyer had been read out. Pa Pearson again passed the letter to Luca to read out – she read that it did seem that the proper procedure was not followed in relation to the required public meeting. But the lawyer's follow-up investigation suggested that challenges to similar infringements have rarely been successful, and this only when there had been a significant public outcry. The summary advice of the letter being that a challenge to the Lyndhurst petition would not be worth pursuing. As she came to the end of the letter Luca's voice was breaking and tears were forming in her eyes. On finishing the letter, she looked towards James in despair.

The usually confident Pa Pearson was unable to speak and just stood looking confused. But his wife Ma Pearson spoke up 'I will put a curse on them – that their lives will be filled with misery from now on.'

Ned stepped forward, anger suffusing his face 'Well, that's it then, we need to confront these two arsehole gorgers.'

James held up his hand. 'Can I just again caution against confrontation Ned. I can easily understand your anger but jail for you and others from the camp will not achieve anything.

These two, Alex Cranfield and Hugh Grenville, deserve any curse you might apply Mrs Pearson, but I have been thinking about the likelihood of a legal challenge not being possible and I can't say that there will be any alternative of saving the camp, but I would like you to give me one week to do some investigations in London. I have already written to ask a London agent who I work with on other business to start looking into this pair and how they spend their time in the city. The second petition notice is due to be pinned to the church door this coming Sunday so we still have almost two weeks before the Commissioners would come to divide any enclosed land.'

'What about the two farmers who have signed the petition?' said Ezra 'I think that we should begin by meeting these two, they seem to be being manipulated. They have lived alongside the gypsies for years and no doubt their fathers before them, so why the sudden change of view?'

'Yes Ezra, I think that speaking to the farmers would be useful. I have been distracted by focusing on Cranfield and Grenville due to something I remember from back in Cerne Parma about Cranfield selling off land.'

So it was that James, Ezra, Luca, and Pa Pearson, called on farmer John Williams later that day. They found him resting following his lunch. When he saw the small party, he invited them in and to sit round the solid oak table in the large kitchen of a successful farmer and asked a maid servant to offer them home-made cider.

Pa went straight into the main point of the visit.

'Why John, when we have been good neighbours for so long have you and Gabriel Casey turned against us and done so without even coming along to tell us how it is that we have offended you?'

The farmer was looking down at table and in a quiet voice for a big man said.

'I think we have been drawn along by others with the enclosure action Pa......that we have been flattered by the attention of local landowners who do seem to have an issue with you. It is only over the past week that myself and Gabriel have come to see that we have fallen in with a couple of quite nasty, vindictive, characters.'

James interrupted the farmer 'These two are we suppose Alex Cranfield and Hugh Grenville.'

The famer was surprised that they already knew the names of the shadow sponsors of the action.

'Yes, these are the two. When they first made contact about six weeks ago it was as if they just wanted the company of the type of farmers who were on the way to becoming more substantial yeomen. At first, we were taken in by their flattery and the chance to meet and mx with the aristocracy of south Hampshire – our wives especially took to the rise of our social position But since the petition has been launched, we have noticed that the invitations have dried up. Mind you, as Gabriel pointed out – our experience of this new social grouping has shown what poor company they are for two working farmers like us. I also agreed with Gabriel when he said he had a sense that some of them were laughing at us behind our backs.'

'Well' said Pa 'That's fine, all you need to do is withdraw the petition.'

'It is not quite as simple as that Pa. we are very concerned about angering these two – they are powerful men and when Gabriel and myself went over to meet with them just three days ago to express our doubts about enclosure, they hinted, no more than just hinted, that if we were to withdraw the petition they would feel let down and so would be minded to persuade our major wholesale dealers in our main crops and in meat on the hoof to stop working with us. And on the eastern edged of both farms, we draw water from a number of the tributaries feeding into the River Beaulieu, and these run through Grenville's estate before they get to us. Lord Grenville said that there is always the possibility to reduce the flow. So we do not seem to have any realistic alternative but to continue with the petition. We are only about four weeks from harvest, this being also the time when we would be selling most animals after fattening them on summer grass…. I am really sorry Pa but we feel trapped.'

'So, you and Gabriel Casey intend pressing ahead and letting us get evicted to save your own skins when it is clear that your overinflated pride led you into such an evil arrangement with those two devils.'

'I am so sorry Pa' said the farmer 'We did think that you might be able to find a new camp site further west or with another group of gypsies, but I now realise that this was probably just wishful thinking.'

As he said this, he was slowly shaking his head and

continuing to avoid much if any eye contact.

The elderly gypsy was clearly quite agitated, looking about to grab the farmer.

Luca spoke up.

'James it is looking like the possible idea that you mentioned this morning, the details of which we don't yet know, is to be our last and only chance.'

James nodded to her 'Yes, let's leave this man to his conscience and when we get back to the camp I will outline what I have in mind....but remember, it will be what we called in the military a 'long-shot.'

And so, the four made their way back to the camp. Evening was drawing in now, and James and Ezra were invited to Pa and Ma's table for dinner along with Luca, Ned, Wicker, and another younger gypsy called Ringer. As was a tradition in the Pearson's family, these representatives of the adult generations of this gypsy family were present to discuss important family business.

Dinner was a muted affair, with each of those present contemplating their own thoughts about what might lay before the group.

Once the table had been cleared of the dinner plates, and ground acorn coffee and home brewed cider had been served, Pa and Luca pointedly looked at James, which he took as his cue.

'I feel that the dismal prospects facing your camp might allow you to think that my idea might save the day, but I really do need to play down such expectations. Before I complete my investigations in London all I have is a hunch.........
My land at Downland is just a few miles from the Cranfield Estate, and over that past year since Alex Cranfield inherited his estate I have read in the auction announcements section of the local paper that he has been selling off land. Now this might simply be due to his having access to more

profitable investments away from farming. But when I add the fact that we know Cranfield and Grenville seem to be the financial backers to a significant smuggling operation I was also curious to know more about Grenville's financial situation. So, I wrote to Simon Gosling in Lymington to asked if he could find out if Hugh Grenville had also been selling land of late and am awaiting a reply.

But for now, I am wondering why at least one of these well-set-up young aristocrats would be selling off land that has been in his family for generations. And why both of them would be involved in what I accept is a potentially highly profitable enterprise but one that is also very risky. If caught they could end up forfeiting their estates to the Crown and even losing their lives at the end of a hangman's rope.

'So, what has this got to do with our plight?' asked Pa 'Even if these two were caught it wouldn't stop the enclosure going ahead, I am thinking that it must be the two farmers who originally signed the petition that need to withdraw.'

'Yes, agreed' said James 'But to get to that point we need to gain some hold over Cranfield and Grenville that is stronger than the hold they have over the two farmers. My thinking is that behind the sale of land, and the risky business of smuggling, might be debt.

I am aware that Cranfield spends as much time as he can in London, and I would assume Hugh Grenville could do the same. I have been in London recently and the gentleman's clubs are becoming notorious for reckless gambling. I intend travelling up to the city on the fast coach from Southampton first thing tomorrow and I should be able to complete my investigations and be back within three or four days, so about the same time as the second posting of the petition notice is due to be made.

Can we leave it there as I am concerned about raising

hopes that can't be fulfilled. And Pa, if you do get evicted, we will do all we can to find a suitable campsite down in Devon.'

Pa looked around him and spread his arms to take in their surroundings.

'See that oak tree over there James, and that silver birch, and that elm, and those larches, and all the other trees around us, their roots go down into the soil of the New Forest. It is the same with us, our roots are deep in this ground – both the trees and ourselves were seeded here and here we have lived together for generations. With the trees providing summer shade, winter shelter, wood to warm us and material for us to work. We are as rooted in this place as are the trees around us, within a forest that sustains us. In that glade over there are buried unnumbered generations of Pearson. Being wrenched from this would mean we would most likely just wither and fade away.'

'I do understand Pa. Let's leave it for now and we will speak again when I get back from London.'

And so, the group broke up with Ezra and James making their way back to the inn.

'This is a bad business colonel – those two titled bastards need sorting.'

'Yes, Ezra. They are people who inherited a form of power that allows them to have control over the lives of others. With power should come responsibility, power ill-used is power abused.'

If we move on for twelve hours, we find James heading toward the capital city. He had set off before sunrise that day, riding to Hythe and taking the ferry across Southampton Water. In the centre of Southampton, he was able to leave his horse at a local coaching inn and, after having paid a premium fare, he took the bright red fast-mail coach along the London Road. He would reach the city by late that evening.

His thoughts were turning to his next steps. First was to call on the agent and see what he had been able to find out about Alex Cranfield and Hugh Grenville and what they might of gotten up to on their extended visits to the city. He had decided to spend the night in the Guards Club in St. James's Street. His having been an officer in the Grenadier Guards qualifying him for membership. Using the club meant that he did not have to arrange for agency staffing for his Hanover Square house for just one night, and it also allowed him to be closer to the staging post for the mail coach back to Southampton the next morning.

Even though it was quite late in the day when he arrived in the city he took a Hackney cab straight to the agent's office in Soho.

The agent, Daniel, could tell by James's somewhat agitated demeanour that this was not to be a leisurely meeting and that it was necessary to get down to the business in hand as soon as a polite welcome and been offered and coffee served. He turned to a file already open on his desk.

'So what have we got Daniel?' asked James

'Well, finding out about these two was much easier than I thought it would be. They are both members of Whites and Boodles gentleman's clubs and for a modest payment to the managers of each club I have been able to find out that these two are heavily in debt to both banks and more so to a notorious moneylender. The managers were forthcoming, not only due to the exchange of money but also to their dislike of the two men. They described Cranfield and Grenville as rude and arrogant and ideally would never again want to see them in their club. So, if the average cliental of these clubs are pretty irresponsible individuals these two stand out even in such unsavoury company.

I have looked into the standard loan conditions usually applied to loans intended to cover gambling debts, and it seems that such money-lenders charge interest at 20-30% per annum depending on their assessment of the risk of the loan not being repaid.

You can see that someone would only resort to a moneylender when they had reached the maxim of a loan from a respectable bank where the annual interest would be 5-8%, again depending on degree of estimated risk.'

'Do we know how much they owe the money-lender and where he can be found?' asked James.

'It is difficult to estimate the level of debt, but I think that we can assume that, based on a very rough estimate I have made of the annual profits of the two estates – which given the poor state of their management are lower than they should be – I would expect that their bank loans would be about £5-£10,000. As to the money-lender, I can't even estimate the debts but here is the address for a pawn shop I understand that he, an Erasmus Blackstock, owns and lives above in St Martin's Lane.'

James picked up the piece of paper from the desk and after having thanked Daniel warmly for his work quickly made his way on foot to the money-lender's shop.

St Martin's Lane was a long winding street running south to north from the more respectable Charing Cross to the poverty of St Giles and then on to the even worse conditions of the Seven Dials. The money-lender's pawn shop was about halfway up the dusty street, if slightly closer to the Charing Cross end. James saw the prominent pawn-brokers sign of three gold balls suspended from an iron fame. A sign that had been used for centuries to indicate a place where goods of at least some value could be exchanged for a cash payment then reclaimed at an agreed later date, with a charge being levied for this form of loan. With the goods being sold if they were not claimed by the agreed time. The three balls are the symbol of St Nicholas who, legend has it, rescued three young women from destitution by loaning each one sufficient gold to serve as a dowry, and so to enable them to get married.

On arrival James opened the shop door and an overhead bell announced the arrival of a customer. As he approached the counter a bright-faced young women turned from a shelf she was dusting and, taking in James's smart clothes said.

'What can we do for you sir?'

'Is Mr Blackstock available please.'

The women was thinking that this looks like another toff who has got himself into financial trouble and is seeking a loan from the master.

'I am sure he will be available sir, let me go and see.'

There was a door to a staircase beside the counter which she slipped through and ran up to the first floor.

She knocked on the frosted glass panel of an office door and received a gruff 'enter'. She opened the door to see her master bending over a dull-varnished desk on which a well-thumbed leger was open. Erasmus Blackstock was short in stature, even for those times, and his legs dangled about two inches from the carpeted floor. He was about fifty years of age with thinning grey hair and pinched face in the centre of which was prominent, red-veined, nose. Beside the leger there was a silver box containing snuff, and from time-to-time Erasmus took a pinch of the yellow powder, pressed it into a nostril and sniffed forcefully. This habit had left a permanent light yellow hue to his nostrils and on the thin grey moustache below. He was pleased to hear that a potentially well-heeled looking customer was on the premises, and he told the women to show him up immediately.

On entering James was surprised that this somewhat shabby office was the centre of a substantial money-lending operation. But this was the man that Daniel had identified as being a principal lender of last resort to fund financially embarrassed gentlemen.

James turned down the offer of a chair and said.

'I will come straight to the point Mr Blackstock, my calling today is due to my understanding that you have provided substantial credit to a certain Sir Alex Cranfield and a Lord Hugh Grenville. Can you confirm this please.'

Whilst Erasmus did not have the burden of any scruples related to client confidentiality, he was wary about being too open.

'Why do you ask sir?'

'I would like to purchase the debt from you – but only if the price is fair.'

The money-lender turned over some pages of his ledger.

'Well, let me see, ah here we are…. Cranfield owes £14,000 capital and £2,500 interest and Grenville £10,000 and £1,800 interest.'

The actual capital amounts were £12,000 for the former and £8,000 for the latter but Erasmus could sense the chance of a premium.

'I assume they are your friends sir, and I have to say that although I am very reluctant to take action I am losing patience with their failure to keep up with interest payments, and I am getting to the point of taking them to the debtors court to obtain bankruptcy orders and so be able to force them to sell assets to pay their debt.'

James had no doubts about the sums mentioned had been inflated but he wasn't in a strong bargaining position.

'Well Mr Blackstock I don't know if you are aware of the present condition of these two men's estates. Each has sold off most of the land belonging to the Home Farms. And most of the other farms on their estates are subject to secure tenancies which, due to the way the landowners have pushed up rents would be difficult to sell.

I accept that under normal circumstances high rented tenancies would be valued assets but, due the poor condition of the land and stock long neglected by hard pressed farmers and by disinterested landowners, the farms are barely viable. A symptom of the poor financial management of these once profitable estates are that over the past two years some of the farmers have just walked away from their tenancies. My own agent's investigations suggests that on the Cranfield estate there are ten unlet tenancies and on the Grenville estate eight. Such are the rent levels and the poor condition of the farms, that I can't see these being let any time in the near future.'

This information did somewhat take the money-lender by surprise as he had received a succession of letters from Alex and Hugh in which they reassured him that they would soon be able to pay the interest due, but just for now can he please bear with them.

On being informed of this, James reflected that he had a pretty good idea of what the means the pair were seeking to gain the interest referred too. But he thought best to leave smuggling out of the conversation.

'I would say that you would be unlikely to see the full amount of the debt repaid and if the banks foreclose on their loans to the pair, then your own money could be entirely lost. Given this, I will offer you £25,000. Which I would suggest is generous.

What do you think?'

Now the money-lender's mind was whirring as he tried to balance the potential loss of interest over future years against the possible default on debts which, after what James had just set out was looking to be a serious possibility.

He was thinking that this could be an opportunity to off-load potentially bad debt and be able to cover a bit more than his original investment, and also gain the interest due. His conclusion being that: 'This fellow must either be mad, or have another agenda, either way, I would be foolish to pass up this offer.'

So, a deal was agreed, and James informed Erasmus that he would instruct his London agent to arrange for a legal agreement to be drawn up and that once it had been signed by both parties, for the money to be transferred from Baring Brothers, his London bank, to the bank used by Erasmus.

'It will take about a week to liquidate some stocks and shares and top up my current bank balance, but the sum agreed should be with you within the coming week.'

James left the money-lender's office having achieved the task he had set himself – he reflected that he had spent pretty much the whole of his liquid wealth on what could well be financially worthless debt. Let's see if part two of my plan can restore my financial prospects as well secure the future for the gypsies.'

As James left the office, the money-lender's eyes were on the closing door and he said under his breath that 'Irresponsibility is good business for me. Bring on more reckless young gamblers.'

He looked out of the dust-coated window and in his imagination he could see the landed estate that he was himself looking forward to owning within the next few years – he had risen from the slums of Whitechapel to now being able to contemplate the prospect of becoming a respected landowner.

Clearly signalling his rising status to the world.

It did not take James long to return to Daniel's office and inform him of the outcome of the meeting and to instruct him to organise the transfer of the sum agree to the money-lender's bank account and to complete the agreement related to the debts.

The evening saw James dining in the wood-panelled dining room at his club, following which he sat in the member's lounge with a writing pad on which he was trying to set out his next move. He was thinking he would soon have control of the debts. But these were still legal agreements, and he could not threaten to foreclose if Cranfield and Grenville were to use the profits from their smuggling trip to pay the interest due. James was unaware that the pair had already used some of the gains made from the maiden voyage to pay of the interest on the bank loans as this was the creditor most likely to foreclose.

His plan now was to hijack the smugglers' cutter when it was loaded with goods. If this move was successful which, given the kind of people they would be taking on would be quite a challenge, then he would approach Cranfield and Grenville with a proposal. It was one he felt sure they would not like, but this was not a consideration that need concern him.

He was also unaware that the smuggler's cutter had that day sailed into St Mayo Harbour on the French coast and over the next few days would be loaded with tons of contraband goods.

After a night spent at his club, James caught the early post coach back to Southampton. Such was the priority given to the mail service over the comfort of the passengers that there was no overnight stay on this journey. The four strong horses would be exchanged for another four of similar condition at the Fox and Hounds Inn on the outskirts of Basingstoke. This urgency suited James as he was impatient to get back to Lyndhurst as soon as he could. As the ferry across Southampton Water did not run during the darkest hours of night he had to put up at the Southampton inn where he had left the horse he had borrowed from John's stable at the Bullfinch. So, it was early the next morning when he set off. Arriving at Lyndhurst mid-afternoon after riding hard through the forest along lanes that were at times mere tracks.

When passing the horse over to the ostler he asked the young lad if after attending to the horse, he would he like to earn an extra sixpence by running down to the gypsy camp and inviting Pa and Ma Pearson, Luca, Ned, Wicker, and Rider, to join them for dinner at the inn that evening. I will write down the names for you and square your short absence with John. This errand arranged, James went looking for John and soon found him in the public bar chatting with a couple of draymen who had just unloaded a dozen barrels of ale and four of cider and were now taking their customary 'drink on the house' with the landlord. James told John about the gypsy guests he was expecting to come along for dinner and asked if they could use one of the two private dining rooms for the evening as there was some confidential business they needed to discuss.

'You and Sarah can of course join us for dinner or, if you can't be spared from the bar and kitchen, then perhaps just for coffee, brandy, and cheese and biscuits, towards end of the meal. I don't want you to be involved in the action I am going to propose tonight John, but I think that you are entitled to be aware of the undertaking as you have been linked to our fight against enclosure from the very start when Wicker rushed into the pub with the copy of the petition that Luca had torn from the church door.'

At about seven o'clock that evening the party had gathered in the dining room and although all of the guests were eager to hear how James had got on in London, he asked them to be patient and to first enjoy the meal following which they would get down to the more serious business of the evening. He also apologised for limiting dinner invitations to just six of the gypsies, explaining the room did not have capacity to seat the whole group and he wanted them to be able to discuss a proposal that he was going to put to them without having to shout over the inevitable chatter of a larger grouping.

A nod from Pa suggested that this was acceptable.

'But if my plan is successful, I can promise that we can have had a full-blown hog-roast celebration in the camp on me.'

With smiles all round at this, the assembled gypsies, along with James, Caleb, and Ezra, applied themselves to the substantial roast dinner cooked by Sarah and served by two agile maidservants.

When the plates for the main course had been cleared away and platers of cheese, fruit, and butter along with shallow baskets of crusty bread, had been laid along the centre of the table, John produced more ale and cider, a bottle of brandy, and he also took a seat at the table.

James looked around at the group, each leaning slightly forward with a look of expectation on their face.

'I just wish I am not misleading them, so raising false hope.' He thought 'There will be a lot to do if my plan is to be successful and there will also be danger to life.'

His look was drawn to Luca and her encouraging smile, mingled with the thought of her being unhappy, gave him both confidence in his plan and the determination to see it through.

He cleared his throat and in an otherwise silent room he gave a brief outline of the result of his and the agent Daniel's investigations in London. How they had found out that Cranfield and Grenville were in significant debt and that currently they had insufficient assets to meet them. Hence their funding of an extensive smuggling operation. Although he had not mentioned the actual amounts involved, he said that he now owned the debt. He paused to allow this information to be considered.

Pa raised his hand to indicate that he was going to speak.

'I see that you have not mentioned any amounts James but, given that each of this pair own large estates I am assuming that the sums involved are substantial. Can I ask how you have been able to afford this – are you now in debt to some bank or money-lender – robbers all in my view? And I assume that if some money-lender was prepared to part with a debt on which no doubt a high rate of interest was due, then he must have thought that he had the opportunity to off-load some pretty risky debt. Risky debt that you now own.'

'Look Pa, I appreciate your concern but please just accept that I have been able to raise the money required from my own resources and if I were to lose it all then I might struggle for a few years but I won't starve.'

He again looked at Luca and his confidence was renewed.

'So, the first part of the plan has been achieved but we can't threaten Cranfield and Grenville with foreclosure just yet as their contract with the moneylender allowed them to get up to two months in arrears prior to legal action be taken. They now have two weeks left to at least pay the interest due. So, if they can run a successful smuggling trip they may well be able to raise the £3,300 needed to cover the interest due. It seems that such enormous profits are available given the size of the boat we believe they are using. Our task is to prevent such an action so that we do have the threat of foreclosure over them and that will be the lever by which we will get them to agree with farmers William and Casey to withdraw the petition and so stop the action to enclose.'

Caleb stood up and looking toward James said.

'Why can't we just find out when the next trip will be and where they are going to land the goods and then report them to the customs officers - I would not normally suggest informing, but we are talking about saving the camp.'

'Yes Caleb, I have considered that alternative, but I think that we can expect that with such a substantial operation as this some of the more senior customs officers could have been bribed to look the other way. If we do as you suggest then the gang will be tipped-off and the trip will just be delayed, or the boat re-directed to a different landing place. But even if there are no corrupt revenue men and they do move against the smugglers, then we need to consider the fate of the crew of the boat and those onshore helping with unloading and transporting the goods. Some of these are no doubt hardened criminals but others would just be local labourers or fishermen endeavouring to gain some much-needed extra income. What would happen to their families if their menfolk were to be imprisoned of even hanged? As Cranfield and Grenville would not be directly involved on the night of a landing, they would certainly escape any punishment. Yes, they wouldn't be able to pay their debts, but they would at least have their freedom.'

'I can see what you mean colonel, I would not want ordinary men like us to suffer, so can I ask what alternative you would propose?'

'Firstly, we need to identify when and where the next landing will be. Perhaps Dick and his fishermen friends in Lymington will be able to help, with this. Then we will need to either intercept the boat at sea or take control of her once she has landed. I would expect that the local men doing the unloading and transporting of the goods would not want to be involved in a fight and would be off home at the first sign of trouble – they would probably assume we were the customs on patrol. But whether we take the boat at sea or once it was moored up, we can be sure that the crew itself would be up for a fight. Bear in mind that they would be thinking that were fighting for their lives. There will be between six and ten crewmen so I am hoping we can find a similar number to go against them and although I want to avoid bloodshed if possible, we will need to be very well armed. Once we have taken control of the boat, it needs to be sailed west along the coast to anchor offshore and remain there until we have confronted Cranfield and Grenville. The second posting of the petition is due for two day's time, so we need to move fast and hope that they have a trip planned for this coming week.

I want you Caleb, Ned, and Rider, to hire a cart and ride to Southampton where it should be quite easy for you to buy muskets and pistols and plenty of gunpowder and shot – here is a list of ideal weaponry, but just do your best. While you are doing this Ezra, Whicker and myself will ride to Lymington to meet up with Dick and see if we can find out the date and landing place for the next smuggling trip. This won't be easy but hopefully Dick will have some ideas. There is no point in planning how we will attack the boat until we know the terrain adjacent to the mooring place or the challenges if we find it is better to take the boat at sea.

Right, so that's the plan then….any questions?'

Ezra was the first to speak up.

'Blimey colonel, you have been giving this some thought and I am already excited by the prospect of action, even if Caleb and me are probably a bit rusty. But my question is that you talk about taking a boat at sea or at a mooring and sailing west and yet, although I have served as a Marine, I could not sail a small dinghy never mind a large cutter.'

'I have thought about this Ezra, and I am again going to rely on Dick's advice. I was thinking that he might have some ex-navy or fishermen friends that, while not being up for the actual fighting, would be prepared to sail the boat for us. We would only need two or three experienced sailors and I am sure that some of us could manage basic crewing.'

Pa had been listening quite passively, but he now stood and looking directly at James he said.

'You sir have come amongst gypsy folk who are at best only barely tolerated in what they call polite society. And yet you have now put at risk your fortune and possibly even your life to help us. I know that you have formed an attachment to our Luca, which I might say is itself a brave thing to embark on, but I feel so overwhelmed at the generosity of you and your friends here. I, like Ezras here, can't wait to see some action. First thing tomorrow I will be cleaning my blunderbuss.'

'Thank you Pa.' said James 'Now, I don't want to upset you but the men required for the action that we are contemplating with need to be agile and to have good eyesight for what will likely be a night-time activity. We need you back at the camp to be able to continue leading the group if the worst happens and we fail.'

The look on Pa's face as he sat down suggested that he, if reluctantly, accepted the sense of James 's comments.

The evening came to an end with James and Luca hand-in-hand as they took a walk towards the campsite on what was a warm mid-August night.

'You have been quiet tonight, Luca.'

'Well, you have given us a lot to take in James. I love you so much that I don't want you to come to any harm – or indeed any of the others. But try as I might, I can't think of an alternative way of stopping the enclosure and all that this would mean for my family.'

He stopped as he drew her to him.

'I also love you Luca and I am hoping that once this business is settled you will come and stay at Downland and in due course, become my wife.'

The pair walked on, parting after a close embrace on the

outskirts of the camp. James to return to the inn, Luca to her summer tent, and for both to contemplate what might lie ahead of them.

'There is not much time to gain the information you are seeking James' said Dick.

We are now back in the ale house on Lymington Town Quay where Ezra and Wicker had previously met with Dick. With James's having been introduced to Dick by Ezra, and his just having explained the reason for their visit.

'Our problem Dick, is that the third posting of the enclosure petition is due in eight days now and once that has happened the enclosure must take place.'

Dick looked up at his visitors.

'So just to summarise: You want me to help you find out when this gang will making their next run and where they are likely to moor to unload the goods?'

'Yes, that's the meat of it' said Ezra.

Dick turned in his chair and called over to an individual leaning on the end of the bar who, given his rough canvas smock worn over fish-oil slicked trousers and with deep leather boots, was probably a fisherman. Dick invited him over and to pull up a chair. If the man's clothes provided a clue to his work then the fishy smell coming from the man certainly confirmed this.

'This is Gideon, he fishes an off-shore lugger out of the town.'

Dick went on to complete the introductions and, after handshakes and friendly nods all round Dick repeated what James had just told him.

Gideon scraped his chair back, walked to bar and asked the landlord to hand him a folded section of thick paper taken from behind the bar.

He then spread out what became obvious was a map of

some sort on the table with the others having to lift their drinks to make room for it.

'This is a sea-chart of a longish section of the south coast of England and takes in the English Channel covering some of the French coast.

Gideon took a draught of his ale and pointed at a place towards one edge of chart.

'There is St Mayo…'

'So why are we looking at France? Interrupted Ezra.

Gideon looked somewhat annoyed at the interruption and Ezra immediately apologised 'I am sorry Gideon just that I am by nature impatient.'

Gideon smiled and continued as if Ezra had not spoken.

'So, as I was saying, this is the Frenchie port of St Mayo and due to a storm in the Channel last week we had to seek shelter in the port to await the storm's blowing through. We were directed to a less busy area of the port and as we tied up we could see that the cutter 'Proud Mary' was already moored and judging by the amount of goods stacked on the quayside she was due to begin the process of loading a very large cargo. I waved to the first mate Tom, as we used to fish together before he took to full time smuggling.'

Seeing James questioning look he said.

'It is difficult to keep secrets in the fishing community sir we each tend to know what all are up too, and bear in mind that most of us have during hard times found space on board for contraband goods. If the opportunity for this seems to have dried up since 'Proud Mary' has been operating.'

Dick looked in turn at James, Ezra, and Wicker, then took over from Gideon.

'So, if we assume that it will take a couple of days to finish loading then we can identify a probable night for the trip across the channel based on when will be the next full-moon, the 'smuggler's moon' as we know it. Given what looks like the size of the cargo, I can't see them landing on an out of the way stretch of shore as Gideon and his fisherman friends would have done.'

Gideon confirmed this with a nod and said 'I think they will be using some store, probably a warehouse somewhere up the rivers Beaulieu or Lymington.'

'So' said Dick 'If we keep thinking along this line of passage, I think that we can rule out the river here at Lymington as the port is pretty busy and the harbour officials do occasional spot checks on both in-coming and out-going cargos – my money would be on the River Beaulieu where it is much quieter.'

'I can't thank you two enough' said James as he placed two gold two-guinea pieces on the table.

'Please do not feel insulted but I want to give some more material indication of how grateful we are. I suspect that times have been quite hard for you fisherman and retired mariners.' Seeing the look of appreciation in Dick and Gideon's faces he decided to go further.

'But I also want you to consider working with us. We cannot sail a boat. We need two or three experienced sailors who do not need to get involved in any fighting over control of the boat but whose skills will be needed to sail her along the coast to anchor off-shore for a few days whilst we visit Cranfield and Grenville. We will of course pay for this work….I was thinking twenty guineas per man – what do you say?'

'Well, I for one am up for this.' said Dick without any hesitation. 'The money will be very useful but the action itself looks to be exciting, and I have been getting evermore bored stewing in my own juice since I have been landed on shore.'

James turned to Gideon 'And what about you Gideon?'

'Well, I can manage without the excitement, but twenty

guineas would be about as much as I can earn at fishing for about three good months. And it will be useful to disrupt this gang who have pushed us out of our own modest activities involving contraband goods.'

'So, what now?' asked Wicker as he looked to James.

'It seems that we have a few days before the 'Proud Mary' will be landing somewhere along this stretch of coast – Hopefully this will be up the Beaulieu River because first light tomorrow we three will ride over to the mouth of the river and start working our way along its banks looking for some large sheds or a warehouse that might be the smuggler's store. Tonight I will write a note to John to go first post tomorrow. I will be asking John to get Ned and Rider, when they have returned from the weapon buying trip, to gather at least six more gypsies. Then, with Caleb and the weapons, to get down to Lymington as early as they can so that they are here for the night we have identified when we think that the trip will be taking place.'

'The fishing has been poor of late said Gideon so how about if I take my boat, the Sally-Ann, up the river to support tomorrow's search. We can cover both sides whereas you can realistically only ride down one side of this wide river. You will need to get up as far as Beaulieu before you can find a bridge across the river and so ride down the eastern side. Perhaps Dick will come along. Even if no or only very light winds we can come in on the incoming tide then run back on the outgoing tide, so we have at least eight hours when we could be searching the river.'

Dick's nod confirmed his willingness to join the search.

'That would be really helpful thanks both.' said James.

With the next step decided, the group broke up, with James, Ezra, and Wicker returning to The King's Head for the night.

Chapter Ten

When they arose, the next day it was to an overcast sky and to a suggestion from the landlord that rain was expected by lunchtime.

It only took a couple of hours for the three to have followed the coastal track from Lymington to the mouth of the Beaulieu River and for them to begin to work their way inland along the western bank.

The going was getting heavy with rain turning the surface of the little-used track into mud. But the three were cheered when they were hailed from the river and turned to see the Sally-Ann coming along at a much faster pace than the horsemen could manage.

It was mid- afternoon when the Sally Anne came back down the river. The fishing boat sailed close to the west bank and shouted to James and the others that just a bit further up-river, at a tiny hamlet called Lower Exbury, they had seen what looked like a newly built warehouse with little obvious activity taking place.

This news lifted the three rider's moods and, after waving the Sally-Anne off on her journey back to Lymington, the three pressed on. It wasn't long before they came to the small settlement and could see what they assumed was the building that had been spotted from the fishing boat.

James was encouraged to see a strip of bushes lining the bank near to the landing stage by the warehouse. His miliary training was already assessing the terrain and so considering a strategy for making an assault on where he would judge the boat could be moored while being unloaded.

He told Ezra and Wicker to stay where they could not be

seen from the building while he went forward to investigate.

On reaching the building he dismounted, and his first impression was that it looked to be deserted. But as he walked along the wooded staging a dog began barking and within minutes a small door set in the side of the building was thrown open and from which a large red-faced, angry looking, individual emerged.

'What the hell to you want?' he shouted at James 'This is private property, clear off.'

James ignored the man's rudeness and calmly said.

'Well, it has been some time since I last rode this way, so I was surprised to see this new warehouse and I was curious to know what it is being used for.'

'That is none of your business, and if I were you I would just ride on.'

This angry man was one of the leaders of the smuggling gang and before being disturbed by James's arrival he had been engaged in preparing the warehouse to receive the next load of goods. When he had time to take in James's quality clothes and his tone of voice, he reasoned that this man might not be intimidated by aggression, so he lowered his voice and said.

'I am sorry to be so rude sir, I have had a busy morning. This warehouse is part of a new business of cereal crop exporters, and we expect business from local farmers who are draining the marshy ground around here and so extending their crop growing. It will now be more convenient for them to sell their wheat, corn, and barley, to our company than to cart it to Lymington.'

James reflected that the man's explanation sounded as if it was a passage learned by rote and read out from memory, rather than being a spontaneous conversation. This only helped to reinforce the suspicion that this was the warehouse they were looking for.

'That does sound like a good idea, and I do wish your new business well.'

With that James remounted and rode away. Then it was back to Lymington and over their evening meal, taken in a small private dining room, the three of them started making a plan of action. They still had another day or so to spend in Lymington waiting for the group coming from Lyndhurst and for the night when their assault on the smugglers business would take place.

Whilst we await the action due to take place on the south coast, we can travel back to Downland and the sad situation of the young farmer Christian Greenwood. Although he was sure from her behaviour towards him that Tess had no interest in him beyond the instrumental, he still pined for her. He had been endeavouring to distract his, if not broken then rather bruised heart, by working hard. This concentration on work had not lifted his mood very much but there had been a noticeable improvement in the crops, and the animal stock had thrived. It was approaching harvest time now and this was usually time for celebration and to look forward to the harvest supper. The communal meal when all the farmers, labourers, and their families, as well as the master and the staff of the Hall would come together for a feast and in celebration of the rewards gained following a year of hard work.

But Christian was even thinking that he might cry off this year. He did not want to see Tess in party clothes looking especially lovely, this would only bring more emotional pain.

Meanwhile Tess had also been concentrating on her work of running the Hall. She would surreptitiously watch Christian when he was making his weekly delivery of foodstuffs grown or bred on his farm. But she had assumed that he had read her letter and she took his silence on this being due to his having learned that she was a 'fallen women', rather than the widow she knew that he had assumed. The spirt of love that had hovered, bow-string taut and arow poised, over Luca and James during the evening they shared in the lounge of The King's Head in Lymington was not to be found here.

Christian's parents still lived in the village where he grew up and, knowing that he would be very busy during the summer months, they decided to make the twenty-five-mile journey to visit him in late August when the harvest would be ready to bring in. This would allow them to spend a few days with their only son, and for his father to help with the harvesting.

On arrival, the matronly Mrs Greenwood was horrified to see the state of her son's cottage and, after being revived by tea and a light lunch following the three-hour bone-shaking journey in their old cart, she set to work on cleaning the house from top to bottom. A task that, as much as she tut-tutted, she knew she would find some satisfaction in doing. She was also aware that this would allow Christian and his father more time alone to talk together about the farm and all of the improvements being made to it.

'This place needs a woman's presence.' she was thinking as she began to lift the mats and bits of carpet from the main living room floor. When she came to the front doormat, she was surprised to find Tess's letter still in place six weeks after Jennie's postal mission. She placed this on the kitchen dresser to been given to Christian later that day.

It would be after a substantial mother's diner that evening when Mrs Greenwood handed the letter to her son. Christian opened it immediately but as soon as he saw that it was from Tess, he excused himself. With a now fast beating heart he walked out into the farmyard, reading the letter while standing in the evening's shadow of the barn. He read the letter once quickly and then again more slowly as he tried to take in its import. Tess had written that although she was developing strong feelings towards him, she needed to clarify her status. The letter continued with an outline of her time at Cranfield Hall and the abuse that she had suffered at the hands of the master. She completed the letter by writing:

'So, dear Christian you now know that I am but a 'fallen women', and so to be shunned, rather than my being the respectable widow that I understand you had assumed. Marriage for us is impossible but friendship might be. – Yours Tess'

Most men of that time would just have, if perhaps reluctantly, accepted the situation and settled for friendship. But that night Christian could not sleep and silently left the cottage and walked in moonlight to the Hall, where he stood and looked up at the broad window of the room that he thought that Tess would be sleeping in.

Christian's thoughts had been in turmoil since reading the letter. The social man could understand Tess's suggestion of marriage being impossible but the natural man within felt how much love he held inside for this woman. Between these two perspectives there is the man of experience who was well aware of the unequal power relationship between masters and maidservants, and how many of the former were only too willing to take advantage of this difference.

His thinking was: 'Why should a young girl forced or enticed into sex within an entirely unequal relationship have to bear the shame for rest of her life, and for an entirely innocent baby, become child, have to do the same?'

His answer to himself was that they should not.....and now that he had arrived at this conclusion his next decision was that he should talk with Tess at the earliest opportunity. With that, he returned home to sleep more easily until the rising sun – the farmer's alarm clock - woke him the following morning. After a porridge breakfast prepared by his mother, he completed the minimum necessary farm work – milking, feeding, and letting out the animals confined for the-night – within just a couple of hours. Then it was back to the cottage to wash, comb his hair, change into his best trousers and smock, and he was ready to go. His parents were enjoying coffee seated in a shaded part of the yard and on seeing his son emerge from the cottage his father remarked.

'It's not Sunday is it Christian, so why are you dressed for church?'

'Not for church father but for courting that I hope will one day lead to a holy bond made within that holy building.'

Mr Greenwood turned to his wife who was looking as surprised as himself.

'Well Lilian, our boy seems to have the wind up his tail.'

'Yes.' agreed his wife 'He also looks to be a sight happier this morning than he did when we first arrived.'

The would-be suiter was fortunate to find the source of his feelings kneeling as she tended a patch of bright-coloured flowers in a sun-bathed corner of the walled garden. He was relived to find Tess there and that she was alone.

As he came up behind her, he held out his hand and said. 'Tess, I badly need to speak with you please.'

Tess ignored his offered hand and stood up asking. 'What is it Christian, is something wrong?'

'Well, yes and no…..Tess when the letter you wrote to me some time ago was delivered, it slipped under the mat by my front door and so was hidden from view. But thanks to the determination of my visiting mother to clean up the cottage she found the letter, that I have now been able to read.'

'In that case' said Tess 'I am relieved to know that your

misunderstanding of my status has now been corrected and that you will now understand why we could never be anything other than friends.'

'No, No, Tess....what I do understand is that it is not right that you should be judged by a past where I can see that you were more victim than willing participant. But it's of no matter what happened, what does matter to me Tess is that your past is for me in the past and if anything, I want you more than ever and would be honoured to be able to stand in as a father for Thomas. That we three can be together as a family.'

Tears were now running down Tess's cheeks and Christian stepped towards her as he reached for her arms she buried her face in his chest.

'How can this be Christian? Do you really want a wife that will cause others to mock you behind your back?'

He gently held her so that he could look directly down at her face.

'Tess, I do not give a damn about anything said behind my back – and I would suggest that over time even the most narrowminded of our neighbours will tire of such gossip, and perhaps will even come to, not just accept our union but to admire our steadfastness, as they will also admire the substantial farm that we are going to build together.'

'Oh Christian.... these last ten minutes have turned my life upside down. But at least I can now release the feeling for you that I have long been suppressing.' She leaned forward to kiss him. As their lips touched a soft tingle of emotion spread throughout each of their bodies.

Looking upwards we can see that the god of love has now appeared, has a self-satisfied grin on his cherubic face, and that the arrow has taken flight from his bow.

Night was closing in as the Proud Mary eased away from

the mooring in St Mayo. The captain could just make out the rigging in the subdued light of a full moon. The creaking of the timbers and the occasional flapping of the sails indicated a boat on the move. Captain Jenkins – or rather Robert Jenkins - had turned to smuggling on being dismissed from the Royal Navy due to negligence following an incident when he was found to be drunk on duty. He had already served 20 years before the mast and had taken part in a number of key naval battles – notable engagements being the battles of Cape St. Vincent, Copenhagen, Camperdown, and the Nile – The thunder of guns, the fear of the enemies broadsides, the carnage caused by the had-to-hand fighting and the general demands of being captain of a large third-rater in the British Navy gradually eroded his courage and undermined his ability to command. By the time he was cruising behind Admiral Nelson's flagship HMS Victory during in the initial skirmishes leading up what would come to be called The Battle of Trafalgar, he was getting through each day on copious amounts of rum and brandy. When the inevitable poor decision on tacking the ship caused a collision, he was relieved of his command and became a mere observer of the naval battle that followed. On being returned to Portsmouth he was court-martialled and immediately dismissed from the service with his pension being cancelled. His financial plight meant that he felt there was little choice other than to take up the offer to captain the Proud Mary. He also considered that he had a certain entitlement to the money gained from evading British customs duties. It was a way of getting back at a government that he viewed as having just cast him adrift after years of dedicated service.

Looking around the deck he could only see some brief movements and the occasional moon-lit face of crew members, but he knew that there were five others sharing this run. He was only 'captain' by title and was only in charge for the actual sailing. It was Jim Drake the leader of the gang who was in overall command of the night's business. When they arrived off the coast of England, the captain skilfully sailed round 'Gull Island', the small peninsula at the mouth of the River Beaulieu, and then the boat slipped easily into the main channel down the centre of the river.

A crew member was placed either side of the main deck, straining their eyes in order to see the river-bank silhouetted by moonlight as best they could given the general darkness. The incoming tide and southerly wind blowing inland allowed the boat to make good progress along the river.

The captain heard a pheasant call near the port side, and it reminded him of a meal he had enjoyed just a week or so ago at the Montague Arms in Beaulieu village. What he did not know was that no bird had made the croaky call. The call was human in origin and was a signal from a gypsy who had positioned himself behind some low growing bushes near the river mouth. He had been told to give the signal when he could see or hear the smuggler's boat making its way towards what was now an ambush. The signal was repeated by a relay of two other lookouts until it reached the warehouse where James and the others were lying in wait.

Early that day the expected weaponry and men had arrived in Lymington and after providing a sustaining meal at the inn for them all, James led the way out of the inn's stable-yard and some way outside of the town where they met Dick and Gideon. They all then gathered round while he explained the strategy for the intended ambush and take-over of the Proud Mary. It did not take long to share out the weapons on the basis of gun type to any known skill, or lack of such. Caleb was a known marksman, and he was given one of the best muskets and two pistols, similar for two of the gypsies. Ezra and Rider were both known for poor marksmanship so each was given a blunderbuss on the basis that if the target was missed then the crashing sound of discharge would quite likely frighten him into submission. The rest of the weapons were distributed on a similar, weapon to suit known aptitude for shooting skills, basis – all were then supplied with plenty of ammunition.

But James emphasized how their best weapon would be surprise, and to ensure this they would need to keep as silent as possible until he gave the order to attack. He was expecting the crew of the boat to be concentrating on their on-board tasks, and so should not have guns to hand. They would have to take control of the warehouse before the boat was due and, according to Gideon, there would be some signal from the smugglers on land to indicate to the boat that the way was clear for them to land the goods.

Gideon also suggest that a usual means of signalling would be the firing of a pistol without a ball in the barrel so just a 'flash in the pan' of the gun. A similar signal should be returned from on-board to indicate that the signal from the land had been seen and that the boat was coming in. The plan was to first capture the warehouse and tie up and gag those taken prisoner, so that those captured could not call out.

James looked around the group of twelve determined looking men and asked if they all understood what was required, the nods and grunts and some grim smiles, suggested that the plan of action was clear and the men ready. Each of the group loaded and checked their weapons and the hooves of the horses were tied in sacking to dull their sound. When all looked ready James gave the order to move off.

As we already know, as the party traversed the track alongside the river, they left a lookout in three places which would allow the bird-call signal to be relayed to the warehouse once the building had been taken and the smuggler's boat had appeared in the river. They then moved on to take control of the warehouse and found that doing this was easier than they had expected. Only one individual was stationed outside and the light from his pipe made it easy to see and so take hold of him, then throw open the double doors and rush into the well-lit building. Taken by surprise, and faced with seven well—armed individuals, (Dick and Gideon had been told to stay with the horses and these had been left about five hundred yards from the building) the gang members immediately gave up, assuming their captors must be customs officers.

The work of tying and gagging the prisoners did not take long, but when the man James had met the previous day saw him, he fired off a range of colourful expletives.

'Get him gagged.' said James 'He can choke on his insults.'

James had the horses brought forward and, along with Dick and Gideon, hidden out of sight in the warehouse.

Now it was a tense time of waiting– the moonlight provided some soft light, a gentle breeze was blowing across the extensive reedbed, from which came the occasional plopping noise of a busy water-rat, and the hooting of a distant owl, providing the background to their vigil.

In parallel with the bird call signals, the Proud Mary also made her way along the river.

As they approached the warehouse, they knew that the moonlight would be sufficient for the watchers on the landing stage to see them. In anticipation of an all clear signal, the captain steered the boat towards the starboard side of the river in order to prepare to turn the boat by a full 180 degrees and so to allow her to come gentle alongside of the landing stage as she eased to a stop due to the force of the incoming tide and the southerly wind.

Ezra and Wicker had laid their blunderbusses on the landing stage and came forward to tie each end of the boat to the substantial mooring posts. The signal was given for the double doors of the warehouse to be thrown open so spiling light over the landing stage and the main deck of the boat as James led the boarding party. As with the taking of the warehouse, most of the crew also gave up without a fight. But Jim Drake the gang's leader slipped unnoticed into a cabin and as the captured smugglers were being rounded up he reappeared with two loaded pistols at his hips.

'Stay where you are and drop your pistols and muskets.' he shouted.

At which point Wicker, who had now picked up his weapon and was just attempting to climb into the boat when he heard Jim's shout, was taken by surprise. He fell back, involuntarily discharging the wide-barrelled gun as he fell. The loud crash of the blunderbuss caused an amount of noise, but of more use for the action on deck some of the shot sent skyward hit the top of the mast at the point where the head of the staysail was attached. This caused the heavy canvas sail to tumble down onto the deck and, favouring the boarding party, the sail covered Drake, with him falling to the floor. Some of the men were soon onto him and, after relieving him of the pistols, they manhandled him to join the other captives who were being marched into the warehouse.

Wicker's involuntary act not only completed the capture of the boat and its cargo, it also provided him with a tale that would, extended and much embellished in the telling, serve for years into the future – the way he bravely saved the day on that dangerous moonlit night on the bank of the River Beaulieu.

The gang were all now gathered in the building, still tied up but with gags removed. James stood in front of them and said.

'We are not revenue officers and do not have a problem with you, but we do have a problem with the people who have provided the capital required for such extensive smuggling. We will be taking the boat along with its cargo. But you will all be free to go, and once you have reorganized yourselves you can perhaps return to the lower level of smuggling that you had being doing in the past. One of you will come with us and once we are a couple of miles away he will be released to return to free you. The lesson for you all is to stick at what you are good at and don't be greedy.'

Before they took their leave, they had to help Gideon, Dick and the volunteer crew of Caleb, Ned, and a gypsy called Christie, to clear the fallen staysail and to prepare the boat for a voyage. It was fortunate that it was only one of the two headsails that had been shot off the mast-head rather than the mainsail, as the boat could still show a turn of speed with the main and the one remaining headsail. These five were to sail Proud Mary along the coast to the sheltered anchorage within the sweeping arch of Hurst Point at the western end of the Solent. Where they would remain until contacted by James. Due to the tide and breeze being against them they would have to tack their way slowly out of the river but once into the Solent they would be able to make good progress west.

When the boat had been cast off the group left on the riverbank, having untied one of the gang to accompany them part way, headed back to Lymington.

After another night at the Kings Head, and settling the bill with the landlord, James and the others set off back to Lyndhurst. The landlord had been curious about this group and their nocturnal activities, but their money was good and as far as he was concerned, their business was their own.

They arrived back at the gypsy camp by mid-afternoon and having gathered the group around the the central campfire James invited Rider to outline what had happened on their Lymington trip. Rider was a man of few words, and it did not take him long to offer an account of how they had achieved the aim of taking control of the smuggler's boat with its hold filled almost to deck level with contraband goods.

Pa stood to speak. 'I must thank you non-gypsies for risking your lives for us, but we still need to confront Cranfield and Grenville, what is the plan for this James?'

James looked round the gathering.

'This should be our final step towards ending the threat of enclosure, so I think it would be appropriate Pa if you come with Ezra and myself, and perhaps Luca can also come along as I understand she has in the past represented the family in dealings with non-gypsy society. But we do need to move quickly now, as the time to the third and final posting of the petition is running out.'

These four set off in the carriage early the following day to cover the ten miles through the forest to the Grenville Estate. By lunchtime, they were driving along the circular gravel drive and drawing up outside the white-washed palladium frontage. With its two tall stone columns supporting an arched portico that provided symmetry in the framing of an impressive front door. The previous evening, James had sent a note to Grenville Hall via a willing Bulfinch inn stable-lad, to say that he and some others would be coming to meet with Sir Alex Cranfield and Lord Hugh Grenville on the next morning. To ensure that the aristocratic pair would meet them the note added that they wished to discuss debts.

When James and the others walked up the steps to the front door it was immediately opened by a Butler who, if with a rather disdainful look at the party, invited them in and showed them into a large reception room with two bay windows looking out over an extensive, if neglected, rear garden. Alex was standing at the side of one of these and Hugh was sitting at a writing desk in a corner. He turned in his chair and said to James.

'I find it impertinent sir that you want to talk about debts. What the hell do you mean?'

James's reply was.

'The fact that we have been invited in suggests that you are well aware that you have debts, and indeed debts which are significant and that you should have been notified that an amount of these debts has now past to a new creditor - I would say that this new creditor is myself.

'You' shouted Alex 'I recognise you now, you are the master of Downland, and it was you who interfered with my relationship with Tess Clare....'

'Yes, I was very happy to have done so sir and by a strange co-incidence of fate we meet again and I have to warn you that I will at first seem to be your nemesis but that you might come to see me as a person that contributes to providing your own and Grenville's financial salvation.'

'Humph' said Alex turning to look out of a window.

'We have not yet been informed of any debt being sold on.' said Hugh 'But even if this is the case, and you are a new creditor, this means little to us. Yes, interest payment is in arrears, but we still have a couple of weeks before this has to be settled and each of us is expecting to be able to meet this demand.'

James picked up on this comment:

'In order to do so I understand that you are expecting to reap the considerable profits to be made from the activity of smuggling..., Tell me have you heard from Jim Drake today?'

Hugh looked surprised and Alex's eyes screwed up as he looked with hatred at James.

During this early exchange Pa, Luca, and Ezra had

just been mute witnesses to a conversation that they were somewhat inhibited from more actively joining. But they could see the puzzled looks on Alex and Hugh's faces.

'What do you mean, why should this Drake fellow have contacted us?'

'As Drake is employed to lead the smuggling group that you two sponsor I was expecting that he would be making contact to inform you that the night before last they lost the cargo they were running, along with the boat that contained it.'

Now the pair looked at each other and the others in the room could for the first time see doubts in their hosts faces.

'In due course, I am sure Drake will have gained the courage to update you on your losses, but in the meantime let's cut to the primary reason for our visit. Shall we all take a seat and get down to business.' said James, as he directed his three friends to the room's comfortable chairs. Alex ignored this suggestion and was now pacing up and down the room.

James continued 'Just now I said that, whilst I would been seen as your nemesis I will also be offering you a chance to begin again, if chastened by your recent experience. I want you to immediately remove the threats that you have made to farmers Williams and Casey so that they can have the petition to enclose the land on which the Lyndhurst gypsies are camped withdrawn. The whole of your debt with me can be written off by our keeping the Proud Mary and its cargo.'

'But hold on.' said Alex 'The boat and its cargo is worth more than we owe.'

'That is just too bad, the alternative to your accepting our offer is that you will not have the money to pay the interest on the debt, nor do you have any easy to sell land available. I can guarantee that if the petition is not removed then I will file for you both to be made bankrupt. So, you have a clear choice between these two – accept the conditions for our offer to clear your debts or face bankruptcy and social disgrace.'

The stark reality of this choice was not lost on Hugh and he buried his head in his hands mumbling that 'Without the boat we won't be able to pay our other debts, so we are lost to disgrace'

'No, said James 'You each have potentially viable estates, what you need to do is to become responsible keepers of the land – efficient management and the introduction of modern farming methods could provide the means to earn your way out of your remaining debts to the banks and to establish a financially secure future for yourselves and any family that you might each have.'

'I for one will accept your offer' said Hugh 'I will go to see Williams and Casey as soon as I can.'

'Thank you Grenville.' said James 'The soon as you can... will need to be very soon, as I expect you to travel to Lyndhurst with us today in order to complete this task.... what about you Cranfield?'

Alex turned to James unable to hide his hatred 'You are a bastard sir....the prospect of becoming a farmer does not appeal to me, but I can't see what we can do here other than bow to your threats. As the gambling phrase goes, 'You have the upper hand.'

James stood up and informed the pair that.

'Prior to our setting off for Lyndhurst, I want you two to write to your M.P. to clarify the changed enclosure situation and to let him know that you no longer have any interest in pursuing this action and will be instructing the two primary sponsors of the petition - Williams and Casey – accordingly.'

This done, there was only one more step to be taken in order to fulfil the plan that James had formulated less than a week earlier.

In order to complete this the four, plus two aristocratic outriders, travelled back to Lyndhurst together. The four friends parted company from the two chastened aristocrats after they had informed each of the relieved famers in turn that they were now free to halt the third posting of the petition notice and to contact the relevant parliamentary representative to inform him of their withdrawing their request for enclosure.

The hog roast that James had promised was postponed for a few days to allow him and Wicker to travel down to Lymington and hire a fishing boat to take them to Hurst Point where they found the Proud Mary swinging gently at anchor.

Once the ad hoc crew had been informed that the task had been competed, and that the threat of eviction removed, James told them that he wanted to talk with Dick and Gideon and he invited Caleb, Ned and Christie, to listen in to what he was going to say.

'I have been thinking Dick. I am looking for a solution to a couple of matters. Firstly, what are we going to do with the Proud Mary now that I have become the owner in return for the cancellation of debts owing to me by Cranfield and Grenville. In addition, there has been another issue at the back of my mind, this being how we can continue to raise sufficient funding to maintain our veteran's emigration project and to expand the number of smallholdings down in Devon.

What I am proposing is that you Dick take over the Proud Mary – I was hoping that, given your contacts with the smuggling community along this stretch of coast, you would be able to pass on the goods onboard to some of these for at least what Jim Drake and his crew would have paid for this with perhaps a premium on top as they would not have to risk the Chanel crossing. That money, less what we agreed with you and Gideon for your part in sailing the boat to this anchorage, will come to me.

Now that leaves a newly renovated fast cutter to dispense with. But rather than just sell it I thought that you could become the permanent master Dick. That you can perhaps find a crew and then use it for the legitimate trade of running cargos from the ocean-going merchant ships that are too big to enter most of the ports in towns along the south coast. I understand that this work pays quite well, and as such there is much competition for loads. I was thinking that, given that Proud Mary is one of the fastest boats of her type, you would have an edge in this business. Obviously you will need some time to think about this proposal Dick, so....'

Dick raised is hand to stop James . 'My goodness, what a turn up. But I don't need any time to think sir.... I would rip your hand off to shake on the deal. She is such a lovely boat. While we have been waiting here we have taken her out into the Solent for a sail and even with her full cargo I found her easy to manage in a strong wind and she is, as you say, a very fast boat. I might prefer her hull to be painted blue or white rather a smugglers' black, but I have had enough of drying out ashore. Moving about on her during the last few days has shown that my leg-wound has at least improved sufficient for me to command this responsive boat. The inshore cargo trade would suit me very well. I am sure that I can get four more sailors to make a reasonable crew. The work would be better paid and more regular than fishing.'

'Can I say something?' said Caleb.

'What's on your mind Caleb' asked James.

'What Dick said just now about our taking her out yesterday was an amazing experience for me. I absolutely loved the sensation of sailing. I felt a sense of freedom that I have not experienced since I was a child. As you know colonel, I will never make a smallholder and I don't particularly fancy emigration, but I can now see my future as a crew member on a boat such as this.'

'Dick stepped forward and held Caleb by the shoulders, you said a boat 'such as this' Caleb, but I would very much like it to actually be Proud Mary that you join. During the night's sail up from the Beaulieu River and yesterday's sail in the choppy Solent you looked to be a natural.'

Gideon raised his hand 'You can count me in as well please Dick.'

The two fishermen who had ferried James and Wicker out to the anchorage had been quietly conferring and they turned to Dick and asked if they could complete the crew of five required for the proposed business.

'Well', said James 'How about that.... It looks like we have established a new business that can offer a decent living for you five, a regular source of funding for our veterans support activities, and if the current cargo sells well then I might even get most of my savings back.'

In contrast to Caleb, Ned and Christie were determined to get back on dry land as soon as possible – a boat was felt by these two as being far from a natural habitat. Both had suffered from sea-sickness, even when at anchor.

With the matter of the boat and its cargo settled the party were soon deposited on Lymington Town Quay and then made their way back to Lyndhurst. The others were talking excitedly about the upcoming hog-roast and associated celebrations, but James was lost in thought of his and Luca's future beyond the party. He had a strong sense of relief after weeks of tension from when Wicker first lumbered into the public bar of the Bullfinch with the copy of the petition torn from the church door, but he was concerned about how he could persuade Luca to marry him and come to live at Downland.

These thoughts continued, if more towards that back of

his mind, during much of the party held on the following evening. But before this he and Pa had to visit farmers William and Casey to ensure that Grenville and Cranfield had assured them of the threats to their livelihoods being removed. So allowing them to take the steps necessary to withdraw the enclosure petition.

James and Pa left each of the obviously relieved farmers with enthusiast handshakes and an invitation to the next day's party.

And what a party it was. The hog had been slaughtered and prepared for the spit that a relay of dusky children had been tasked to turn slowly under the watchful eyes of a couple of elderly gypsy matrons. John and Sarah had supplied copious amounts of beer and cider. The musicians had tuned up and the whole group, plus their guests from the Bullfinch, were intent on a good time. It was to be an evening that was to be spoken about for generations to come.

The ashes of the central campfire were still smouldering the next morning when James arrived to join Luca for a day's walking and to enjoy each other's company. They followed a similar route to the first walk they had taken together and as they reached the place where woodland gave way to heathland the same passion-fuelled co-mingling of their bodies happened. In due course, they lay side-by-side in the mossy grass.

James sat up and holding Luca's hands he said.

'Dearest Luca it is the end of August next week and this is the time for the harvest supper at Downland. My manager, Joe, has written to say that this has been a bountiful year for cereal crops and the market prices of stock animals has been high. Joe writes of there being a surge of enthusiasm for modernisation across our farms and that the farmers and their families are looking forward to my being present at the harvest supper in a week's time. Over the past few weeks, I have come to learn about and to understand the ways of your people and of the land that you roam. I would very much like you to come with me Luca and meet more of my friends and see the place that I have made my home.'

Luca raised her eyes to James's.

'I am uneasy to leave this place. Apart from very occasional trips to nearby towns, my whole life has been spent in the forest. But I do love you so much James and when we are apart I ache for your company. I think that it would be selfish of me not to travel with you to your home.'

She was smiling as she said. 'I will view it as an adventure for me to go amongst the gorgers of Dorset!'

And so it was that towards the end of the following week, the carriage that had set off about a month earlier with James, Arthur Gordon, Ezra, and Caleb, turned from the main highway into the long gravel drive of Downland and round to the stables at the rear of the Hall.

Luca was struggling to take in the size of the house.

'Is this all yours James?' She asked.

'Yes, but bear in mind that legal owners of such places as Downland only own it for one life, we are more caretakers of the land and as such we do have responsibilities towards its well-being.'

Their exchange was interrupted by seeing Joe, Mary, and Tess hurrying to greet them.

Luca was almost overwhelmed by the fuss made of her and, while James and Joe were soon in close discussion about the estate business, Tess took Luca on a tour of the house. While Mary returned to her cottage to finish mixing the ingredients for a special cake she was baking for what she knew would be James's coming birthday.

Since meeting James, Luca had spent time in what was for her the over-comfortable bedrooms of inns, but the bedroom she was shown into as being for her was truly sumptuous.

'Well, I suppose sleep is the same wherever the night is spent, so I ought to be able to manage. I just wonder what Pa and Ma would think of this.'

Within but a couple of hours of their being together, Luca and Tess were forming a nicely relaxed bond. It was encouraging for Luca to learn from Tess how much James was appreciated by all of the staff of the Hall.

James was soon able to settle back into life at Downland. Although he did have mixed feelings when Joe told him that Tess and Christian were engaged to be married, an event due to take place in the Dissenters Chapel in Dorchester. On the one hand he was really pleased for the young couple – it did seem to be a perfect match for each of them. But then he was assuming that Tess would soon become a full-time farmer's wife and so leave her post of housekeeper running the Hall. A job that she had grown into and now carried out to perfection. When he raised this with Joe over coffee one morning he was put somewhat put at ease. Joe said that Tess had informed him that she would continue to work mornings at the Hall and the rest of the day at the farm, at least until any babies come along. And that during this period she would, with our permission, start training Susan to take over as housekeeper. It seems that Tess has seen the potential for Susan to rise from senior housemaid to the more substantial role of housekeeper. Joe was also able to update James on the general progress of the estate's farms as they were now so obviously benefiting from implementing the range of advice provided by Arthur Gordon. It seems that even farmer Bedlow was, if grudgingly, coming to see the potential of modernization in terms of improving profitability.

After coffee they took a leisurely walk around the walled garden to see the progress being made here, and then on to the row of tied cottages that had been undergoing a process of renovation.

'Well Joe, in my absence you have certainly been getting on with the work here. And I have already seen some of the excellent work that Amos has been doing in the Hall.'

'Yes, and now that Ezra is back to assist him, he is to have the work in the Hall completed by the end of the year, when they can then move on to help with the cottages.'

'That's good' said James 'If we are looking forward to the next few years, I also have ambitions to build a school for village children. With Tess, her brother Jude, and now Susan, we have been able to see the potential in the children of the so-called lower classes to learn and so, at least in economic and social terms to rise. Once when I was out walking with Luca, she was telling me about her own early learning experience, and of a motivational quote that has stayed with her - that 'knowledge is power'. If this is so, then we can offer the opportunity for local children to be exposed to knowledge in the school-room and so have the power to lead more fulfilling lives.'

During the first week after James's return to Downland, life settled into a steady routine. But throughout the whole estate there was a rising undercurrent of excitement about the coming harvest supper. The annual social recognition of a year's hard work.

As the day of celebration approached, the gardeners Jake and Michael, along with Amos and Ezra, were engaged in preparing the large Home-Farm barn for the event. A line of stout trestle tables was set down the middle of the barn, along with a collection of chairs of various styles, from rustic to crafted. Even-spaced down the centre of the line of tables were shallow bowls of water in which the flowers of both white and pink-tinged water lilies floated. Between these were placed earthenware pots containing bright-coloured stocks, sweet-pea, and cornflowers. Each side of the barn was lined with solid bales of hay, and on some of these were piles of fat yellow and orange pumpkins and some elongated green marrows. There were also a number of freshly painted wheelbarrows filled with carrots, potatoes, turnips, and other such fruits of the soil. Along the beams and down the walls trailed hop vines donated by the two farms that grew the crop. And barrels of beer flavoured by the same locally grown hops, as well as flagons of cider, were placed where they would be within easy reach of the diners.

Left to the men the barn would have been full of such produce all piled high and in something of a disordered jumble, but order and indeed tasteful design had been introduced by the forceful direction of Mary and Tess. On the evening before the supper, the men and these two were able to stand back and view the completed setting with some satisfaction of a job well done.

The following day dawned misty and warm, with the level of excitement building throughout the morning as the mist slowly lifted. Cook oversaw the preparation of various kind of egg, sausage meat and chicken pies, while Susan took charge of the transport of these, along with broad platters of cheese, bowls of butter, baskets of crusty bread and large jugs of milk, from the busy kitchen to the similarly busy barn. The wives and older children from the farms joined the Hall and Home Farm staff to carry out these tasks. As he and Luca watched the activity, James was thinking that all the preparation and anticipation were a big part of the celebration.

The pair walked to the side of the barn where the more substantial meat cooking was being progressed. Here a wide shallow pit had been dug and over its hot coals a whole side of beef and of a large pig were being slowly roasted. Looking into the barn itself, Luca was amazed at the care that had gone into the decorations – celebrations at the gypsy camp tended to be more makeshift affairs.

In one corner of the barn they could see that a group of musicians, booked for the day, had arrived from Dorchester and were setting up. While being intently watched by a group of small children curious to view this novel collection of individuals going about their musical business.

I am sure that the reader can imagine how the rest of the day would have gone. Prodigious amounts of food were consumed, washed down with similar amounts of drink. Noisy conversation flowed around the barn as smoke drifted up into the rafters. Following the feast, the tables were cleared away – the musicians struck up their instruments to provide the rhythms and beats that most of those present danced too. If at times the dancers were out of step with the music. The older men and women seated themselves on the more comfortable seating and in their minds' they relived aspects of their own youth while watching the happy throng in front of them. As the afternoon turned to evening, with more candles being lit, most of the younger children fell by the party wayside as they curled up on the hay bales with heads in their mother's laps.

Such was the Downland harvest supper of late summer 1820.

In the following week James did all that he could to show Luca the estate. To some extent his enthusiasm was infectious for her, but he had noticed that she was becoming quieter and at times he had to repeat some comment due to her not listening. He was reassured that the intimacy of their nights together was as passionate as ever. But he could sense that something important was on her mind.

On a day on which they rode to the highest ridge of

the valley they dismounted to enjoy the lunch prepared by cook. As they took in the view of northern Dorset spread out in front of them James shared his thoughts.

'Luca I have noticed that over the last week your naturally happy disposition has softened quite a bit, is something bothering you?'

'Oh dearest James, I have been trying to settle to life at Downland, but I do feel like a fish out of water. And I so miss my family – I do love you, but I need to go home.'

'It was probably too much for me to expect that you could easily move from life in the gypsy camp to such a different life here Luca. When we get back to Downland I will arranged for the carriage to be prepared for us to travel to Lyndhurst as soon as possible'

So it was that two days later they set off for the New Forest.

About midday, they stopped for lunch at a place where a slivery stream ran alongside the road.

After they had eaten Luca took James by the hand and led him a little way along the bank of the stream.

She turned to face him saying 'James, I have a baby in my belly.'

A stunned James just looked at her then his face formed into the broadest of smiles. He pulled her to him.

'That is such good news....does this mean that you will now agree to marry me?'

'Let's leave marriage on one side for now James. We need to consider the implications of our bringing a new life into the world.'

During the rest of the trip Luca dismissed James's suggestion that the baby should be born at Downland where they could more easily arrange for a Dorchester physician to be present.

'It might be selfish of me James, but I am a gypsy woman

and I want our child to be born in the same place where generations of its gypsy ancestors first saw the sun.'

James reluctantly agreed to this arrangement and the pair looked ahead to a time when the baby become child would grow up alternating its time between Downland and the Lyndhurst camp. And during the period of pregnancy James would visit Luca as often as business at Downland and in London allowed.

It was spring the following year when Luca felt the first stomach gripping pain of impending child-birth.

By some elusive woman's instinct, Luca was sure that the conception of the baby had taken place on the very first occasion that the two came together. She used that date to assess the time that the baby would be due, and so James was able to travel down to Lyndhurst in the week that Luca had correctly identified as leading up to the birth.

He was excluded by the gypsy midwife from the tent within which Luca was confined, so left to pace up and down outside, himself feeling the pain of each of Luca's cries. As these cries ceased a gentler, if more persistent, cry took its place, the first cry of Luca and James's daughter.

The midwife emerged from the tent wiping her hands on a blood-stained cloth as she also held the tent flap open and indicated for James to enter. He ducked into the tent then went down on his knees beside the low bed on which Luca was sitting up with a tiny bundle of life wrapped in a small blanket. As a smiling Luca handed the baby to him James had tears in his eyes and a deep love in his heart for both Luca and his daughter.

All went well for the first two weeks, so James reluctantly returned to Downland to help with planning the estate's business for the coming year. But one morning in late May he received a letter in the first post – the letter was from John at the Bullfinch. He read that Wicker had come to the inn to say that Luca was unwell and asked that I write you to say that Luca wants you to get down to Lyndhurst as soon as possible.

By the time James reached the camp on the following day, he was in quite an agitated state, not helped by the obviously low mood of Pa, Ma, and the other gypsies that came forward to greet him.

'You must come straight to see Luca.' said Ma as she guided him to Luca's tent.

On entering the tent, he was shocked to see how unwell Luca looked, with heavy-lidded eyes hardly able to keep awake. The baby, Taliya, was nestled in a small cot beside Luca who was gently holding the sleeping baby's tiny hand.

For a brief moment when she first saw him, Luca brightened.

'Dearest James, thank you for coming. As you can see I am not doing too well – I have an infection cause by milk-fever, and I can feel myself getting ever weaker. I don't think that I am long for this world.'

Now James was in tears, and he tried to reassure Luca that she will soon get better and that all will be fine.

'All you need is rest and plenty of good food and drink, I will arrange for a doctor to come along'.

'No James, last night whilst asleep I dreamt of my body being covered in a white shroud and this is my future. Please don't cry for me my darling…. The past year since we met has been the happiest time of my life, and having Taliya has brought me a joy that I would never have known without you.'

She had become quite breathless and so paused to rest, but before James could speak, she held up her hand.

'James, I do so want Taliya to know her gypsy heritage even if you do take her to live at Downland.'

James lifted his head to look into Lucas's eyes.

'Dearest, if anything does happen to you, she will grow to be a gypsy woman just like her mother and I will tell her all about you and your traditions. She will be living here and will only visit Downland from time to time, at least until she inherits the estate, then she can choose where her home will be.

'Thank you, James. My people will bury me in the family cemetery over yonder, and it is a comfort to know that Taliya will be playing on the same dusty ground and in the same wild woods as I did as a child.'

The pair held hands and, as the day wore on Luca's breathing became ever shallower.

It was late afternoon, as the sun was sinking in the west when Luca closed her eyes and with a gentle sigh she passed from this life.

Postscript

If we roll the time on for about five years, we see that James and Joe have developed Downland to become a model collection of productive farms and so an estate that benefits both the landlord and the tenant farmers equally. The stock of farm worker's housing has been improved and extended by the work of Amos and Ezra and a small team of builders whose work they oversee. They have also been able to build the small non-denominational school that it had been one of James's ambitions to set up in Cerne Parva.

Tess and Christian's family has been increased by a set of twins and with Susan's support Tess has continued to manage the household of the Hall as well as fulfil her responsibilities on the farm. It will come as little surprise to learn that Alex is dead. It was perhaps inevitable that his reckless riding style would lead to a broken neck, and so it was. Was this an accident, or the result of the gypsy curse cast by Ma Pearson?

Hugh Grenville had seen the error of his ways and had come to realise how susceptible he had been to Alex's influence. He was now married with two small children and had settled to life as a substantial landowner as he endeavoured to improve the financial viability of the Grenville estate.

Taliya had enjoyed spending time alternating between Downland and the Gypsy camp at Lyndhurst. When at Downland she enjoyed outings riding beside James on a small pony that had been a gift for her fourth birthday. Father and daughter would ride for hours with Red lopping along beside them.

When in the Lyndhurst camp she would soak up the culture of the nomadic tribe – Hearing the tall tales told by the likes of Pa and Wicker, learning earthly wisdom from Ma and learning about the animals and plant life of the forest with her gypsy playmates. As she grew up she also developed a love of the natural world. Having access to the collection of drawings and notes made by her mother also stimulated her interest in medicinal plants and she would in due course establish a physic garden in a sheltered corner of the wall-garden at Downland. This being modelled on the one established in 1697 in the London village of Chelsea by the Worshipful Company of Apothecaries.

Dick, Caleb, and the rest of the crew running Proud Mary out of Lymington had slowly built a successful business in the carrying trade. Providing sufficient income for themselves, as well as funds to invest in buying more land in Devon, and also to support a new settlement in west Wales.

The world turns and with it the lives of the people whose times we have been sharing and who we now leave to experience whatever futures await them.

9 781803 699226